Saving Her Name

by

Rebecca Byrne

Saving Her Name

Cover Art by *Kristian Norris*

The Wild Rose Press, Inc.
PO Box 708
Adams Basin, NY 14410-0708
Visit us at www.thewildrosepress.com

Publishing History
First Edition, 2024
Trade Paperback ISBN 978-1-5092-5477-4
Digital ISBN 978-1-5092-5478-1

Published in the United States of America

Dedication

To Baider, Mary, Thomas, and Sarah—you are the best husband, parents, and sister I could ask for. And to Claire, my found family who always reads what I write.

Chapter 1

Sofija

Eleven million dollars.

I kept repeating it in my head, a light at the end of the tunnel mantra, as I let in the younger of the two FBI agents. He was a strikingly handsome thirty-something man whose last name was Velasquez, according to the badge he held up. He walked gingerly past me and into my small apartment, almost like he was afraid that if he touched anything, it would break.

Velasquez's older partner showed no such hesitance. After flashing me a badge that had "Cantrell" printed on it, he moved brusquely past me and installed himself on one of the thrifted chairs that I had painstakingly painted to match my table. Once Cantrell was seated, Velasquez followed suit. Almost as soon as he sat, he looked from side to side. When he seemed to realize that there were no more chairs, he abruptly stood up and gestured toward where he had been sitting.

"Please, take this seat. I'll stand."

It was only a few words, but the quality of Velasquez's voice sent frissions through me. There was something impossibly rich to it, like the honey whiskey color of his eyes but in acoustic form. If he noticed my small shiver, he didn't give any indication.

Gorgeous, considerate—and here to investigate me,

I silently lamented. "Don't worry about it. I prefer standing," I assured him. Leaning forward, I rested my forearms on the yellowing linoleum countertop in my kitchen and stared at the two men.

If I were less nervous, I might have felt embarrassed by my apartment's lack of decent furniture.

These men weren't guests, though. They were law enforcement.

That much was especially clear as I studied Cantrell. He reminded me a little of my grandfather insofar as there was something vaguely military about him, a combativeness that had gradually faded, probably smoothed by years in the suburbs spent hosting backyard barbecues and driving his kids to soccer.

But I could sense that there was still something steely and severe running through him. It made me uneasy. He seemed to know the effect he was having, because he arched his eyebrow expectantly and drew his mouth in a line when he caught me studying him. His expression seemed to say, "I know that you know why we're here."

Tearing my gaze away, I shifted it to the younger man. Cantrell intimidated me, but Velasquez was so handsome that he almost overwhelmed me. I had to remind myself that gawking at an FBI agent who saw me as a suspect and who was about to question me would *not* help my situation.

And it was a situation that needed to be resolved as seamlessly as possible. My reputation depended on it. So did the eleven million dollars.

Well, not quite eleven million, I silently corrected.

Eight million two hundred and fifty thousand, once Adam got his share.

Four million one hundred and twenty-five thousand, once I split what I had in half with Jesse, like we had agreed.

Still. Four million plus some. It was enough to make me dizzy. It was hope, for the first time in a long time.

Ever since my mom died, and especially since my dad's stroke, I'd done what was expected of me. The right thing, according to our circle of family and friends back in Malta and at church. I'd stayed near my dad in our same small town in central Massachusetts and enrolled in the local nursing program instead of leaving for medical school four states over. My brother was currently chasing that dream, not me. He would be a great ophthalmologist. I was proud of him, if a little jealous.

For a while now, I'd expected to continue working as an in-home nurse, probably until I was too old to truly enjoy retirement. If I were lucky, somewhere along the way I would be able to afford a small house, or maybe half of a duplex. In this economy, I wasn't picky.

But four million dollars changed everything—as long as I was cleared of guilt and allowed to keep it.

I had to do things in the right order. If I signed for the inheritance now and accepted the money before I was cleared, things might blow up in my face. My patients' families might find out and drop me. Admissions boards might catch wind and reject me. And maybe after all that, the FBI would decide I was guilty, or Adam would hire a powerful lawyer and take it all away from me. Then I would be ruined and left high and dry.

If I were patient, though, my name would be cleared and I would have more money than I had ever thought possible.

My future would be boundless, maybe for the first time in my life.

I could afford to go to nurse practitioner school. I could move out of my musty apartment and into one that had been built within the last three decades and was closer to the train. At the very least, I could get a nice set of chairs. A matching new table too, if I were feeling like a real spendthrift.

My daydreaming was interrupted by a gentle cough. Snapping back to the present, I watched as Velasquez opened his notebook and clicked his pen, so deliberately, so carefully. His hands were veiny, but not in the same way as my patients' hands, the blue conduits of their blood eerily visible as they crisscrossed under the milky pale of aging skin. No, Velasquez's hands were smooth and powerful, the veins evincing a strong heartbeat and good blood flow.

Looking at them made my own heart beat a little faster.

Velasquez glanced at Cantrell, who gave him a short nod, like a go-ahead.

"I'm Agent Mateo Velasquez," he began.

"And I'm Agent Derek Cantrell," his no-nonsense partner barked out.

Velasquez paused, as if waiting in deference to see if Cantrell had anything else to add. When it was clear the older agent did not, he resumed. "So, Ms. Zammit—"

"Sofija," I blurted out reflexively. Velasquez looked up, clearly taken aback. "Sorry," I apologized. "I prefer going by Sofija. But I guess I can't stop you from calling me what you want. It's your investigation," I rambled, gesturing awkwardly in their direction.

Nice, Sofija. So much for being calm and wrapping this up quickly.

The two men exchanged glances, then looked back at me with matching furrowed brows. The coordination was comical, almost like a buddy cop movie where the fledgling young apprentice finally acts in sync with the gruff mentor. I snickered at the thought, which I realized was a mistake as soon as I saw their confused frowns deepen. I hurried to explain myself.

"It's just that Zammit is a really unusual name. There's not too many Maltese around here. I got teased so much in school about it, because it sounds too much like 'dammit,' you know? I'd mess up and classmates would say, 'God Zammit, Sofija!' " I winced at the silence with which my explanation was met. "I guess that's not what you meant yesterday on the phone when you said that you wanted to come here and get some biographical details about me, though," I quipped.

"No, it was not," Cantrell confirmed matter-of-factly.

My joke seemed to land better with Velasquez, who offered a brief, small smile before quickly resetting his face into a neutral expression.

"Sorry," I muttered. A beat of uncomfortable silence passed. I couldn't stand it. "Can I get you anything to drink? Water? Coffee? Tea? Soda? Kombucha?"

Cantrell wrinkled his nose. "Just the answers to our questions," he said bluntly.

His younger partner politely replied, "Nothing for me either. But thank you."

Dammit. I had been hoping that one of them would want something, because I would have taken the opportunity to casually pour myself a drink too. I was parched, but I didn't want to draw attention to the fact. Guilty people had dry mouths.

And I wasn't guilty.

I hadn't planned for any of this to happen.

"Agent Velasquez can sit on the couch. Feel free to sit at the table across from me, so we can hear each other better," Cantrell said. It was clear from his tone that this was more of a strong suggestion than an attempt to be considerate.

My temper got the best of me. I drew myself up to my full height—all five feet and barely two inches—and crossed my arms. "I'll stand, thanks. My voice is plenty loud," I said firmly.

Cantrell's expression soured. I bet he was used to intimidating suspects into submission. It was nerve-racking, watching his reaction, but asserting myself felt good.

Velasquez, on the other hand, was all politeness. "Whatever makes you more comfortable," he said with an accommodating smile. "Now, Sofija, we didn't go into too many details on the phone, but you understand why we're here, right?"

I shifted from one foot to the other before I forced myself to be still. "I have an idea, yeah."

He nodded, a strand of thick, silky black hair falling over his eyebrow. He quickly smoothed it back into place. Everything about him was impeccable, I realized appreciatively.

I had always wondered what was underneath people like that. People who were so carefully put together that every action seemed perfectly deliberate. Maybe behind the façade of control they burned brighter and ran hotter, like monks who channeled megawatts of religious ecstasy and divine love into careful meditation. We'd learned in a biology class about Tibetan monks who tolerate ice cold water for extended periods of time by raising their body temperature with just their mind and breathing exercises. They might look placid, but I had to believe that just beneath the surface, something fierce and intense simmered.

Reading about those monks had fascinated me because they were my opposite. I usually broadcasted my emotions at maximum volume. When I was happy, there was no question about it. When I was sad, crying gave me away. And when I was overwhelmed with anger, I tended to be snappy.

But maybe Velasquez wasn't completely monk-like. After all, he had smiled at my lame attempt at a joke just minutes ago. He might just be nervous—he was clearly the more junior agent of the two, and this might be one of his first assignments. If it was, he was probably scared to mess up in front of the intimidating lump of frowning muscle that was Cantrell.

I had been staring blankly above their heads with glazed over eyes. Refocusing, I looked at Velasquez and realized he was waiting for me to indicate that he could start the questioning. I gave him a small nod.

In his deep timbre, he began. "Sandra Armitage is the second elderly woman who was in your care to leave you the majority of her substantial assets, even over her own children."

"Why is this an FBI concern?" I asked, more defiantly than I had intended.

Velasquez didn't appear fazed or upset by my tone, answering smoothly, "Well, the first patient to leave you her assets—Bea Coventry—lived in Connecticut, and

Sandra Armitage lived here in Massachusetts. That makes it a multistate matter, meaning that it gets escalated from local jurisdictions to a federal level. That's where we come in."

At the mention of Bea Coventry's name, my stomach plummeted. *They know about Bea?* I fretted.

Before I could dwell on it, Cantrell curtly added, "And also because it's a question of millions of dollars."

Velasquez cleared his throat lightly, like he'd swallowed something irritating and wanted to hack it up but couldn't because he was at a posh dinner for diplomats. He said, "Yes, that too. We're just doing due diligence."

Sighing, I kept my arms crossed as I carefully fiddled with the ring on my finger, the one that Sandra had given me. Memories flooded me, a post-storm deluge in a dry canyon, threatening to drown me. I tamped them down and met Velasquez's amber gaze.

"I'll answer whatever I can for you. What do you want to know?"

Chapter 2

Mateo

"What do you want to know?" she asked.

Are you scared of me because I'm an FBI agent here to question you? Do you think I'm like Cantrell? If I had said yes, that I wanted the coffee you offered, how would you have prepared it? If I'd met you at a bookstore or a bar or on a run instead of during an investigation, what would you think of me? What would I think of you?

Who are you really, Sofija Zammit?

All of the things I wanted to say in response to Sofija's question—none of which were appropriate—raced through my mind at a dizzying speed as I tried to recalibrate.

Sofija already fascinated me, subverted my expectations. Within the first ten minutes of our entering her apartment for official questioning, Sofija had refused Cantrell's suggestion that she sit, instructed us to use her first name, and attempted to joke with us. Most people didn't act that way with the FBI in their home. It was intriguing. It was hard to believe.

What was equally hard to believe was that the petite nurse, who was currently studying me with luminous green eyes framed by dark curls that were endearingly large on her tiny frame, was the calculating manipulatrice that Adam Armitage had made her out to be.

Standing in front of us with her arms crossed, her body projected confidence, but her hands betrayed her. She was fiddling agitatedly with a ring on her middle finger, the glittering opal standing in stark contrast to the warm olive-brown skin of her hand. A hunch struck me.

"That's a lovely ring," I observed.

Sofija's face crumpled for a second, her mouth wavering. It looked like a small tear escaped and slid down her left cheek before she recomposed herself. "Thanks. Sandra gave it to me—but a long time ago." She quickly swiped at her face with her left hand, confirming what I thought I had seen.

Interesting. The memory of Mrs. Armitage makes her sad. That, or she's a fantastic actress.

Just as I was preparing to follow that line of inquiry, Cantrell butted in. "How'd you convince her to give it to you?"

Clearly indignant, Sofija retorted, "Sandra gave it to me as a birthday gift. I would never, ever ask patients for any of their personal possessions. I didn't become a nurse to take advantage of people, contrary to what you clearly already think of me."

Cantrell appeared to be gearing up for an equally provocative follow-up question that might make Sofija so mad that she shut down, which would render the whole evening a waste. So, even though I expected to get an earful from him later for doing so, I interjected.

"We didn't mean to give that impression. Just covering our bases."

At my words, Sofija's expression softened. I took that as a promising sign and continued. "So, Sofija, if you don't mind, why don't you tell us why you became a nurse?"

She looked surprised by the question. "Umm, I guess it was a combination of my parents' expectations and my own goals."

Nodding encouragingly, I urged, "Go on."

"Well, my parents wanted me and my brother to become doctors. My mom's parents brought her over from Malta when she was a baby, and my father immigrated here from Malta when he was eleven. Their families were friends back home, so my grandmothers introduced them in their teens. They got married young and had me young. Neither of them had college degrees, so they struggled financially. My dad joined the Army and got permission from his command to also work a part-time night shift at a car rental to help make ends meet. My mom balanced raising us and working as a secretary at a small law firm, but she died when I was twelve." Sofija gulped, and this time there was no doubt she was crying as fat tears slid down her cheeks.

"Take your time," I said gently.

"Thanks," she whispered thickly. After a deep sigh, she resumed. "Needless to say, they wanted my younger brother and I to get jobs that offered more financial security. My mom's dream was for us to go to medical school. That was making it in her eyes. In my dad's too, I guess, but back then I didn't know what he was thinking half the time. He was always busy at one job or the other. And now, he's—well, the point is that being a doctor equaled success for them, you know?"

Do I ever, I thought as I formulated the best reply to her question.

Cantrell disliked sharing any personal details whatsoever with suspects, but I didn't think that his approach was the most effective. Before I joined the FBI, when I was working as a lawyer, I found that strategically revealing something about myself led the people I was interviewing to drop their guard and talk more freely. Of course, I had still been in charge of the valve, deciding how much information to release and when. I had still been careful, in control.

But now, listening to Sofija, I realized there was something more: I genuinely empathized with her and her all-too familiar story. It wouldn't be hard coming up with the right thing to say, because it would be the truth.

I nodded and said sympathetically, "I'm familiar with the pressure. My parents also worked unforgiving jobs and had similar hopes for me. They weren't exactly thrilled when I went to law school and then joined the FBI instead of becoming a surgeon. Immigrant parents— they just want the best for you, but it's *their* idea of what's best."

Sofija responded with the first genuine-looking smile I had seen from her yet. "Right," she said. "Except in this case, it *was* actually what I wanted to do. It was my dream to be a doctor. I majored in biochemistry during undergrad and got very good grades. Took the MCAT, did well—not, like, stellar, but definitely good enough to get into middle-tier schools."

"But you didn't go?" I prompted.

She gave a pained smile and shook her head. "My dad had a stroke early in my senior year of college and only made a partial recovery. You know, his mind is still there, but it's harder for him to move around and he's a lot grumpier. I think it made him feel mom's absence even more. He was afraid that when my brother and I were off at school, there would be nobody there to take care of him, to keep him company."

Lip quivering, Sofija paused and then asked, "Sorry, is it okay if I grab a drink? I'm really thirsty all of a sudden."

Cantrell grunted his assent, and I assured her, "Of course."

I tried not to stare too obviously as I watched her shuffle over and open the fridge. She seemed exhausted, like the world was draining her of all the patience she had managed to drag with her into adulthood.

It rattled me, seeing someone young already so defeated.

Clutching a swing top bottle full of something purple in one hand and a glass that she'd retrieved from the cupboard in another, Sofija trudged back over to the counter. A hissing sound escaped the bottle as she opened it, followed by a strong smell.

"That alcohol?" Cantrell demanded with a disapproving frown.

Sofija shook her head as she poured the liquid into the cup. "Not really. It's kombucha. There might be trace amounts as a byproduct of the fermentation, but I kept this one at a slightly cooler temperature, so it's probably not even one percent. I drink it for the taste and the caffeine."

She took a sip of the drink and made a small, satisfied sound. Something about it made me grip my pen harder in one hand and curl the other into a fist.

The kombucha seemed to perk her up, because she straightened and continued without any prodding. "Anyways, after my father's stroke, I decided to stay nearby so I could help him out. I only applied to local medical schools, which narrowed it down to two options.

Unfortunately, they're both super competitive, and I knew they would be a stretch. So I applied to an ADN program around here as a backup."

"ADN? What's that?" I inquired.

"Oh, right. Associate Degree in Nursing. In the end, I didn't get into either medical school, so I had to go with the ADN option. Took me sixteen months and cost much less than medical school, so I guess it's for the best. It was the right thing to do. Plus, it made it easier for my brother to afford medical school—he's in his second year right now, out in California. Wants to be an ophthalmologist, if he can." She gave a wan smile that made my heart lurch.

"I'm proud of him. And besides, I might actually go to nurse practitioner school soon, if I can afford it." She blanched at the end of the sentence, an unnatural paleness draining the color out of her tawny skin.

"Which you certainly can now. Pretty convenient, I'd say," Cantrell remarked. I felt reflexively angry at him, though I knew it was an illogical reaction. What he was saying was the truth.

"I guess so," Sofija said nervously. She again began to fiddle with the ring Sandra had given to her. "But you can't imagine I would do anything illegal or unethical just to go back to school."

"So what do you plan on doing with the money, if not school?" Cantrell asked sharply.

"I—I mean, I'll certainly use it for nurse practitioner school, if I get in."

"Unless I'm very mistaken, no graduate program costs eight million dollars, which is what you're set to inherit. Combined with the money you inherited from Bea Coventry—" Cantrell pressed before Sofija cut him off.

"It seems like you've done enough research to find the court case against me that Bea's monster of an ex-husband filed before I could hire a lawyer to figure out how to decline or donate her money, so I don't know how you missed this crucial detail; I didn't keep that money," she practically spat at Cantrell.

So she's self-sacrificing but with a bit of a temper, I mused as I considered the vitriol in her retort.

"That so?" Cantrell asked skeptically.

"Yes, *that's so.* I just didn't want Bea's ex-husband to get his greedy, lying hands on it. As soon as the money was mine, I gave it all to Bea's cousin and great niece. That won't be in the court case transcripts, though," she sneered.

Huh. Adam certainly didn't mention that little detail.

"That's our fault," I said apologetically. "Pretty big oversight on our part. We haven't had a chance to really dig into things yet. This is all preliminary. We're just trying to get a lay of the land," I said, attempting to soothe her. "If you could give us the name of Bea Coventry's cousin and great niece so we can confirm this, we'd appreciate it."

Sofija shrugged, obviously still miffed. "I'm sure it's something you could use your super sleuthing skills to find, but sure. Happy to help," she said in a clipped tone. She grabbed a pen and sticky note from a pad from the counter, jotted down two names, and thrust it at me. As I reached out to take it, our fingers grazed. It felt like a small shock of lightning coursed through my hand, up my arm, and down my upper spine. Quickly, I withdrew my hand.

Cantrell, evidently, wasn't ready to let the line of

inquiry go. His foot nudged mine rather sharply under the table. I looked at him and his eyes flashed dangerously. He gave a nearly imperceptible jerk of his chin toward Sofija.

Stifling a sigh, I turned my gaze back to her. "So, Sofija, if you didn't accept the money from Bea, why are you accepting the money from Sandra? If that's your intention, that is."

That seemed to throw her for a loop; she began gnawing on her lip. I felt heat suffuse me as I watched her teeth capture her full bottom lip. I wondered what it would feel like against my own lips, between my teeth, under my tongue.

Focus, I reprimanded myself.

Finally, Sofija answered. "Because Sandra doesn't have any living relatives other than her sons, and her oldest, Adam, is already a billionaire. He'll be fine. Plus, it's now clear to me that I won't be able to save up for nurse practitioner school with my current salary alone. And I clearly need to buy some new furniture," she joked half-heartedly, gesturing to the worn table at which Cantrell and I sat like judges.

It was obvious that Sofija was hiding something, but before I could work that angle with any degree of finesse, Cantrell jumped in.

"Again, that certainly isn't going to eat up all eight million. Got any other plans?" he badgered.

Sofija reached for her glass of kombucha and knocked it over. Purple liquid spilled all over the counter. "Dammit," she muttered.

I sprang up and instinctively moved to help her. When I realized what I was doing, I paused. Cantrell and Sofija's bemused expressions were boring holes into me, so I sat back down.

Control yourself.

"Do you need help?" I offered in what I hoped was a vaguely indifferent voice. Out of the corner of my eye, I caught Cantrell giving me a reproving look. I couldn't blame him. It wasn't like me to be so reactionary, but something about being around Sofija made me feel like a livewire.

"I'm okay. Thanks for the offer, though," she added with a grateful smile.

"You were about to answer?" Cantrell pressed.

Sofija blushed. "Right. The answer is, I'm—I'm not keeping all eight million. I'm splitting my share in half with Sandra's other son, Jesse. After that, I'll use the rest to pay off my brother's med school debt. Then…I don't know. Charity and new furniture, I guess. Maybe I'll move someplace closer to the train so that I don't have to take so many buses to reach my patients," she concluded with a shrug.

"And you're splitting this with Jesse why? Out of the goodness of your heart, like you did with Mrs. Coventry's relatives?" Cantrell asked skeptically.

I saw something close off in Sofija in response to his question. Drawing her full lips into a firm line, she said, "What I do with money that is legally mine is surely my business. Now, gentlemen, I'm willing to talk more about this with you at a later date, but it's six in the evening and I've had a long day. I'm too tired to answer anything else."

"I see," Cantrell replied, irritation evident in his voice. "Well, we'll need to set that up as soon as possible. We'd certainly like to know more about your relationship with Mrs. Armitage and her sons."

"Understandable," Sofija acknowledged stiffly. "I'll be happy to hear those questions when I'm feeling better rested. And maybe with a lawyer present."

A disgruntled humph escaped Cantrell as we rose and walked the short distance across the compact apartment toward the door. Sofija followed.

Cantrell was already out the door by the time I turned to face her.

"Thank you for your time, Sofija. I'm sorry for your loss—I know this must be difficult for you."

As soon as the words left my mouth, I knew that it was a strange thing to say. I had no way of knowing for certain how emotionally invested Sofija had been in Sandra. Cantrell seemed to think not at all.

But as I stood watching Sofija's reaction, I got the feeling that Cantrell was wrong. She sniffed, her delicate nose briefly scrunching up. This time, no tears escaped, but her lips trembled.

"Thank you, Velasquez. Sandy was so much like my mother. Or at least, how I remember my mother. I can't believe that now I've lost her too," she whispered morosely.

"I'm sorry," I repeated lamely. "If you think of anything else, here are the numbers where you can reach us." I held out a simple business card with my name and work number on it. Out of the corner of my eye, I could see Cantrell fishing around for his, finally finding it and slapping it into Sofija's outstretched hand.

She looked a little startled, turning the cards over as if she couldn't believe what was happening to her. When she finally looked up, I gave her a reassuring but professional smile and said, "We'll be in contact."

I'll call you, I imagined myself saying. In a different

world, I was telling her goodnight after an electric first date, restraining myself from asking to spend the night tangled up with her because it was too soon. I was already calculating when would be the earliest that I could call her without seeming pushy. I was analyzing every word she'd said over the course of our meal to pick out her likes and dislikes so that I could plan the perfect second date.

But that wasn't the world we lived in, so instead, I pivoted neatly and walked away. Sofija's voice floated after me on the gentle evening breeze: "I'll be waiting."

****

"Seemed a little like bonding, what you did in there with the suspect," Cantrell said gruffly as he slid behind the wheel and I took my place in the passenger seat. "That whole bit about being the kids of immigrants and parents' expectations."

Parched all of a sudden, I grabbed my water bottle and unscrewed the top. Though I was tempted to gulp, I took small sips. Eventually, I responded.

"I was just trying to create common ground with her so that she'd loosen up and answer our questions," I explained. "She was very closed up at first. You saw her body language."

"Yeah," Cantrell conceded, before adding, "But I didn't spend *too long* looking at it, if you take my meaning."

I nearly choked on the water I was drinking. Composing myself, I said calmly, "I'm not going to let that kind of thing influence my investigation."

"Good."

"But," I added, "She doesn't seem like the type to do something like fool her elderly patients into signing away their fortunes. If what I saw today was genuine, she cares for Mrs. Armitage. And there was no evidence of foul play, not in either case."

"She lives in a shitty apartment and needs to come up with thousands of dollars for school. She has motive," Cantrell argued.

"I agree," I said, proceeding cautiously to avoid giving Cantrell the impression that I thought he was off base. "That being said, don't you think she seems emotionally attached to Mrs. Armitage? She kept playing with the ring she gifted her. She even teared up about it."

"What, Velasquez, you don't think that pretty young women can fake emotions? Trust me, the longer you stay in this job, the more you'll realize that anybody can play games," he said sternly.

Unable to think of a response, I gazed out the window, away from Cantrell, and cracked my knuckles. It was the only nervous habit I couldn't seem to break.

After a minute without talking, his voice, softer this time, broke the silence.

"Look, I get the appeal. She's easy on the eyes, clever, a little quirky, vulnerable. At one point or another, most of us have felt pulled to people like that. She probably knows it too. So you've got to be extra careful to keep things professional, okay?"

"You're describing the manic pixie dream girl trope, and I'm not convinced that's who Sofija Zammit is or is trying to be," I countered.

"What the hell is a maniac pixie?" Cantrell asked with a deep frown.

Don't laugh. Do NOT laugh at your senior agent partner on day one of this case, I ordered myself. I bit the inside of my lip until the pain pushed away the urge. "It's not important," I managed to say with a straight face.

"Maniac pixie. Half the things you young people come up with are plain gibberish. I blame social media. Stupid memes spread like wildfire there. Especially on QuikQlips," Cantrell declared.

Before I could point out to him that I was actually a generation above QuikQlips's main demographic and that I'd never used the app myself, he resumed talking.

"Anyways, Velasquez, all I'm saying is, don't get yourself thrown off a case and maybe out of the force for a woman who quite possibly preys on the elderly."

Things were getting uncomfortable, so I turned to humor to diffuse Cantrell's intensity. "Well, when you put it like that, I guess I should at least make a pros and cons list..." I joked.

Cantrell snapped his head toward me and looked like he was about to yell something when I assured him, "I'm kidding. Of course I wouldn't jeopardize my career. If I left the FBI, I'd probably have to go back to being a lawyer."

"God forbid," Cantrell said with a faint smirk, his eyes back on the road.

"Yeah, exactly. God forbid," I echoed, staring out the window again. The trees were the color that comes with mid-May: a beautiful, light jade. I'd seen it every spring for thirty-three years, but today, it seemed prettier than ever.

In fact, it seemed impossible that I'd ever had a favorite color other than green.

Chapter 3

Sofija

Like every time I was about to see Jesse, my
stomach started somersaulting. It was Pavlovian for me,
at this point.

While I waited for him in the diner the morning after
the FBI agents' visit, I traced the rim of my coffee cup.
Something about how smooth and perfect it was
bothered me today. Searching the table for something
else, my eyes landed on the crumpled turbinado sugar
packet that I had emptied into my coffee. I drank good
coffee black, mediocre coffee with sugar, and horrible
coffee with sugar and some kind of milk. The coffee here
was extremely average, but it was affordable.

More importantly, this diner was where Jesse and I
had gone on our first date—if I could call it that—so it
had a special place in my heart.

I flattened the empty sugar packet and placed a
fingertip on top of the metal straw in my glass of water,
suctioning it up. Next, I positioned it over the packet,
lifting the pad of my finger ever so slightly until the
tiniest drop of water ballooned out. It quivered there, like
it was waiting for its fate.

Suddenly, I felt impatient. I shook the straw and the
drop splashed onto the packet, soaking into the recycled
paper and turning the light brown dark as it bloomed out

toward the edges.

I replaced the straw in my water glass and picked up the dampened packet. Slowly, I began to rub it between my pointer finger and thumb, relishing in the feel of the wrinkled, fibery texture of the wet paper as it disintegrated.

"Coffee that bad, huh?" came a familiar voice.

Snapping my head up, I was greeted by Jesse's confident smirk.

"Hi," I blurted out eagerly, hating myself just a little for how excited I sounded. I couldn't help it.

Jesse reached down and stroked his thumb over my chin. My heart sped up. He sat down, jauntily throwing one arm over the back of the booth. Then he stretched out his legs out toward me and crossed them at the ankles.

His shoes were spotless—even the soles. They were always like that, as if he never walked on the streets here. Every winter and early spring, my own boots became filthy from trudging through the aftermath of New England's lumpy snow mounds as they melted and released the dirt they had accumulated during the colder months. Jesse avoided the mess because, as far as I could tell, he never took the train. No walking to and from stations for him. Over the last few months, I had noticed that he even used TripHitcher, the ride hailing app popular in our area, much more than he drove his sports car. He was dropped off exactly where he needed to be.

"So, how'd it go, babe?" Jesse asked. To most people, his voice probably would have sounded casual. But I knew better. I could hear the forced nonchalance in his question, just as clearly as I could hear the annoyance of the waitress at the table behind us as she read the specials for the second time to a boisterous family of five.

How did it go, really? I silently reflected. It hadn't gone extremely well, but I didn't want to worry Jesse. I wanted to care for him, reassure him. It was the same impulse I felt when my patients felt anxious.

Gazing into his deep blue eyes, I offered a smile that I hoped reached my own. "I think it went okay, Jesse. One of the agents is kind of a hardass. His name is Derek Cantrell. The other one, Mateo Velasquez, is very easy to talk to. I don't think he's the kind of guy to find somebody guilty just for the sake of it."

Some of the tension that had been in Jesse's shoulders visibly dissipated as he slouched a little and ran a hand through his dark blond hair. "And did they ask about us? About you and me?"

"Not in so many words," I answered carefully.

He plucked a butter knife from the utensil holder and spun it around on the empty plate in front of him. "In how many words did they ask, exactly?"

"They only asked why I was splitting the inheritance with you. Adam must have told them. They didn't ask me why Sandra didn't leave you anything, or why she left Adam some but not as much as me, or about—about our romantic involvement. Though to be honest, I doubt that Adam neglected to tell them about it."

Jesse nodded. "All right. Did you deal with the question?"

I nodded. "For now. I said I was too tired to answer more questions and they left. They did say they'd be back in contact, but I hinted that I might have a lawyer present next time they want to talk. I don't actually have one, but it seemed like the right thing to say."

"Good girl," Jesse said with a wink as he leaned forward to capture and squeeze my hand.

"Thanks," I replied as I squeezed back.

"Now," he said, clapping his hands. "Let's get some food in you. I know you're not eating right, now that Frannie isn't regularly stuffing you full of Roland's cooking."

At the mention of Sandra's talkative house manager and talented cook, I chuckled. "I miss your mom the most, but Frannie's chit chat and Roland's cooking second and third."

"I bet you do."

"You know, when she had spare time, Frannie ate lunch with me and Sandra. Then she'd sit there and entertain us with funny stories while I checked Sandra's vitals. It was nice." The memory made me smile.

Jesse hit the table with his hands, making me jump. "I know what we're going to do then," he announced.

"Oh?"

"Forget lunch here. We're going to split a dessert— pick whatever you want—and then we're going to drive back to the house and invite Frannie to eat with us. We'll have whatever Roland's cooked today."

Perking up at the idea, I exclaimed, "Dessert before our meals?!"

Jesse offered me a charming grin and instructed, "Put aside your impulses as a healthcare worker and indulge a little. You survived an FBI interrogation. You deserve to have a treat."

Laughing, I said, "I don't know if I'd call it an interrogation, but you don't have to convince me. I miss Frannie. I've only seen her a few times since Sandra died." I sobered up on the last words.

"I know," Jesse said gently. I watched as he signaled for the waitress.

Once he caught her eye, she traipsed over. "Whad'ya have?" she asked tiredly.

Jesse looked at me expectantly. I grasped the laminated menu and scanned it. "Sorry, I haven't really looked. Jesse, just—you can just order for me."

"Great. We'll have a large strawberry milkshake with a shot of vanilla syrup and extra whipped cream. And some sliced strawberries on top. Sound good?" he asked me.

Beaming, I said, "Sounds decadent."

The waitress grunted in affirmation and started to pivot to put in the order, when Jesse called out, "Oh, and coconut milk instead of dairy milk, please."

The waitress gave him a look bordering on disbelief. "We don't have coconut milk," she stated plainly.

"Macadamia milk?"

"No."

"Cashew milk?" he persisted.

"I've got real milk, almond milk, and soy milk. That's all," the waitress said in an exasperated tone.

"All right. Almond milk, I guess," Jesse conceded. He turned back to me and gave me a what-are-you-going-to-do expression. "Not great in terms of water usage, but soy is bad for men."

"You'd have to have a lot more than half a milkshake's worth of soy milk to be in any real trouble," I gently chided.

He was quiet for a second before he let out a chuckle. "Yeah, you caught me. I just prefer the taste."

"Me too, it tastes better," I echoed. I wasn't sure why I said it, because it wasn't true—I didn't have a strong preference. Maybe I didn't want Jesse feeling guilty by himself.

"Anyways," I said. "I'm excited to see Frannie!" Suddenly, a troubling thought occurred to me. "Wait. The last time I was at the estate, I overheard Roland say that now Adam is living there part time so that he can inspect things before the will is executed—or something like that. Is that true?"

Jesse shrugged dismissively as if this were a non-issue, something of so little concern that it hadn't even occurred to him. "Maybe a couple nights a week Adam sleeps at the estate. But he still lives at his and Xiaoming's place, and he's at his company for the better part of most days and some nights. You know, his typical workaholic behavior. Doubt we'll see him. And even if we do, it won't be worse than last time. He'll say something judgy to me and ignore your existence, then he'll jet off."

"Okay," I said, pursing my lips.

"One almond milk strawberry milkshake with modifications," the waitress said, setting the creation down on the table a little too forcefully. "Enjoy."

Jesse pulled the vintage glass full of pink liquid toward him and took a quick sip. "Mmm. Delicious," he hummed. "Just checking it for poison. All safe." He pushed it back toward me.

The joke had me rolling my eyes, but I smiled. I liked cheesy humor. "Always looking out for me, aren't you?"

His expression turned serious. He grabbed both of my hands and ran his thumbs over the bed of my fingernails. "Always, Sofija."

I held his gaze for as long as I could before I blushed

and looked down. Directly below me was the milkshake.

"Try it," Jesse urged.

I opened my mouth and closed it around the straw. Sucking, I waited in anticipation for the first burst of flavor. The cold liquid hit my tongue, and it was sweet. Too sweet. I raised my eyes ever so slightly, without tilting my head up. I could just barely see Jesse, who was watching me with a strange intensity.

"Do you like it?" he asked.

I swallowed. "It tastes a little like a ten-year old's idea of the perfect milkshake," I replied truthfully.

Jesse's face fell ever so slightly, and I quickly added, "And that's exactly how I prefer it. Skip me with the trendy artisanal ice cream sweetened with monk fruit or some bullshit. This is how a real milkshake is supposed to taste."

My words had their intended effect, because Jesse looked smug and happy. He nodded at the glass, as if encouraging me to keep going.

And so, I put my head down and sucked down several more gulps of the sickly sweetness before it felt safe to come up for air.

Chapter 4

Mateo

As I readied myself to head into the office the day after our interview with Sofija, I was overcome with dread. I hadn't felt anything like it in the mornings before work since my days as a lawyer. It was unsettling to experience it again; I thought I'd kicked the habit with my career change.

I pulled into my parking spot in front of the nondescript concrete building, early as always. After I turned off the car and along with it, the podcast I'd been listening to, I glanced up at the mirror to inspect my face. I hoped that I looked like I'd gotten my usual seven hours of sleep. In reality, I had tossed and turned through nightmares of a young, green forest that had been set ablaze and consumed by fire, leaving me standing covered in soot and burning embers.

There were slight dark circles under my eyes, but nothing too bad. "This is as good as it's going to get," I muttered aloud. I set my face in a practiced neutrality and hoped that Cantrell wouldn't pick up on anything out of the ordinary.

Grabbing my lunchbox, I exited my car and strode over to the building's heavily guarded entrance, locking the door over my shoulder.

Once I'd made it through the metal detector and the

rest of security, I took the stairs two at a time to the fourth floor. I was usually one of the first ones in at the office, but as I rounded the corner of my cubicle, I was surprised to see Cantrell sitting in my chair, looking at me expectantly.

"Morning," he said with his usual terseness. I knew he meant nothing by it—it was just how he talked—but along with his unexpected presence, it made me bristle.

Composing myself, I offered him an easy smile. "Good morning, Cantrell. You're up and at it early, no?"

He shrugged. "Real interested in this case," he said. "Wanted to dive in as soon as possible. You're looking kind of tired there, Velasquez."

Mentally cursing, I set my bag down on my desk. "It's the change in seasons—it makes me sleep poorly. Nothing coffee can't fix." Hoping that Cantrell wouldn't follow me, I walked briskly to the office kitchen and put my bento box lunch in the fridge.

I made my way over to the coffee machine. The smell of slightly burnt grounds suffused the air as I opened the container and ladled two heaping scoops into the filter. After I pressed brew, I closed my eyes and leaned against the counter.

Sofija. Sofija. Sofija Zammit, I chanted to myself. She didn't seem like the type to deliberately hurt her patients, much less the elderly ones.

Compared to Cantrell, I was a very junior agent, but I had honed my ability to sniff out guilt while I'd practiced law. My instincts screamed that Sofija was innocent of crimes like elder abuse or theft by deception. Nevertheless, I had a strong sense that she was hiding something significant. It would take finessing to figure out what exactly that was.

The impulse hit me again; I wished that I could know Sofija. I wanted to learn everything about her, not just what was pertinent to the case. The glimpses she had shared of her childhood, her family dynamics, her goals and dreams—they had piqued my interest and made me feel a kind of camaraderie. It was the most self-indulgent type of fantasizing, though, so I tried my best to push it aside.

"Coffee's done." Cantrell's loud voice echoed through the small kitchen, slicing through the veil of my secret thoughts. My eyes snapped open and I saw him pouring the piping hot liquid into his World's Best Grandpa mug. I smiled to myself. Little things like that softened Cantrell for me. He held up the pot, poised to pour for me.

"Thanks," I said, extending my cup. Cantrell filled it to just below the brim and we began the walk back to my cubicle.

"I'm thinking that we look into the Zammit girl's story, the one about what she did with that other old woman's money," Cantrell suggested.

"Sounds like a good place to start," I agreed. "I can follow up with Bea Coventry's cousin and great niece to make sure that Sofija's story checks out."

"Sofija, is it?" Cantrell asked sharply.

Flushing, I defended, "She requested that we don't call her Ms. Zammit."

Cantrell grunted. "Can't blame her, I guess. Kids can be little shits, and I bet you they did tease the hell out of her for a name like that."

"Right. Anyways, I'll do some research into the Coventry matter. After that, maybe we should look into interviewing the staff at Sandra Armitage's estate, as well as her sons."

"How about I confirm the story with the Coventry cousin and niece, and you go to the Armitage estate to interview whoever's available today?"

What? He can't have meant that. Blinking, I shook my head and refocused my eyes on Cantrell. He was looking at me with the faintest smile playing across his normally serious face. I felt equal parts incredulous and giddy as I replied, "I'm sorry, I could have sworn I was dreaming. I thought I heard Agent Derek Cantrell say that I could take the lead on interviewing without supervision. Give me a second to mainline this coffee and wake up."

Cantrell chuckled. "You heard me right. I trust your abilities, Velasquez. Get it done and get it done right. We can regroup and exchange notes tomorrow."

"Thank you—it means so much that you trust me to do this on my own. I'll do it exactly like you taught me," I said earnestly.

He gave me an almost fond smile and said, "No, you won't. But that might be a good thing. Use your charm and emotional intelligence, or whatever it was the Behavioral Science Unit called it in that longass seminar they made us attend."

"I'll do my best," I promised.

With a short nod, Cantrell took off to his cubicle. I checked my watch. It was barely 8:30 am—much too early to pay a visit to the estate.

Since I had a little time to kill, I turned on my computer, got through the dual factor authentication, and opened the case notes. The whole thing had been thrust upon us pretty abruptly, and what with the other assignments we were working, I'd only skimmed through the case notes. Now, I had time to do a thorough read through. I set an alarm on my phone for 10:30 am, when I would call the Armitage estate to inform the residents that I would pay a visit sometime in the afternoon.

First, I pulled up the intake form that the employee who had taken Adam Armitage's initial call had filled out. As I read through the transcript section, I could almost feel Adam's indignation radiate through the computer screen.

"Sofija Zammit, the nurse, has cared for my mother for—what, around three years? And then my mother decides to give her three quarters of what should have been our inheritance. It rubbed me the wrong way. I only got twenty-five percent. Jesse got next to nothing. I think the provision was something like $250 a month for the rest of his life. You can't even afford to rent a broom closet in this state with that.

I mean, don't get me wrong, I don't need the money. And Jesse is a profligate drifter who's never taken a job seriously in his life—but he's still her son.

You know, he's oddly calm about all of this, which makes no sense given that our mother was the one who financed pretty much everything for him. But that's beside the point. Fifty percent of her assets should be his, even if he would just piss it away on useless purchases and half-baked ideas.

Anyways, once our mother's will was read, I looked into Sofija, really dug deep. I even had some of my more tech savvy lawyer friends help out. What do you know, we found out that this isn't even the first time something like this has happened with her! There's a court record from a hearing in Connecticut that's pretty damning.

One of Sofija's wealthy patients—Bea Coventry—left Sofija all of her money upon her death. That didn't seem to sit right with Bea's ex-husband, so he took Sofija to court over it. He didn't win, but the record's there.

I mean, think about it. What are the chances? Within the span of a few years, two rich, older widows with declining health leave most of their millions to the same nurse? It looks like elder abuse to me—elder abuse across state lines, which is why I'm calling the FBI.

It's just wrong. People shouldn't grift vulnerable, elderly women. Look, I'll admit that I haven't been the perfect son, but I loved my mother. I hate to think of someone taking advantage of her, much less at the end of her life."

The transcript ended. I read through the biographical details that Adam had provided and finally made it to the end of the document.

Next, I navigated to Hartford County's digital repositories and downloaded the court records for the Bea Coventry asset division hearing. They revealed that Ms. Coventry's ex-husband Preston had accused Sofija of being a manipulative con artist guilty of elder abuse and medical malpractice. Sofija had responded that Preston had practically written himself out of the will by constantly cheating on and neglecting Ms. Coventry during her final years. Occasionally, the judge had interjected to ask a question or to demand that they keep things civil. In the end, Sofija had declared that Preston would not see a single cent of the inheritance. The judge had affirmed her right to decide this, as Ms. Coventry had been of sound mind and under no duress when she had signed her updated last will and testament. Preston had declared that he would appeal, and then the hearing apparently ended.

No actionable information here.

My chair creaked as I leaned back in it and picked up a pen, twirling it expertly between my fingers. Cantrell had volunteered to confirm that Sofija had indeed given Ms. Coventry's wealth to her distant relatives. There was no need for me to do any research into that.

Might as well learn more about the Armitage sons.

I decided to start with Jesse, since I knew the least about him. Plus, Sofija had reluctantly admitted that she planned to give half of her share to him, but nothing to Adam. I found that strange.

To start, I opened up Konnectly, a professional networking platform that everyone seemed to be on. Once I had logged into the dummy profile that FBI agents used in our investigations, I searched for "Jesse Armitage" and scrolled through the results. Almost immediately, I found a profile of someone based in Boston. The Armitage estate was in Springfield, but I figured that it was close enough. The profile picture was that of a man with blue eyes, dark blond hair, sharp cheekbones, a strong jaw, and an aquiline nose. There was no doubt that Jesse was classically handsome.

I bet Sofija thinks so too. The thought made me irrationally jealous.

Poking around his page revealed that, assuming he hadn't skipped any grades or been held back, he was about thirty-two—just a year younger than me. He had graduated from a top ten university with a Bachelor's of Finance and had spent the subsequent years at a series of companies which he had founded or co-founded. All of them were related either to crypto or to what seemed to me like specious health products.

I clicked on his current company and was redirected to a page that had a sleek logo and a buzzy, if vague, description. The company size was zero to five employees and there was no city listed as headquarters. After clicking through Jesse's previous ventures, I noticed that each one was the same—few employees, no headquarters.

Intrigued, I dug a little deeper, opening the Konnectly page for the first job listed on Jesse's profile: a business called "KryptoGrafer." A quick search revealed its ChitterChatter page as well. The Konnectly posts and ChitterChatter feed for KryptoGrafer were frequent and packed with trendy language and hashtags. Then, on June 8, 2019, they abruptly ceased, as if the person in charge of the company's social media had been summarily fired.

Even though I expected a 404 error, I opened the link to the KryptoGrafer website. Surprisingly, the domain name hadn't yet lapsed. What I saw matched my other findings: there had been biweekly blog posts related to crypto and replies to guests' comments up until June 2019, at which point the site seemed to have been abandoned. I navigated back to the employment history section of Jesse's page, and my hunch was confirmed; his end date at KryptoGrafer was June 2019.

I repeated the process for each of Jesse's companies and found that the pattern held, without exception. The man's entire professional career had been as a founder of failed startups.

As a final step, I cross checked the companies against LLC listings on the Massachusetts Secretary of State website. Sure enough, Jesse's name was attached to all of them. I noticed with some interest that his brother Adam wasn't listed on a single one.

So Jesse is a serial entrepreneur, but a bad one. I thought back to Adam's words from the intake form. He had called Jesse a "profligate drifter" who "pissed away" money. Adam had also implied that their mother Sandra had been bankrolling Jesse's companies.

Jesse must be panicking right now. The tap of money that had been flowing to him all his life was about to be shut off.

But Sofija had said she was planning to split her eight million with Jesse. That meant he would soon have four million dollars in his bank account. It wasn't the fifty percent that he had probably been expecting, but it was a lot better than nothing. He'd still be a millionaire.

I wondered why Sofija would be willing to do something like that for Jesse. Besides, if she wanted to deal evenly with the two brothers, she would keep four of her eight million to herself and give two million and seventy-five thousand to Jesse. Then, he and Adam would inherit the same amount. But she wasn't giving anything to Adam.

Why is that?

Surprisingly, a search for Adam Armitage on Konnectly yielded no results in Boston or anywhere in Massachusetts. I widened my search to include profiles matching the criteria in startup meccas like New York, San Francisco, Miami, and Austin—still to no avail.

Frustrated, I tried searching his name on Trawlerr. This time, my search returned several hits. I clicked on the first result and found myself staring at the profile of a company called Alleleprint.

Its logo was a double helix that unwound at the top,

the strands branching into lines of code. The description read:

Alleleprint takes privacy to the most personal level. Our easily-installable products use proprietary gene sequencing technology to generate locks for everything from devices to buildings that only your DNA, exhaled on our sensors, can open.

A little creepy, but ingenious. The rest of the page revealed that the company had approximately thirty-four employees, was headquartered in Somerville, and had received Series C seed funding for $71 million less than two months ago.

A picture was coalescing, slowly but surely. Adam seemed set; he probably wasn't hard up for cash and didn't need his mother's money for anything anymore. Most likely, it really was the principle of the thing that led him to report Sofija.

My mind turned to her again, remembering how her eyes had turned into liquid jade pools at the mention of the late Mrs. Armitage—and had just as quickly glinted with something like defiance when Cantrell had asked her why she was sharing her portion of the inheritance with Jesse.

Was I too ready to think the best of Sofija? I would be unbelievably disappointed in myself if a pretty face was biasing me in my work.

But there was something more underlying my impression, I was sure of it. Sofija's surface fragility belied an underlying strength, a strength shared by so many first-generation Americans who had to care for their parents while simultaneously living up to their expectations. Sofija seemed like the type to tap into that strength and work for her success, not take a shortcut by manipulating lonely old women.

Of course, I might be reading my own experience and worldview onto her. Maybe our ethics were completely different.

I couldn't eliminate that possibility without more investigation. Due diligence was important to me as a lawyer and continued to be as an FBI agent. Nothing and nobody could make me discard that by the wayside, no matter how tempting.

This time, I searched for Sofija Zammit on Konnectly. I got one hit in Massachusetts and four in Malta.

Scanning her page, I saw, with some relief, that her story from last night seemed truthful. She had gotten her ADN from a local school, after which she had worked at a hospital for about seven months. After that, she had begun working for a home visit nursing service. She was coming up on the fourth anniversary of that.

I clicked on the Posts section under her profile. She mostly reshared feel-good stories of healthcare workers who had gone above and beyond, as well as the occasional scientific article.

Searching for her name yielded a few hits, almost all related to graduation and honor roll lists. She had also been the recipient of a test score-based merit scholarship and college scholarship for Maltese-Americans, so there was a feature on that in the local news, dated to about ten years ago. In the accompanying picture, she looked very similar to how she did now, but the brace-filled smile gave away that it was old.

She seemed so happy and hopeful in the photograph. Her energy practically radiated out, a pure ray of light from the otherwise mechanical glow of the computer screen. Smiling a little, I was jerked out of my reverie by my phone's alarm. It was time to call the Armitage estate and let them know I was coming.

I opened up the contact folder in the casefile, found the number I needed, and dialed. The phone rang several times until a woman with a strong Boston accent, the kind that was rare in anyone younger than fifty, answered, "Armitage residence, this is Frannie McDonnell. Who's calling?"

"This is FBI Agent Mateo Velasquez. We're investigating a few things regarding the beneficiaries of Sandra Armitage's last will and testament. Would her sons, or at least some of the house staff, be around today if I were to swing by and ask some questions?"

Ms. McDonnell sounded miffed as she replied, "Don't know who invited the feds to come and investigate the inheritance situation. That's something that the people who were close to Mrs. Armitage should work out without you all butting in."

I said gently, "I can certainly understand why you'd feel that way. Money is a sensitive subject, especially after a death."

She sniffed loudly. "That it is." After a beat, she continued. "Anyways, if you really have to talk to us all, then I can tell you that Jesse often comes over for lunch. Not Adam. Adam comes and goes according to his moods. No telling when we'll next see him. Could be today. Could be days from now."

"No problem," I reassured. "And the staff?"

"There were only four of us, and Talia, one of the maids, just quit. Said she wasn't sure if there would be stable work for her here, now that Mrs. Armitage is gone. Hey! She's probably the snitch who called the FBI, isn't she?"

When I gave no answer, Ms. McDonnell huffed. "You aren't allowed to say, are you? Fine. Anyways, the other three, myself included, stuck around. To be honest, we also weren't sure we'd have jobs after Mrs. Armitage's passing, but Jesse hasn't stopped spending lots of his time here. So we're in the clear for now, unless he starts up with his old jet setting lifestyle again. And nowadays Adam stays here a couple nights a week, though he really ought to list his address as his company headquarters, if you ask me. In any case, we still have a house to run. Who knows what will happen once they sort out all the inheritance business. Me, I'll be staying until I'm not needed."

"Makes perfect sense. And would it be fine if I came around one this afternoon?"

"Sure, sure. Two of us, me and Roland—he's the chef—sleep in the house. The other maid has her own place, but she usually doesn't leave till around 5:30 p.m. So we'll all be here."

"Fantastic. Thanks, Ms. McDonnell. I'll see you soon."

"One thing, Agent Velasquez. You oughta park away from the house, just inside the gate. There's a parallel mulched path through the woods you can walk on."

"No problem. Do you mind if I ask why?" I asked.

"The driveway pavement is all messed up. Might tear up your tires. Jesse hired someone to resurface and pave it last summer, and she did a shoddy job. Can't believe the woman calls herself a professional. Was wicked expensive too—think Mrs. Armitage had to pay $40,000."

I nearly dropped the phone. "I'm sorry, that's forty thousand? Four zero zero zero zero?"

"Four with four zeros, forty K, however you want to say it. Total con artist, if you ask me. Jesse felt so bad about it. Spent a month apologizing to his mom. Of course, Adam mocked him for weeks. Called him a bum who couldn't even hire people to do a job right. So different, Mrs. Armitage's sons. You'd hardly know they were related, were it not for their last name."

Despite her professed distaste for federal law enforcement, Ms. McDonnell was turning out to be a fountain of information. Though there was a certain thrill to subtly coaxing the truth out of laconic suspects, it was nice to have a few chatty ones on each case.

"Well thank you so much, Ms. McDonnell. I really appreciate the tip about parking. I'll see you all in a few hours."

"All right then. We'll be waiting."

Chapter 5

Sofija

It turned out that Jesse had busted out the six-figure car for our date at the diner, so he took us back to the Armitage estate. It was such a treat, and not just because he rarely drove me anywhere. There was just something magical about riding around with your boyfriend on a nice day, no strict agenda, basking in the sweet ecstasy of a new relationship.

Jesse and I had only been romantically involved for about four months, but we had gotten to know each other increasingly well when Sandra had fallen ill a year ago. I started spending more hours caring for her at her estate, and Jesse came back from whatever country in Southeast Asia he'd been living in that year.

When Sandra really took a turn for the worse and I started to realize that I would lose her soon, Jesse began to step up and fill the hole that was inevitably forming in my life—and it was a big hole. I had loved Sandra, and she had loved me.

No matter what that grumpy asshole Cantrell implies, I thought defiantly.

Jesse knew how much me and Sandra cared for each other. He later told me it was one of the things about me that first attracted him.

Still, while Jesse had referred to me as his girlfriend

around his friends on the rare occasions that we went out with them, he had never called me that in front of Adam, and certainly not in front of Sandra. In fact, he had insisted that we hide our romantic involvement from them—which wasn't hard to do when it came to Adam, since he was barely around.

Strangely, in the relatively short time since Sandra's death, Jesse had at least once paraded our relationship in front of Adam.

A few days ago, Jesse let me into the estate so that I could pick up my belongings. I had been keeping toiletries and a few outfits there for my night stays, which had become frequent toward the end of Sandra's life when she had needed constant supervision.

****

I barely made it through the door before Jesse pushed me up against the cherry wood panels under the stairs, pawing at me and moaning. Adam walked down the stairs, shot us a nasty glare, and spat, "I don't want to see or hear that. It's a big house—get creative."

"Nice to run into you too, brother," Jesse sarcastically replied.

Of all the days for Adam to be here, I thought ruefully. But Adam's reply surprised me.

"Come on Jesse, you knew I'd be here. I told Frannie I was coming for lunch so that she could have Roland make something spicy for me. We both know she'd warn you about that."

Jesse knew Adam would be here? And he still acted like he was going to take me against a wall, knowing that Adam might see? I was beyond confused.

When I tried to ask Jesse about it later, he explained his change of heart earnestly.

"Sofi, I just don't want to hide *us* anymore. I regret not telling mom earlier, before her death. She would have loved to see me with someone wonderful like you—she was always telling me to date what she called, 'A woman of quality.' That's what you are. The reason I wanted to wait seems so silly to me now."

When Jesse had initially talked to me about the need for secrecy, he had claimed that he just wanted to get his latest company better-established before he told his mom that he was in a relationship.

"My mom loves you so much, Sofi. She would kill me if she thought I was just playing with you...and I worry she would think that. I don't have a great track record when it comes to commitment," he confessed. "If we wait until my company is doing a little better, mom will see me as a serious person who can stick it out through difficult times. Then she'll believe me when I say that I'm serious about you," he explained as we sat on the bank of the Armitage estate's pond, drinking grapefruit-flavored fizzy water.

"I guess I understand," I replied a little skeptically between sips. *At least he's honest about who he was in the past.*

"Come on, I'm sure your parents were like that. Immigrant parents always are. I bet you had to show them that you were killing it in school before you felt comfortable telling them about your first serious boyfriend."

"That's true," I conceded. "But you're not exactly in the same position, are you? Hasn't your family been here since, like, the *Mayflower*?"

"Actually, it was the *Anne*, but close enough," he corrected with a grin.

Rolling my eyes, I said, "My mistake. But what I'm trying to say is, your family doesn't exactly have to prove that you can make it in America."

"True, but I have to prove that I'm a worthy link in the chain of wildly successful Armitages who came before me—including my older brother. I'm not a genius like him."

"Hey," I had said, setting down my drink and stroking the top of his hand with my thumb. "Don't get down on yourself. You're trying to build something, and just because it doesn't yet have a valuation like Adam's company, doesn't mean that your effort isn't just as admirable. And nobody is as smart as Adam, except his fellow nerds from the engineering department. You're smart enough for me, and I'm no dummy. Besides," I added, "I like *seeing* you. If you were like Adam, we'd get together, what? Twice a month? That would suck."

Jesse twisted to look at me appreciatively. "Thanks, Sofi. Your opinion is the one I really care about," he whispered before giving me a long, languid kiss.

****

I thought back fondly to that day now, as the gentle New England summer breeze ruffled my curls while Jesse carefully guided the car along the winding road toward the Armitage estate. Weeks ago, on the only other occasion that Jesse had driven me to the estate instead of ordering us a TripHitcher ride, he had taken the curves at twice the posted speed. After I had screamed and told him it made me uncomfortable, he had slowed down and apologized. It made me so happy that he remembered to go slowly this time.

Looking over at Jesse now, I smiled. The afternoon sun hit his profile just right, creating a halo of summer light.

"Sometimes, you don't even look real," I blurted out. *Dammit Sofija, that sounded like it came straight from a cheesy YA romance.* I tensed, waiting for him to laugh or dismiss what I'd said.

Instead, his face split into a dazzling smile that made him look even more like someone I'd dreamed up as a teen.

"Thanks, babe." He reached out and rubbed my shoulder. My heart felt swollen, like it was too much for my chest and was trying to escape my body via my throat.

We parked just after the gate. Jesse hustled around the front of the car to my side and opened the door. Snaking his arm around my waist, he planted a kiss on my nose and led us up to the house.

"I've got to say, Jesse, that contractor you found did a truly shit job of paving this driveway. No offense," I said as we walked over the uneven pavement.

Groaning, he said, "Don't remind me. I was doing penance for a month after that debacle."

"Let's just use the side path," I suggested, tugging him off the pavement.

Once we made it up to the house, I detached from his grip and sprinted in front of him. "You got the car door, so it's only fair that I get the house door," I teased.

A piece of me, an echo almost, felt guilty for being so happy while approaching Sandra's home. I *did* feel a lot of sadness, knowing that I would go inside and wouldn't be able to see Sandra's sweet smile. Wouldn't be able to tell her that I liked—or was it loved?—her son. Wouldn't be able to see what I was sure, despite Jesse's concerns, would have been her happy reaction to the news.

But the joy of being with Jesse out in the open outweighed the pain of Sandra's absence.

"Such a gentlewoman," Jesse said as he inclined his head toward me in thanks and swept through the entrance. I followed and pulled the heavy door shut behind me.

The scene that greeted us stopped me right in my tracks. It was like an old Western standoff, but in a bougie setting.

"Adam," Jesse said coolly.

"Jesse," Adam drawled. He was so obviously making a point of ignoring my presence. It made me angry.

"Sofija," I mimicked sarcastically. "Look, Adam, I get that you're angry, but pretending I don't exist? Don't you think that's a little much?"

"Eight million dollars of money that isn't yours? Don't you think that's a little much?" he retorted, finally making eye contact. I almost wish he'd go back to ignoring my presence. His dark stare burned through me, unblinking and full of disdain. I could see what he saw when he looked at me: a woman who had conned his dying mother.

A knock at the door interrupted our stare down. I heard something clatter a few rooms over as Frannie flew in and fretted, "Oh, I'm so sorry, but I forgot to tell you—see, I got caught up with housework, and then Roland wanted—"

"Frannie, never mind that," Adam cut in. "What did you forget to tell us?"

Clearing her throat and blushing, Frannie said, "That an FBI agent is coming over to interview all of us who are here today. Something about an investigation into the inheritance situation. None of the FBI's damn business, in my personal opinion. I bet it was Talia, that maid who up and left us, who contacted them. Clearly had no sense of loyalty. She probably didn't even think twice about gabbing to the feds about a family situation."

"Nope, Frannie, it was me," Adam said with a deadly calmness. "I called the FBI."

Gaping, I cried out indignantly, "It was *you*!? Adam! We haven't even executed the will yet! Why wouldn't you at least talk to me before getting law enforcement involved?"

Before he could answer, the knock came again. Instead of responding to my question, Adam sidestepped me to open the door. I whipped my head around to see who would be on the other side, though I had a gut instinct about it.

The door seemed to open in slow motion. "Hello, I'm Agent Velasquez, FBI," I heard a familiar voice say.

"Come in," Adam replied.

For the second time in two days, I was gazing at Agent Mateo Velasquez as he stood on a doorstep, waiting to be let in to investigate.

Chapter 6

Mateo

Just as Frannie McDonnell had instructed me, I parked at the gate and walked up the mulch-covered trail that ran parallel to the driveway. Eventually, the Armitage estate appeared before me and the path ended, so I crossed over onto the driveway. I paused for a minute and took in the view; it was undeniably beautiful.

An imposing, federal style residence sat at the top of a gentle swell in the ground. It reminded me of the homes I'd seen in the old towns that we used to stop in for gas and snacks on our summer trips to the ocean. Curved-arch Palladian windows were set into peach brick. Swooping iron railings flanked the steps up to a large door, which was topped by a half oval window and framed by two bone-white pillars. Hydrangea and rhododendrons in full bloom lined the front of the house. The rest of the property consisted of spacious stretches of lawn occasionally interrupted by red maples and eastern red cedars. I could just barely make out a pond in the distance.

My foot caught on something and I nearly tumbled to the ground. Regaining my balance, I looked down. A huge crack in the pavement gaped up at me. As I surveyed the rest of the driveway, I saw that it was warped and littered with cracks.

Ms. McDonnell was right. Whoever Jesse had hired to redo the driveway had done an awful job.

Carefully, I walked the rest of the distance to the front door and knocked. A minute, and then two went by. Though I could hear a muffled but clearly heated exchange unfolding inside, nobody opened the door, so I knocked again.

This time, the door opened abruptly and I stood facing a towering man who I recognized to be Adam. Dark gray-blue eyes peered out from a long, pale face framed by perfectly cut black hair that stopped about two inches below his ears. He was dressed sharply, as I suspected he would be. His dark black sweater and business casual jeans were high caliber and perfectly fitted.

"Hello, I'm Agent Velasquez, FBI," I greeted, showing my badge.

"Come in," Adam invited, opening the door.

As I crossed over the threshold into the house, I saw her and I faltered. *What was she doing here?*

"Agent Velasquez!" she exclaimed. She seemed as taken aback as I was.

"Sofija?" I gasped.

"What are you doing here?" she asked.

"And why are you on a first name basis with her?" Adam asked pointedly, disapproval coloring his tone.

This damn question again. I was racking my brain for the best way to phrase my answer and dispel any impression of favoritism toward Sofija when she jumped in.

"Come on Adam, you know I don't like it when people call me by my last name," she said, shooting Adam an annoyed look.

"You've said that, yes," Adam admitted, sounding a little mollified.

Relief flooded me. "Yes, she informed me and my partner of her preference during our first interview. And on that note, would you prefer that I call you Adam or Mr. Armitage?"

"Adam is fine, but it's Armitage-Chen. My husband and I hyphenated our last names. That's a mouthful, though, so you can call me Adam. Now," he said, gesturing behind him at a seemingly endless hall of doors. "Where do you want to conduct the interviews?"

I started to reply when Jesse cut me off. "Actually, Agent Velasquez, my brother failed to consult me about the timing of this interrogation, as did Frannie," he said, shooting the woman a frown. "So Sofija here, she and I made plans to have lunch. You can interview me after that," he declared, tugging Sofija by the waist so that she was nestled against him.

"Newsflash, Jesse, the FBI doesn't have to accommodate your eating schedule. Just wait, it won't ruin your precious date," Adam said heatedly.

Jesse narrowed his eyes and taunted, "Forgive me if I don't take dating advice from a workaholic who probably sees his husband twice a week."

Adam opened his mouth to reply, but I intervened before the situation spiraled further out of control.

"All right!" I cried, clapping my hands. I tried to modulate the sarcasm in my voice, but some of it bled through. Besides, it was time to assert some authority. "I really don't care who I interview first, and I don't care what the rest of you do while I'm busy with one of you—eat lunch, trade stocks, or whatever you do for fun around here—but I need to talk to you two Armitages,

Ms. McDonnell, Roland, and the maid."

Out of the corner of my eye, I saw Sofija smirking at the dressing down I had given the brothers. I knew that I should feel ashamed—it had been an inexcusable lapse in control on my part—but couldn't deny that it felt good to discover that Sofija thought I was witty.

"You're going to talk to all of us, but not to Sofija?" Jesse asked in a strange tone.

"My partner and I have already conducted a preliminary interview with Sofija, though we will need to do a follow-up with her after we speak with everyone here. Let *us* worry about when that is, though," I said with a note of finality.

Adam pursed his lips, arched his eyebrow, and nodded. Ms. McDonnell crossed her arms defensively but said nothing. Jesse, however, smiled and said, "Understood, Agent Velasquez. Before we delve into the interviews, I would like a private word with my brother. Up until now, I didn't know that he was the one who called the FBI."

I looked at them warily. There was always a chance that Jesse would try to convince Adam to fix their stories, but that didn't seem likely, given the enmity between them that I had just witnessed. Still, it wasn't desirable to have interviewees conference together ahead of time.

"This is a condition of me talking to you. Otherwise, feel free to come back with a warrant if you really want to chat with me," Jesse insisted.

Sighing, I acquiesced. "Fine. Make it quick."

"Five minutes, tops," Jesse reassured, dragging his surly brother down the hall and disappearing behind a door.

I turned to Ms. McDonnell, but she was already

scurrying off too.

"Ms. McDonnell! I was going to start with you!"

"We'll talk, Agent Velasquez, but you scared the daylights out of me with your knocking. Made me jump, and I knocked over a huge platter of veggies and dips that I was setting out for lunch. Gotta clean that up. We'll talk after you're done with the others."

With that, I was left standing alone in the giant foyer with Sofija. I walked to an old leather divan along the right wall and sat down, cracking my knuckles in agitation. My first solo attempt at on-premise interviewing was not going well. *If you don't turn this around, Cantrell is going to be beyond disappointed. He won't trust you on your own again for months, at least.*

"You seem upset," Sofija said, approaching me with tentative steps before she stopped a few feet from me.

I could hear muffled shouting from down the hall. Instead of answering Sofija's observation directly, I said, "This family...they're difficult, aren't they?"

She shook her head vehemently. "Not Sandra. She was an angel. Opinionated. Not afraid to give tough love. But absolutely golden-hearted."

It was touching, watching Sofija soften while talking about a patient. "I meant the brothers," I clarified.

Her face fell. "Oh. Well, there's always been tension, but it's really come to a head since Sandra died. The boys are honestly much better company when the other one isn't there." She paused, then added, "At least, Jesse is. I just learned that Adam was the one who called the FBI about me, so I'm not eager to say anything nice about him right now. Maybe I'd better keep my mouth shut—I don't want to give you an unfair impression of him."

Raising an eyebrow, I regarded her, impressed. "That's mature of you. We'll investigate everyone fairly and come to our own conclusions, so don't worry too much about that."

A little exhale escaped Sofija's nose, barely audible, and she nodded. The shouting from down the hall once again spiked in volume. "Can I sit there too?" she asked, pointing to the divan.

Too close. Swallowing, I commanded my heart to stop racing. "Sure." I scooched to the opposite side of the furniture, putting as much distance between us as possible. It wasn't enough to mute the sweet, clean smell that clung to her curls, perfuming the air around her. I gripped the leather on the side of the divan with so much force that it squeaked when my palm lost traction and slipped.

Focus, Mateo. Use this situation to your advantage. Learn something you can take back to Cantrell.

Clearing my throat, I said, "Anyways, unless I'm mistaken, you don't have to ask permission to sit on your own furniture. It is yours now, isn't it? The whole estate?"

Sofija tilted her head at me and frowned. "Sandra didn't divide the house into inheritable sections, if that's what you mean."

"So Adam's twenty-five percent comes in the form of bank accounts and stocks? You've inherited some of that, plus the whole estate, no?"

Fidgeting, she said, "Sandra stipulated that in her will, yes. Though I haven't technically inherited it yet."

This caught my attention. "Oh?"

Sofija took a piece of paper out of her pocket and proceeded to twist it and roll it between her fingers. "I haven't—I haven't signed anything yet. The asset transfer isn't official without my signature."

My thoughts raced a mile a minute. Once I had reordered them, I asked, carefully, "And when you do, you'll transfer half of that to Jesse, won't you? Kind of like what you did with Bea Coventry's fortune, except this time you'll keep some."

She didn't respond verbally. Instead, she nodded and furiously rubbed the twisted paper together, like she was trying to turn it into dust.

"Sofija, did Jesse ask you to give him half of your share?"

Her bright green eyes widened and met mine. "What? No! No, he didn't ask me. I offered. Why would you think that?!"

"My mistake," I placated. "So you offered. You're dating him, aren't you Sofija?"

My instincts, plus the possessive tug around the waist that Jesse had given Sofija just minutes ago, meant I already knew the answer. All the same, I held my breath and prepared for the stomach acidifying impact of hearing her confirm it.

"I am, I think." She wet her lips. "Yes. I am. We are dating," she said with a little more confidence, straightening up. "We were going to tell Sandra, but she died before we could."

Something about that set alarm bells off. "How long before Mrs. Armitage's death had you two been seeing each other?"

Sofija's olive skin flushed so deeply that it was obvious even in the dim light. "Well, when Sandra got sicker about a year ago, Adam and Jesse came by more and more—and so did I. Sometimes, I even stayed the night. I started running into the brothers more frequently. Adam always intimidated me...he gives off a grumpy giant vibe."

A bark of laughter escaped me in spite of myself. I coughed to cover it up. "Sorry. Please continue."

"Jesse, on the other hand, was really friendly. Pretty soon I was nursing—no pun intended—a crush on him. From what little I knew of him, though, he was a serial dater who went out with PixABoo influencers and models in their early twenties. I didn't think I had a chance with him, and I definitely didn't think that he would ever want anything more than a fling."

"Seems like you were wrong about that," I said. "Why do you think Jesse's behavior changed like that when it did, around the time that his mother became ill?"

Sofija crossed her arms and replied testily, "I don't know. Maybe his mother dying put things in perspective."

She's closing up. Time to turn up the charm.

"Or maybe he realized that he loves endearingly cheesy nursing puns," I said with a smile.

Sofija's scowl dissipated and her hunched shoulders went slack. "Maybe so. I *am* the queen of those. Anyways, my crush turned into something deeper the more we talked. I started to really care about him. We spent a lot of time out on the grounds here. I was still too hesitant to make a move, though. Normally, I would—but he was the son of one of my patients. I thought it would be inappropriate."

"So he initiated the relationship?" I asked.

"I guess you could say that. One night, after Sandra was in bed, he asked if I wanted to stay and play pool. I was off duty, so I said sure. I thought that's really what he wanted, since we'd played before. Once we were in the pool room, though, we—he wanted—" she faltered and blushed.

"I understand," I said quickly. I did not want to hear about her first hookup with Jesse. With anybody, really.

"Right. So that was about four months ago. I wanted to tell Sandra, but Jesse wanted to keep it a secret. At least, from her and Adam. He was fine introducing me as his girlfriend to his friends."

"That's a little strange. Do you have any idea why he wouldn't want Mrs. Armitage or Adam to know?"

Again, Sofija looked down. "Yeah. He wanted to get his company better established first."

"And how exactly does that impact his relationship with you?" I probed.

"Jesse thought that if he could show Sandra that he was taking life seriously, running a functioning business, she would believe that he could be serious with me too." Sofija sounded almost defensive. "Like I said, he was kind of…untethered for a while, and he was worried that was how Sandra still saw him. Maybe *someone* was encouraging her in that view."

Sofija's emphasis on *someone* stood out. I suspected that person was Adam, but I would need to do some digging. In the meantime, I decided to press a little further, unearth any underlying sore spots. That meant switching tactics to something a little more underhanded, something I wouldn't feel fully comfortable trying in front of Cantrell.

I stretched, using the opportunity to turn and look directly at Sofija. Parting my mouth just a little, I adopted an entranced expression. It took embarrassingly little acting, but I didn't dwell on the fact.

Sofija met my gaze. Her pupils dilated and she bit her lower lip, looking almost alarmed, like she couldn't quite believe her own response. I shook my head, looked away, and swallowed, as if I were struggling to control a powerful impulse.

"I still think that's just a little strange," I murmured half an octave lower than normal.

"What is?" Tension reverberated through Sofija's voice, clear as a bell on a cold day.

"That someone could date you and hide it."

"What do you mean?"

I turned slowly to look at her again. "You're well-educated, caring, beautiful, good with the elderly," I enumerated. "Pretty much everything that parents want to see in their child's partner. If someone brings a woman like you home, it's pretty obvious that it's serious, no? I bet Mrs. Armitage would have known that and would have been thrilled for Jesse."

My words had the intended effect, but it still hurt me to watch them hit home. Sofija's face crumpled, her full lips quivering, viridescent eyes spilling tears. Voice wavering, she said, "I *always* wanted Sandra to know. She said I was like the daughter she never had, and I thought it would make her so happy to know that I care for her son. That I believe in him. But now it's too late. We'll never see her again."

She cried and clumsily swiped at her damp cheeks with the back of her hand. I felt an overpowering urge to dry them myself, to rub her back, to comfort her, but I knew that I couldn't. Instead, I extended a pack of tissues to her. Sniffling, she accepted one and added, "I think the other thing that hurts is that Jesse has come around on that. After Sandra died, he had a complete change of heart about Adam knowing. I wish he'd gotten to that point sooner, when Sandra was alive."

I was trying to work out the implications of what Sofija had just said when Jesse and Adam burst out of the room where they'd been arguing and walked over to us.

Jesse took one look at Sofija's tear-stained face and accused, "You made her cry? What the hell is wrong with you? Come here, Sofi," he commanded. She complied, and he curled his arms around her and buried his nose in her curls as she leaned her head against his chest.

"I'm sorry," I said honestly.

I couldn't say more than that, which was a good thing. The apology script that was running through my head would have been wildly inappropriate, even if I hadn't been investigating her.

Sofija, I'm so sorry. I want to kiss away your tears, on your cheek, down your neck to your collarbone where the drops merge and spill into the valley between your breasts. I'll kiss you until the only wetness on your skin is from my mouth.

I blinked hard and gritted my teeth, frustrated at my wildly inappropriate and undisciplined stream of consciousness. Brushing my pant legs for nonexistent wrinkles, I stood up. "Who's up first?"

"I'll go," Ms. McDonnell's voice came from down the hall. "Let the three of them eat lunch."

"I'll have to take lunch to go," Adam said.

Ms. McDonnell nodded and said, "I'll pack it up for you now and leave it in the dining room. As for you, Agent Velasquez, I'll meet you in the library in five minutes. It's the third door on the right," she said, indicating it with a thumb jerk over her shoulder. Pivoting neatly, she walked off.

I furrowed my brow at Adam who replied to my unanswered question unapologetically. "I'm going to be late for a meeting if I don't leave."

"When is the next time you'll be free?"

Adam opened his phone and scrolled. "I should be home with my husband, Xiaoming, tonight at 7:30 p.m. The next week and a half after that, I'll be in San Francisco for some business meetings. I'll be back not this Wednesday, but the next."

I keep later nights at this job than I did as a lawyer. Resigned, I said, "No problem. I'll come by tonight then. Here's the number you can reach me at, if you get delayed." I held out the card with my work number.

Adam pocketed it without a glance. He said, "I'll tell Xiao to let you in if I'm running late." With that, he took off toward the kitchen.

It's like herding cats. Stifling an exasperated sigh, I turned back to face Sofija and Jesse. The sadness still apparent on Sofija's face shot a pang of guilt through me.

"As for you, Jesse, I'll speak with Ms. McDonnell, Roland, and—what's the other maid's name?" I asked.

"Marly," Sofija quickly supplied as Jesse shrugged.

"Marly—thanks. I'll speak with those three while you two eat. Jesse, once you're done, please come to the library."

Jesse gave a lazy nod and a disinterested-sounding "Mmm" as a response.

Entitled ass. I knew his kind, or what I suspected was his kind. I had seen plenty of legacy students in law school, flush with old money and connections. Some were truly gifted and had every right to be there. Others

61

acted indifferent to everything, especially when they knew they would go straight to work at their mother or father's big law firms upon graduation, free of student debt. They had nothing but the world ahead of them and a cadre of people to help them shape it to their liking.

"Agent Velasquez?" Sofija said. My attention shifted to her. "If you're done questioning me for the day, I'd really like to go home directly after lunch. I'm pretty tired."

"Of course, get some rest. Thank you for your cooperation today. We have more questions for you, but we will get in touch later. Just keep your phone handy."

She rolled her eyes and gave a faint smile. "Yeah, yeah, and I won't skip town either."

I grinned, not because it was especially funny, but because I was relieved to see that she wasn't too melancholy to joke. "Much appreciated. Enjoy your lunch," I said as I walked off toward the library door.

Many great FBI field agents—or great detectives, for that matter—have a sense about slices of reality that are unseen to them, the things that unfold that they don't witness. It's as if they tap into the cosmic fabric and feel when the strings of matter and emotion are pulled, stretched, bunched, and twisted. That tangled web vibrates, and they feel it and zone in on the origin.

I didn't have this ability the same way my sister Rita had it. She could practically fool people into thinking she was clairvoyant. I wasn't totally convinced that she wasn't.

But I did have a smattering of the gift, enough to know that there was a single pair of eyes boring into my back as I walked toward the library.

Chapter 7

Sofija

Walking through the door into my apartment had never filled me with so much relief. I shucked off my shoes and collapsed on my couch. It was a little threadbare and very lumpy, but right now, it felt like a bed of clouds.

Today had been unexpectedly draining, and that was saying something, because I knew what tired was.

Nursing was often exhausting. Unappreciative relatives would occasionally blame their loved ones' deterioration on me and my inability to perform biology-defying medical miracles. I tried not to internalize it. But when expectations rose only to be shattered—that's when I bore the brunt of their worst anger, and it always hurt. It always sucked the energy right out of me.

Even my sickest patients would have good days from time to time. Their minds would emerge from the oppressive fog of Alzheimer's and their muscles would cooperate long enough to move them from room to room unassisted. Fate could be a bitch, though, and sometimes the next day or week the same patients would once again be lost or immobile. Then their families, hurt and confused by the capriciousness of disease and aging, would order me to "do something," even though I was doing everything.

When that happened, I would stare pleadingly at my patients, silently, irrationally hoping that they would try harder. I would do this even though I knew that faltering synapses, unraveling myelin, atrophying muscles, and glitching proteostasis were not things they could just be willed away.

And then it would start. A family member would make a snide remark about paying me money just to see no improvement. Another would question my competence and say something along the lines of, "This is why we should have gotten a doctor." Once, a patient's son publicly berated me in the parking lot of an assisted living facility. I stood there, humiliated, while the elderly residents and the tired staff stared on.

I knew these were normal reactions for family members who had to watch someone they loved slip away slowly, sometimes in excruciating pain.

It's mortality they hate, not you, Sofija, I would repeat. I would try to remind myself that I had felt the same irrational anger when the oncologist couldn't save my mother from cancer. All of this, I knew it was part of the job when I signed up to be a healthcare worker.

But on rare occasions, when families said something especially cruel—like accusing me of caring about the money but not about my patients—well, then I didn't just resent them. I resented the patient too, wrong as it was. I wished beyond logic that their sick body would heal itself, not only for their family's sake and their own, but also so that I could catch a break from the constant stream of blame.

When these emotions overwhelmed me, I felt like a shit nurse. The guilt was an acid that ate away at my insides.

After one particularly rough day, I had called my brother to talk about the problem. I was worried, I had confided, that I was unfit to work in healthcare. He had laughed and told me that at some point, everyone in the medical field felt flashes of resentment toward patients and families. Hell, he was only halfway through residency and he'd already experienced it a few times, he had reassured me with his good-natured patience. The important point was making sure it didn't impact the quality of care I gave, but he knew that I would never let it do that. He always sounded so confident.

Intellectually, I knew that was the truth. I took excellent care of my patients *and* I cared about them. I even came to love some of them, like Sandra. When they died, or worse, when they slipped so far down into the layers of their shrinking gray matter that they no longer recognized me, it tore me up.

I was a good nurse—a great nurse. I loved what I did.

Still, it was tiring.

What I felt in this moment was even worse. It was more than just my hurt and outrage at being suspected of elder abuse. It went beyond my fear of how this could impact my career if my patients or prospective nurse practitioner schools caught wind of the controversy.

It was the loneliness of enduring it by myself. I missed Sandra so much. With this accusation hanging over me, I wanted a mother to comfort me and tell me that I would make it through. Sandra had become like a mother to me.

But she was gone, and I couldn't talk to my dad about something like this. Most days, he was already tired and sad. As for my brother, I didn't want to drop this on him while he was busy with residency, on the cusp of realizing his dream career. The last thing he needed was to have to comfort his older sister, a nurse accused of conning her patients. I had considered talking it out with friends, especially my best friend, Keiko. In the end, I couldn't bring myself to do it. I was too ashamed. What if she doubted me? Besides, picking up the phone and explaining the situation seemed like it would require a Herculean effort, and right now, nothing about me felt Olympian.

Then there was this small, nagging thought. It tugged insistently at my consciousness as I tried to ignore it. In the end, I couldn't, so I finally acknowledged it: I was upset that Velasquez didn't seem to be totally convinced that I was innocent. He had still questioned me like a suspect today—to the point of tears.

He was doing his job. I knew that, but I still felt awful. Deep inside, I felt an insuppressible need for Velasquez to think well of me.

I didn't want to examine why. It made me feel guilty, being so drawn to someone while I was already with Jesse. The only thing that assuaged the guilt was knowing that Velasquez, being actively involved in investigating me, was so off-limits and unattainable that he might as well have been a fictional character.

There was probably no harm in having a sort of celebrity crush—-as long as I never actively fed it.

Lost in my own worries and reassurances, I barely registered the push notification that sent a little chime ringing through the air.

It was a story from the local paper. As I took in the headline, I felt an unpleasant electricity thrum through my body. Little white dots speckled my vision.

Local Nurse Twice Accused of Elder Abuse.

I sat in stunned silence, in so much shock that nothing seemed real. It felt like I might be in a simulation.

After who knew how long, my surroundings came into sharper focus. My eyes landed on my phone, which must have clattered onto the table in front of me.

Dreading what I would see, I looked at the screen again. The same slanderous words blared across it. I could feel my vision starting to narrow, the telltale sign of the rare but terrifying stress-induced syncope that I suffered from. I shook my head and sat up straight.

Stay awake, Sofija, and get someone over here now.

Speed dialing Jesse's number, I prayed he would pick up. After a couple of rings, he did.

Rather loudly, he greeted, "Hi baby, did you just make it home? What's up?"

The voice that answered didn't sound like my own. "Jesse, someone leaked the story to the local paper. It's—it's going to be everywhere."

Immediately, Jesse soothed, "Oh, Sofi, I'm so sorry. I'll come straight over, and I'll bring some leftovers so you don't have to cook for the next few days. Let me take care of you, baby."

"Thanks, Jesse," I sobbed, voice cracking on his name as I hung up.

Not five minutes later, my phone's loud ringing shattered the silence in my apartment. I glanced down. It was an unknown number. I almost considered ignoring it. I wasn't in the mood to deal with telemarketers or scammers.

But something like intuition pushed me to pick up. "Hello?"

"Sofija, hi, how are you?" came Velasquez's rushed but unmistakable voice.

"Well, if you've seen the news…" I trailed off.

"I have."

"Then you can guess," I said wryly.

"I'm very sorry you're distressed," he said, sounding genuinely sympathetic. He cleared his throat, and something in his tone changed as he recited impersonal advice about how to contact local law enforcement if at any point I felt like the press was harassing me.

It disappointed me, the sudden detachment. I felt the urge to ask, "And what would you do for me, Agent Velasquez, if I called you and asked for help?"

Instead, I simply said, "Thanks."

He then informed me that he and Cantrell would need to speak with me again, given certain details that had come to light during the interviews with Jesse and the staff of the Armitage estate.

I told him that I was too tired tonight, and that tomorrow was a packed workday for me. I suggested a compromise; I would take the train to my first patient, and then he and Cantrell would pick me up from there and drive me to my second patient. They could ask me whatever questions they had during the ride.

Velasquez agreed, so I instructed, "Meet me at the Rosegrove Residences in Worcester. You know where that is?"

"In Worcester? As in, Worcester, Massachusetts?" he asked, his shock clear even over the phone.

Pursing my lips, I replied, "Agent Velasquez, contrary to what you and your partner think, I don't only work for wealthy divorcees and widows. Grifting people isn't actually my source of income. Caring for them is."

He assured me that he didn't mean to imply that and apologized profusely. I accepted, and we agreed that he and Cantrell would pick me up from Rosegrove Residences at 1:30 p.m.

Our conversation had come to a natural conclusion, but suddenly, I was terrified of being alone with my thoughts. I wanted to keep him on the phone just a little longer, so I feebly joked, "You know, if it means I get to skip the train and have the FBI chauffeur me to work, maybe I should make myself a person of interest more often."

There was a pause, before he replied breezily, "Better to not make a habit of it."

That's what you get for making lame jokes.

Embarrassed, I mumbled, "You're right, better not. Driving's bad for the environment, anyways. Bye, Agent Velasquez."

I hung up the phone and stared around, the silence crushing me. While I waited for Jesse, I knew I needed to distract myself.

First, I did a HIIT workout, which took a little of the edge off, but not enough to really relax. Then, I showered and did my nails in a calming seafoam color. When that didn't work either, I tried painting on the little wooden easel that my father had built for me years ago. Too late, I realized that my nails were still wet, and that I had smudged them while wiping my fingers on my apron. Frustrated, I walked back to the bathroom and scrubbed away the ruined coating. The stringent acetone smell infused the humid shower air, stinging my eyes.

Defeated, I nestled under a blanket on my couch, fired up my laptop, and logged onto my brother's

Streamii account. I put on something mindless and opened the top drawer of the tiny side table.

The scent of cinnamon wafted up to me, and I felt a little calmer. My mom had taught me to chew on cinnamon sticks when I was stressed. Her father, my *Nannu*, had smoked his entire life, and mom had wanted to make sure I wouldn't pick up the habit.

Some of the clearest memories of Nannu that I had were of him hacking up a lung every morning when I would bring him his coffee. He would wheeze out a "*Grazzi, ghaziz*"—thank you darling. "*Mhux problema, Nannu*," I would reply. Then I would sit next to him and wait until the coffee had warmed up his raw throat enough to talk to me. I would listen with rapt attention as he told me stories about his life in Malta. When he ran low on coffee, I would refill it, and when his stomach grumbled, I would grab him some *pastizzi*. I had loved taking care of him.

One day, Nannu had been coughing so much that he couldn't talk—the coffee hadn't helped. My mom must have heard, because she had come in with a steaming cup of hot water with lemon and honey for him. Then she had dragged me to the kitchen and had placed a jar in front of me.

"Sofija, you don't want to end up like Nannu, right?"

I had shaken my head forcefully. "No, mama. I like my voice."

She had given me a relieved smile. "That's right. When you get stressed, Sofija, go run outside, play soccer with your friends, read, paint. But if someday that isn't enough and you're still upset, take a cinnamon stick, a good long one, like one of these." She had lifted the lid to show me what looked a bit like a bouquet of the brown, aromatic sticks. "Suck on it or chew on it. Never pick up a cigarette. Do you understand?"

"Yes, mama," I had replied.

"Good girl. You, me, and your Nannu, we're anxious people, but that doesn't mean we all have to be smokers."

The memory comforted me now as I grabbed a stick from the little uncovered box that I kept in the couch side table drawer. I rolled it between my fingers before biting down on it, just enough to barely break the fibers of the bark and release the flavor. A spicy sweetness hit my tongue, and I laid back and took imaginary puffs from the stick.

I watched the show playing on my laptop with glazed over eyes. It was raunchy and action packed— perfect for distracting my mind from the horrible headline.

The lead actor looked familiar. I vaguely remembered seeing an interview with him in which he said that his grandmother was Nahua. But there was some other reason he was striking such a chord with me.

Suddenly, it hit me: the actor had the same amber eyes that Velasquez did, the same thick, straight, jet black hair. It explained the strange pull I felt in my stomach as I watched the actor approach the lead actress and snake one arm around her, using his free hand to push her hair away and kiss her neck.

Heat crept up me, from my lower back to my cheeks. I felt tight and somehow *achy*.

Just then, the doorbell rang.

"It's me, babe," came Jesse's voice.

I slammed my laptop shut and ran over to the door.

When I opened it, Jesse set a large, covered aluminum tray on the ground and swept me up in a hug.

"Baby, I'm so sorry. How are you holding up?" He pulled away to study my face, concern etched on his own.

"Better now," I said. "Thanks so much for coming over and bringing food."

"Anything for my girl. Let's get this tray into the fridge and then we can talk."

Nodding, I opened the door widely enough to accommodate him and the giant tray of food. While he put it in the fridge, I settled back on the couch and waited.

Because Jesse had insisted on keeping our relationship a secret from his mother and brother for so long, we had spent a lot of time in my apartment. I knew it wasn't as high-end as the things he was used to, but he didn't make me feel bad about it—never on purpose, at least. Occasionally, I would see him grimace as he looked at my couch, or play off his disappointment when he asked for a specific food or drink and I only had the cheap brand.

All of this was playing through my head as he rummaged around in the fridge.

"Want anything to drink?" he offered.

"No, I'm fine."

"Do you have any kombucha in here? Honeyflower or HealthSpring?"

"Sorry, no. I have my homemade stuff though. There's some ginger-orange—I know you like that combination. You should try it! I'm really good at brewing," I suggested hopefully.

"I'm okay, thanks though, babe. I'll leave the special

stuff for you. I'm just going to have a beer."

I felt a twinge of disappointment. As he walked toward me, beer in hand, I blurted out, "Jesse, would you still be with me if I didn't have your mother's money coming in? Or, if I did, but I didn't plan on sharing it with you?"

Jesse laughed and rumpled my hair. "Of course I'd still be with you. You'd just have to be the one who pays on our dates."

Relief flooded through me. *You were silly to doubt him, Sofija.* "Thanks, Jesse," I whispered, burying my head in the space between his head and shoulder.

"Sofi, never doubt how I feel about you." He pressed a kiss into my curls, and I finally felt myself start to relax.

Out of nowhere, a crash sounded from off to our left. I started, hitting my head on Jesse's chin.

"Sorry!" I squeaked as I hopped up and ran to the source of the sound.

The left windowpane was shattered, glass scattered around a brick that had a note attached to it. Poking my head out the window, I looked from side to side. There was nobody in sight, so I came back and crouched down by the brick.

Jesse hovered above me. "Don't touch that, Sofija," he instructed. He jogged off to the kitchen and came back with my rubber dishwashing gloves.

"Do you want me to read the note?" he offered.

I gulped and shook my head. "This was clearly intended for me, so I'll do it." I took the gloves from him and slipped them on.

Carefully, I untied the string affixing the letter to the brick. With trembling hands, I unfolded it.

What I saw was like something from a detective

novella. Letters of different fonts, sizes, and colors had been pasted onto the paper in uneven lines. Some were glossy, like they were cut from a magazine, and some were matte, maybe taken from a newspaper. Together, they spelled out an ominous message:

STAY AWAY FROM OUR GRANDPARENTS, BITCH.

"What does it say?" Jesse asked from behind me.

I walked over to the couch and collapsed, letting the letter flutter down beside me. "See for yourself," I said.

Jesse's brow furrowed as he scanned the letter. "What does that even mean?"

I shrugged listlessly. Worrying about this, on top of everything else that was happening—it was too much. "Who knows? It's probably just some asshole teen who thought it'd be a funny prank."

"Maybe," Jesse said. "Hey, Sofi...you and your family aren't secretly part of the mafia, are you?" he teased in an obvious attempt to cheer me up.

Glaring, I playfully swatted him on the shoulder, though I was grateful that he was trying to lighten the mood. "That's Sicily, not Malta. Also, that's racist."

Jesse scooped me up, twisting and then sitting so that I was on his lap. "*Mi dispiace.*"

Rolling my eyes, I kissed his cheek. "Italian, but close enough."

"Really?"

I laughed. "No, but it's the thought that counts."

Jesse's expression turned serious. He said, "Sofija, you should report this to the police. Maybe to those FBI agents."

I gnawed on my lower lip. "I just don't have the emotional bandwidth to talk to the police right now. I'll file a report tomorrow. And why would I call the FBI? Do you think this has something to do with your mom's inheritance?"

"Who knows? But I can't think of any other reason, can you? Especially now that the story is in the news."

"That would be super fast work. Like, the story breaks two hours ago and someone is already harassing me? Also, why? What could they hope to gain from it?"

Jesse shifted beneath me. "Like you said, it's probably some shithead teenager who thought it would be a cool thing to brag about doing. But as long as you're living in this bad area in an old apartment, you should be on your guard. Just in case."

It was a little insulting, but it was reasonable advice. "You're probably right," I agreed.

"And Sofija?" he said hesitantly.

"Yeah?"

"I do think you should hurry up and finalize things. Just sign for the inheritance already. It's what my mother wanted."

Stiffening, I said, "I don't see how that will stop shithead teenagers from harassing me."

Stroking my hair, Jesse said, "You'd be rich enough to move somewhere with better security and more privacy. Or into the estate. Nobody would bother you there—it's gated. Just be done with the whole thing and move on. People will talk, and then they'll forget it all when something more scandalous makes the news."

Sighing, I said, "I see your point. Look, I don't plan on delaying it forever, but if I finalize the inheritance before the FBI publicly clears me of suspicion, I can kiss my credibility goodbye. My patients' families, the admissions boards at prospective schools, they'll all be convinced that I grifted your mom. At least for now, since I haven't actually accepted any money, some people might give me the benefit of the doubt. Plus..." I trailed off.

"Plus what?" he asked gently.

"To be honest, there's an irrational part of me that is scared to finalize it because when I do, Sandra will really be *gone*. The most substantial thing I'll have left of her is her money. It's going to feel so...so real. So irreversible. I know this sounds ridiculous. Also, I'm sorry that I'm crying to you about it. I mean, she was *your* mother, not mine." My eyes were misting up.

Jesse wiped my tears with the soft pad of his thumb. "It's more touching than anything, Sofi. I love that you loved my mom. But that's not a good reason to put the future she wanted for you on hold."

I sniffed and nodded. "I know. But even the logistics of the whole thing are intimidating. I'm in way over my head."

"What do you mean?"

"I need to make sure I handle it right. I've got to research good lawyers and tax advisors and then at least do a free consultation with a few of them before I sign all the documents. I don't want to rush over the details and have this bite me in the ass later on."

Jesse gave me a wolfish grin and nipped at my jaw. "I'll be the only thing to bite you, on the ass or anywhere else. Don't worry Sofi, nothing will go wrong. I won't let it."

I really wanted to believe him, and pretty soon, he had kissed away most of my doubts.

Most of them.

Chapter 8

Mateo

Unfortunately, the interview with Roland didn't yield much useful information. He seemed to know little of the goings on at the Armitage estate beyond people's food preferences. About that, he was talkative.

"Adam loves spicy things. I try to work with the Szechuan and Andhra Pradesh spice palates for him. Jesse is a tricky one, because he likes to keep fit and goes through those 'clean eating' phases," Roland said disdainfully, making air quotes and rolling his eyes. "But the man really likes sweet things too. With him, there are weeks where it's all smoothies and salads and then a week when it's burgers and milkshakes. Really unsophisticated palate, if you ask me." He blanched, his eyebrows shooting up toward his receding hairline. "Don't tell him I said that."

I waved off the comment with my hand. "You don't have to worry about that. This is confidential."

Roland looked relieved, and launched back into his recitation. "Now Mrs. Armitage had quite a nice appreciation for food, if you ask me. She liked Continental cuisine, like—"

"Mr. Courville," I gently interrupted. "I'm sorry, but I was hoping for more information about the dynamics of the people here. Can you tell me anything about that?"

"Oh." Roland frowned, looking disappointed. He unscrewed the top off a metal water bottle and emptied it in several huge gulps, not breaking to take a breath. When he was done, he swiped the back of his hand across his mouth. "Sorry," he wheezed out. "I've been thirsty as a fish the last few days."

"No problem. You were saying?"

"Right. Look, sir, I spend most of my time in the kitchen, and if not there, reading on the porch just outside the kitchen door. I'm not so up-to-date on family dynamics. Not like Frannie is, at least."

"Anything you can share would be useful," I practically begged. The results of this day were not shaping up to be the type that would impress Cantrell.

"Well," Roland said slowly, just as I was ready to give up. "Obviously, the boys do argue about what to eat all the time now. Sometimes, I end up having to cook two separate meals. It's really increased my workload," he complained.

I cocked my head. "It wasn't always like that?"

Roland shook his head. "Jesse didn't use to spend much time here. Adam has always had a crazy schedule, what with that company of his. But he always managed to stop by the house for dinner one night a week to eat with his mother. It's been that way for years now."

"And Jesse?" I prompted.

The chair Roland was sitting in creaked a little as he leaned back. "Jesse," he mused, "would pop in about twice a year, for a couple weeks at a time. Then he'd be off."

"How was he with his mother?"

Roland shrugged. "Can't say that I saw them together too much, but from the glimpses I got, he seemed like a good son. Doting, polite, that kind of thing."

"How was Mrs. Armitage with him?"

The chef gave me a blank stare. "I don't know. Motherly?"

Sighing, I pressed pause on the recording device and clicked my pen closed, placing it carefully on the blank part of my paper pad so as not to smear any ink. "Thank you for your time, Mr. Courville. This has been helpful," I lied.

Heaving himself up, he said, "Glad you thought so."

He was almost to the library door when, seized by an impulse, I called out, "Mr. Courville!"

Swiveling to face me, he said, with a note of impatience, "Yes?"

I swallowed and asked what I knew was unnecessary. "What does Sofija like to eat? I mean, when she started staying nights here, were her tastes easy to accommodate, what with you already balancing the preferences of the two brothers and Mrs. Armitage? Or was that a source of tension?" I tacked on the last two questions quickly, trying to cover my interest with the veneer of thorough investigative work.

Roland's eyes lit up and he beamed. "Well, Sofija isn't picky. She'd always eat whatever I made for the rest of the house and never complained. But on her birthday last year, I asked her what she wanted, if she could have any dish in the world. You wouldn't believe what she picked..." he trailed off. I could tell he was trying to build suspense.

It was working; I was champing at the bit. "Yes?" I asked eagerly.

"*Ftira!*" Roland said with a bemused chuckle, as if

it were inconceivable that someone would ask for that on a birthday.

I looked at him, nonplussed. "What is that?"

"Maltese bread baked into a ring shape. You slice it up and stuff it with tomato, tuna, onion, capers, olives…ingredients like that. Really, it's just a simple sandwich with a funny name."

"A sandwich? For her birthday? That *is* an unusual choice," I agreed.

Who are you, Sofija?

"I told her, I said, 'Sofija, I can make you something fancier, like that braised rabbit that's so popular in Malta.' But she just smiled and she said, 'My mom used to make *ftira* sandwiches, and they remind me of her. I always try to recreate them, but I just can't get the breadmaking part of it right. Show me how to do it, and that will be the best birthday meal,' " Roland finished. He looked at me expectantly.

I wondered what kind of reaction he expected. In truth, it was so touching that I felt a kind of pressure in my chest, as well as an overwhelming urge to call my own mother. I should tell her again how much I appreciated the homemade *conchas* she sent me off with every time I drove over to see her.

"Anyways, if that's all, I've got to prep food for tomorrow," Roland said, calling me back to the present.

"Of course. Thank you for your help. Send in Marly, please."

Roland yanked open the old wooden library door and hollered, "Marly! The FBI needs you."

A tall redhead in her mid-twenties appeared in the doorframe and gracefully ducked under Roland's outstretched arm while he held the door for her. When she reached the old chair, she almost seemed to flutter down onto it.

She smoothed her floral print dress and said, "My name's Marly. I'm a maid here. What would you like to know?"

"Hello Marly, I'm Agent Velasquez. To start with, you could describe for me what you do here, as well as your relationships to everyone—including the late Mrs. Armitage. Then I'll ask you a few questions about the dynamics between people here. Easy stuff," I said conversationally.

"That's it?" She sounded unimpressed. "We couldn't have done that over the phone?"

I leaned forward and poised my pen over my notepad. "These things typically work better in person."

"Well, you're the one with the badge," Marly said. "I took this job as a way to save up enough money to open my own sustainable fashion company. Mrs. Armitage let me live here for free—meals included—and paid me a decent salary. I was saving a lot. A year more of this and I'll only have to take out a loan for about ten thousand to produce my first round of inventory. Mrs. Armitage, she was generous."

"Sounds like it," I agreed. "And would you say she was generous with the other employees?"

Marly pursed her lips then replied, "To the best of my knowledge. I mean, I know she was good to the staff. We all feel that way." Her face twisted into a wry smirk before she added, "I'm sure Sofija more than most."

"Do you see that as unfair, or undeserved?"

Marly examined her cuticles, seeming to formulate a careful answer. Eventually, she said, "I don't think any of us would deny that Sofija was there for Mrs. Armitage in a way that nobody else was, not even her kids. She gave Mrs. Armitage her meds, sat with her for hours talking and playing cards, walked with her and then eventually pushed her in her wheelchair around the grounds. Sometimes I'd walk by the library and hear Sofija reading to her. Toward the end, Sofija even gave her sponge baths and changed her bedpan. I can see why Mrs. Armitage liked—I guess, loved—Sofija. Still, though."

"Still, though?" I pressed.

Marly gave me a knowing look. "I can understand that Mrs. Armitage wanted to take care of Sofija. Leave her enough for school or something, you know? But seventy-five percent of her inheritance? That's absurd. I understand why Adam is pissed."

"Was Mrs. Armitage not generous to her sons?"

Marly slowly shook her head. "I wouldn't say that. Mrs. Armitage gave Adam the money he needed to get his company off the ground, though it's doing great now. I think this past year it even turned a profit, and that's on top of all the new investor money. Mrs. Armitage did the same for Jesse—multiple times. She gave him most of the capital that he used in his various startups. None of them have been as successful as Adam's company, though."

"Current will and asset division aside, do you think that during her life, Mrs. Armitage gave more to Jesse than to Adam?"

Nodding vigorously, Marly answered, "Oh, definitely. Especially if you factor in the money that Jesse lost on all those botched repairs and maintenance jobs."

At this, I leaned in. "I thought it was just the

driveway?"

A derisive scoff followed by a snort escaped Marly. She looked appalled and quickly apologized. "Sorry. If only it were just the driveway! Jesse has had spectacularly bad judgment when it comes to contractors. For the first two years I worked here, Jesse wasn't around much—maybe a few weeks at a time, twice a year. But when he came, he'd go on "fix-it" sprees. I can't even remember everything the people he's hired have screwed up, but Frannie would know."

I made a mental note to follow up with her about that. "I'll make sure to ask her. One more question for now."

"Sure."

"Do you have any idea why Sofija would share some of the inheritance with Jesse, but not Adam?"

Marly shrugged. "That'd be a question for Sofija. Maybe it's because she clearly has a thing for Jesse. Or maybe she thinks Adam's lifestyle won't be impacted one way or another. His company is worth billions. They say it's going to IPO soon."

"Interesting. Do you think Jesse's lifestyle would?"

"Would what?"

"Change drastically, if Sofija didn't plan to share."

Marly laughed. "Maybe Jesse would think it's a drastic change, but he'd still be doing just fine compared to you or me. He's got all kinds of stocks. Plus, he seems like the type to find a wealthy older woman to pay for him if things ever actually turned dire. Worst case, Jesse just won't have the capital to waste founding failing companies. He'll have to build something worthwhile and attract seed funding."

"You seem well-versed on Adam and Jesse's

business ventures," I commented.

Marly beamed. "Like I said, I want to start my own company, so I try to learn lessons wherever I can. I don't have an MBA, but the real world is full of lessons. I mean, Adam and Jesse are practically case studies of what to do and what not to do."

"Seems like you have the expertise to create something really special," I flattered. "Well, thank you so much for your time. Here's my card, in case anything else occurs to you. Would you mind letting Ms. McDonnell know that I'm ready for her?"

"Sure thing, I'll send her in now." With a swish of her dress, Marly whisked out of the room.

As I was standing up to stretch, Ms. McDonnell walked in.

"Ms. McDonnell, hello," I said, resuming my seat.

She held up a hand. "Please. Frannie is fine. I'm not thrilled that you're here, but it's no fault of your own, so let's be friendly."

I nodded. "So, Frannie, tell me a little about yourself. How long you've been here, how well you know the staff, the boys, Sofija."

Frannie launched into a detailed explanation that confirmed and added texture to what the others had said. I took diligent notes and thanked her.

"If that's all, I've got to get back to work," she said.

"Just one more thing. On the phone, you mentioned the driveway—thanks for that warning, by the way."

Nodding sympathetically, Frannie said, "Just awful, isn't it? We're planning to have it fixed in late June. Though I guess that'll be up to Sofija now."

"Awful might be an understatement. My eight-year-old niece Claudia could have done a better job with her

Play Clay," I said with a conspiratorial grin. Frannie smiled back, and I knew I was in. "I'm given to understand it's not the only time Jesse has had bad luck hiring for maintenance jobs."

"Oh, it's like a parade of idiots when he's in charge!" Frannie exclaimed. "In the last five years, we've had issues with the driveway, mold in the basement, maple tree fungus, bad wiring, and the roof. It's an old house. Every single contractor that Jesse has hired charged a criminal amount and did, at best, shoddy work. He's a good-hearted young man, but he can't pick a decent company—to invest in or to hire—to save his life. Hasn't got a shrewd business mind like his brother."

"Poor guy," I said with feigned sympathy. "It's like that with me and my sister. She's got all the math savvy. That was never my thing, so medicine and engineering were out. I became a lawyer. It was the most palatable alternative for my parents, though they weren't thrilled."

"Well, you can't be an idiot if you graduated from law school," Frannie comforted.

Chuckling, I said, "You'd be surprised, Frannie. There's no shortage of clowns in law school. You've seen some of the billboards we put up."

By now, Frannie was grinning, and I felt like we had more than a tenuous rapport. "By the way, Frannie, do you happen to have the receipts for those jobs that Jesse gave to contractors? Or at least the company names?"

"I could certainly get them. Why?" she asked, though she didn't sound suspicious. I took that as a win.

"Since we're already here investigating, we might as well look into these companies to make sure they're not ripping people off or violating standards. No company responsible for the driveway outside should be allowed to continue paving," I added jokingly for good measure.

Frannie nodded in agreement. "You're telling me. Sure, I can get them for you. Could I email them?"

"Of course. Let me give you my card," I said as I pulled one out and handed it to her. "Feel free to email or call if anything else that you think is worth sharing comes to you."

"That I will. And I'll get the receipts or name of those companies to you by tomorrow," she said.

"One more thing. You said there was another maid who worked here, one who quit shortly after Sandra died. Can you tell me her name?"

Frannie nodded. "To be honest, Agent Velasquez, I'm feeling guilty about badmouthing her earlier, seeing as it was Adam who called you all in. She's really a nice woman. Hard worker too. And she was more than a maid—for all intents and purposes, she was also a groundskeeper. Her name is Talia Portnoy."

I scrawled the name down and said, "Thank you so much for this and for your time, Frannie."

"My pleasure. Should I call in Jesse?"

"You read my mind."

"First time I've sat in a room with a lawyer and he hasn't charged me an arm and a leg after our talk," Frannie quipped, standing and walking toward the door.

Jesse was waiting on the other side as soon as it swung open.

Had he overheard us?

I was a little worried. I didn't want to tip Jesse off about any suspicions or nascent theories that I had.

Before I could get a word in, he said, "Agent Velasquez. Why don't we go across the hall? The library isn't my favorite place. It smells like moldy pages."

"Wherever you're most comfortable," I acquiesced. It was good practice to put interviewees in environments in which they were most likely to let their guard down.

Jesse led us across the hall and into what appeared to be a room built for billiards and cigar smoking, if the pool table and velvet jackets were anything to go by.

This place is a murder mystery game board come to life, I thought as I looked around.

"Do you play pool, Agent Velasquez?"

A Machiavellian idea occurred to me, a way to get Jesse to drop his cool exterior and say what he felt, unfiltered. "Not much at all, but I'm not a total novice," I lied. "I've enjoyed it, the few times I've played."

A grin that didn't quite reach his eyes crossed Jesse's face. "How about we play a round while you ask your questions?"

"That's not really how this is supposed to work," I said with feigned reluctance.

"You're one of those types who can't break a rule without permission from a higher up, aren't you? Guess that comes with working for the government. That's why I like being my own boss. Nobody tells me what to do," Jesse bragged. He stretched like a satiated cat across the pool table and began racking the balls. When he saw me watching, he smiled and said, "Well, go ahead. Ask away. I'm going to shoot a little while you do, but suit yourself."

"You know what? I'll take you up on your offer."

Jesse grabbed a cue and tossed it to me, followed closely by the chalk. I caught both neatly. "I'll be solid and you can break," I said.

He shot a clean shot. "What is it you want to ask,

Agent Velasquez?"

"I've heard that you were a bit of a globetrotter until about a year ago. Were you close with your mother, even though you spent so much time apart?"

Jesse looked sad. "I should have been closer to her. We had a good relationship when I would come back and visit, but that wasn't more than a couple times a year. She wasn't a fan of video chatting either. Looking back, I should have spent more time at home. I would have, if I had known how close the end was for her. For years, though, I wanted to get all of the traveling and partying out of my system before I settled down."

"You're not the first person to feel that way," I said, taking my turn. I made sure it was a little sloppy, so that what should have been an easy shot only barely fell into the pocket.

Jesse gave me a smirk. "Close one. What else?"

"Did your mother fund your companies?"

Screwing up his face in concentration, Jesse hit a perfect shot and sunk a striped ball. He straightened and said, "Yes. Honestly, I haven't had the best luck there. I'm feeling really good about my latest venture, though. I think we're on the cusp of something."

Slowly, I circled the table until I was where I wanted to be. It was a difficult shot, but I could potentially sink two balls. I made a point of lining up my cue and considering it, before shaking my head and opting for the simpler, single ball shot. I sank it.

"Nice job," Jesse said, a little condescendingly.

"Thanks. So—correct me if I'm wrong—but it's my understanding that your mother only left you with $250 a month. Why do you think that is?"

Jesse poked his tongue out of the side of his mouth

and lined up his cue. "If you ask me, she was under the impression that I'm irresponsible, and that cutting me out of the will would force me to make better decisions. Lead a more serious life, be a more serious businessman, that kind of thing. Maybe she thought she was doing me a favor. I was trying to show her that I had changed, but maybe someone was telling her that I hadn't. Who knows?" He took his shot. Two more striped balls rolled into the pockets.

"Do you have any idea who might have been giving her that impression?" I paused and leaned against the edge of the table.

Shrugging, Jesse said, "I have plenty of ideas, but they change every day. I have no way of knowing. Your turn, agent."

This time, I hit the trickiest shot I knew how, sinking two balls at near impossible angles. Jesse gaped at me, and I struck. "And Sofija is going to share her portion of the inheritance with you, correct?"

"She—that's what she's told me, but that's entirely her decision, so you'd have to ask her," Jesse deflected, clearly knocked off balance. There was an undercurrent of hostility in his voice now.

"And when and why did you start dating Sofija? How did it start?"

Jesse tossed his cue to his other hand and walked toward me, deliberately, quietly, like a hunter ready to spear a jungle cat in a tree.

"Why do you think, Agent Velasquez? You've met her. Would you need a lot of convincing to want a smart woman who looks like that and is good to your mom?"

"No," I admitted, figuring that honesty was the best option. Anything else would so obviously be a lie that it would be suspicious. "No, I suppose I wouldn't."

"Not to mention, Sofija is like nobody I've ever had before. The way she fusses over me. So pliant and willing. So grateful for it when I give—"

"This has veered into information that is no longer pertinent to the case, Mr. Armitage," I gritted out. *He knows exactly what he's doing. Maybe I was too transparent today in the foyer,* I silently fumed, all while keeping my face as unaffected as possible.

"Just trying to answer all of law enforcement's questions thoroughly," Jesse said with a shrug. "As for the how—I saw someone I wanted to be with, and I went after her. Sofija was only too willing to reciprocate."

I was focused on not betraying my emotions when Jesse's phone rang and he picked it up. "Hi Sofi, did you just make it home? You need me for something, baby?" he asked. His voice was worried, but there was a triumphant gleam in his eye as he stared at me. I looked away, but kept listening. The voice coming over the phone was clearly distraught.

"Oh, Sofi, I'm so sorry. I'll come straight over, and I'll bring some leftovers so you don't have to cook for the next few days. Let me take care of you, baby." Jesse hung up and turned to me. "That was Sofija. She has a problem, so I've got to go. Sorry to cut our game short."

"What's happening?" I asked with forced calmness.

Jesse shot me a disdainful look. "You're the federal investigator. Hop on the internet and search her name and you'll see it."

All right. Enough. I stood up straighter and looked Jesse dead in the eyes. "I can, and rest assured that I will—along with all other details that have been shared with me today that require fact checking"—at this, he seemed to purse his lips infinitesimally— "but right now, I'm asking you."

Jesse clenched his jaw and then typed something into his phone. He flipped it around and held it up to me.

Right on the landing page of the city's news outlet, the headline shouted its accusation in loud, unforgiving font:

Local Nurse Twice Accused of Elder Abuse

My stomach plummeted, in much the same way that I suspected Sofija's had when she first read the damning words.

"I have to call my partner. Please wait here," I instructed, standing up.

Jesse sprang up. "No, you stay and make your call. I've got to go see Sofija. We can pick this up later if you still have questions. Frannie or Marly will let you out." With that, he walked out of the room and closed the door rather forcefully.

Taking my phone out of my pocket, I prepared to call Cantrell when my phone rang. It was an unknown number.

"Hello?" I answered cautiously.

"Agent Velasquez," came Adam's booming voice. "It's a good thing you gave me your number after all. Something urgent came up, and I've got to get to San Francisco tonight. My plane leaves in less than half an hour—I'm already at the gate. We'll have to reschedule our interview for when I'm back. Should be not this Wednesday, but the one after. I can maybe take a call or two out West, but I'll be busy and my schedule won't be predictable."

Groaning internally, I replied, "This isn't ideal, Adam."

"Sorry. It is what it is," he said. He didn't sound very sorry at all.

Clearing my throat, I replied, "Fine. We'll be in contact as soon as you're back. Wednesday, did you say?"

"Yes. 11:30 a.m. EST."

"Thank you, Mr. Armitage."

"Speak to you then." He hung up the phone.

I took a steadying breath and called Cantrell. He picked up after two rings.

"Velasquez, I've been wondering why you haven't checked in yet. How's it coming?"

Gripping down on the cue stick I was still holding, I said, "It could be better and it could be worse."

"Like herding cats, isn't it?" Cantrell said with a sympathy that I hadn't expected.

"Something like that. I'll get it done though, and share what I have so far tomorrow at work. But Cantrell?"

"Yes?"

"Search Sofija Zammit's name."

I heard him mutter and curse to himself. I knew he was trying to navigate his phone to open the web browser app while staying on call with me. I smiled to myself. He was a great investigator, but a bit of a Luddite.

"Damn," came Cantrell's voice after a minute. "That's going to make this investigation a circus."

"Right? It's not great," I agreed.

"We need to talk to the Zammit girl as soon as possible. See how she's taking the news before she's had too much time to process it. See her raw reaction, you know?"

"Sure, if—if you think that's necessary," I faltered.

"Get that scheduled, and make it ASAP. We also need to press more on why she's sharing her seventy-five percent of the inheritance with Jesse and not with Adam."

"Got it. I'll set something up now."

"Good work, Velasquez. See you tomorrow."

Once Cantrell hung up, I stared at the phone. It felt like invisible arms belonging to the ghost of a previous maid or butler that haunted this ancient boys' club of a room were restraining me. Like they didn't want me to dial Sofija's number just to set up another round of questioning.

Forcing the thought out of my head, I called her. The phone rang and rang. Just when I was about to give up, the line picked up and an unsteady voice said, "Hello?"

"Sofija, hi, how are you?" I rushed.

"Well, if you've seen the news..."

"I have," I said apologetically.

"Then you can guess."

Her voice, so broken, made what I was about to do even harder. All I wanted was to comfort her, to tell her it would work out. I swallowed and struck a balance between that and what I knew I had to do.

"I'm very sorry you're distressed. I know the publicity must be unpleasant. If at any point reporters or other people start violating your privacy for an interview and make you feel threatened, you can inform local law enforcement." I rubbed my temple, hating how callous and detached my advice sounded.

"Thanks," she said softly.

"In the meantime, Cantrell and I have a few more questions to ask you. Just small things that have come up since we last spoke."

"Which was earlier today," she whined. "How long is it going to be like this?"

"I'm sorry, Sofija, I know it's tiring. But we do need to speak with you as soon as possible."

I heard her sigh loudly. "It's too late today. Tomorrow, I work from 9:30 a.m. to 6 p.m., but I'm at two different patients' residences. They're both on the orange line, so I take that. But if you and Cantrell want to pick me up from my first patient and drive me to my second, you can interview me during the car ride, I guess."

Quickly weighing the pros and cons, I decided that Cantrell would prefer a non-standard interview setting over a delay. "That's fine."

"Okay. Meet me at the Rosegrove Residences in Worcester. You know where that is?"

"In Worcester? As in, Worcester, Massachusetts?" I asked incredulously.

There was a pause before Sofija responded in a tight voice, "Agent Velasquez, contrary to what you and your partner think, I don't only work for wealthy divorcees and widows. Grifting people isn't actually my source of income. Caring for them is."

"Right, I'm sorry for how that sounded. I didn't mean to imply that," I stated calmly, professionally. *I want to believe you, Sofija. I think I do.*

"It's fine," she said tiredly. "I'll see you tomorrow. Come by around 1:30 p.m."

"We'll be there."

I thought that she would tell me goodbye, but instead, she said, "You know, if it means I get to skip the train and have the FBI chauffeur me to work, maybe I should make myself a person of interest more often."

Sofija's playfulness in the face of an investigation that was clearly hurtful was more than a little admirable to me. She was tough.

"Better to not make a habit of it," I said lightly. *I'd drive you anywhere, if I could. Wherever you wanted.*

"You're right, better not. Driving's bad for the environment, anyways. Bye, Agent Velasquez."

After she hung up, I shivered. The room was as cold as death, but I hadn't noticed until now.

Chapter 9

Sofija

My alarm pierced the cold apartment air with jarring clarity. Jesse shot up next to me, looking disconcerted, his normally perfect hair squished against the left side of his head. He looked vulnerable and endearing. It made me feel a little giddy.

"Sofi," he moaned. "I hate that thing."

I laughed and pushed against him to propel myself off the bed. "Some of us aren't our own bosses. I'll get coffee and toast started. Maybe that will lure you out of bed."

"What if I just stayed here all day?" he suggested, stretching on top of the sheets like a satisfied cat. "I brought my laptop. I could work from here and heat up the food when you're on your way home."

"If you want to do that, of course you can, Jesse. But I have to make a police report about the brick through my window, so you'll have to deal with cops if they come by today."

He wrinkled his nose and rose. Wrapping his arms around me, he kissed my neck and said, "Sorry, hard pass on that. I had the distinct pleasure of interacting with law enforcement yesterday, and I think once was enough."

"You mean yesterday, with Agent Velasquez? Come on, he's nice."

Jesse shot me an arch look and I blushed.

"He made you cry yesterday, Sofi."

I wracked my brain for a response. For some reason, I was willing to defend an FBI agent who I had met a grand total of two times. It didn't make sense, but it felt natural. Like instinct. Finally, I said, "Listen, Jesse, he didn't mean to do that. He just asked a sensitive question. Probably didn't even realize it would hurt me that way."

"What was it that he asked you?" Jesse asked sharply.

"Thought it was the FBI who was supposed to interrogate me, not you," I retorted.

Jesse breathed in slowly through his nostrils and looked at me. "You're right. I'm sorry. I just didn't like to see you upset."

He engulfed me in a hug. Slowly, the tension seeped out of me.

"It wasn't much of anything, Jesse," I finally managed. "He just asked why you wanted to keep our relationship a secret from your mother."

I felt Jesse stiffen. His arms tightened around me, like he was afraid I would pull away. "It's something I truly regret, Sofi," he said earnestly, brushing the curls out of my face. "But you explained to him why I did what I did, right?"

"Of course," I reassured.

"Good girl," Jesse whispered, his lips ghosting along my ear. I shivered and he gave me a knowing smirk. "I'll go put on the coffee and toast. You just focus on getting ready for work."

"Thank you," I said a little shakily. Jesse knew how to use words and little touches to tap into my hardwiring and short circuit me.

I walked into the bathroom and ran the hot water, soaping up a bar between my hands and gently rubbing circles with the foam over my face. After I rinsed it off, I put on my dual sunscreen moisturizer, brushed my hair and my teeth, and applied my makeup—with more care than usual, I realized, and I knew why.

It made me feel a little guilty. I wondered what kind of person could be drawn to two men at once, even if one was just fantasy. I fell into my habit of chanting mental reassurances to soothe my conscience.

So what if you're going to see Velasquez today? You put on makeup every day. So what if you put a little more effort into it today? It's just makeup. You always put on makeup for work.

Staring at myself in the mirror, I felt as though I still looked tired. Quickly, I applied a dab of concealer under my eyes and massaged it in until it seamlessly blended with my olive skin. On an impulse, I added a splash of cranberry colored lip gloss. Satisfied, I turned off the lights.

As I rounded the corner into the living room slash kitchen, I gave Jesse a big smile. He had set out a mug of black coffee for each of us, as well as a plate of toast topped with raspberry jam and fried halloumi cheese.

"Jesse!" I exclaimed, bounding up and kissing him. "You made me halloumi toast!"

He pulled me flush against him, his blue eyes sparkling. "You've only mentioned how much you love it on every food-related date we've ever been on. And you've turned me on to the stuff too—I can't get enough."

Happily, I sat down and took a huge bite. Crumbs stuck to my freshly glossed lips. Jesse picked up a napkin and wiped my mouth clean. I put a hand in front of my mouth and said, "S' really good."

He chuckled. "I see that. So, what are you doing today?" he asked casually as he sipped his coffee and munched on his toast.

"Well," I managed between mouthfuls. "I'm going to swing by the police office and file a report. After that, I'm taking the train over to Worcester for my first patient of the day. Then agents Velasquez and Cantrell are picking me up and driving me to my next patient because—"

"What?!" Jesse interjected. He looked stunned. "Why is the FBI driving you from patient to patient?"

I took a long swig of my coffee and cleared my throat. "I was told that they needed to question me again, as soon as possible. I said that I was too busy to come by the FBI office today, so if they really need to talk to me so soon, the only free time I have is when I'm in transit between patients."

"Well, at least it will be a short round of questioning," Jesse mused, seemingly more to himself than to me.

"I hope so." I polished off the rest of my breakfast and got ready to clear up the dishes. "Done with your toast, or still working on it?"

"Oh, I'm not that hungry. Ate a lot at the house yesterday. Roland knows what he's doing."

"He certainly does. I'll put yours in the fridge just in case you want it before you head out." I stored Jesse's nearly-full plate before washing and placing my own in the drying rack.

The police station wouldn't open for another hour, and given what he'd said earlier, I assumed that Jesse would be gone long before the police could get to my place. I didn't want to leave behind anything valuable in my apartment while the window was broken, so I slipped my laptop and small portable speaker into my messenger bag.

"Why are you bringing those to work?" Jesse asked.

"I'm going straight from the police station to my first patient and I don't want to leave anything too valuable in here."

"Why not just wait here until the station opens up and call them?"

"Because I'd be late for work. The police station doesn't open till nine, so I'd have to wait till then to call. Then I'd have to wait for officers to arrive, explain everything to them, and walk to the train. I wouldn't make it to my first patient until 10:30 a.m. at the earliest."

"Is it a big deal to be a little late?" He sounded genuinely surprised.

I worked to keep from smirking at his naivete. "In my line of work, yeah, it is. Patients need to be given medications on a schedule. Anyways, I've timed it so that if I walk, I'll get to the police station right when it opens. I'll make the report and leave from the train stop across the road from it. Besides, I'm probably going to have to come into the station and make an official report and answer questions anyways. Might as well get it over with now."

Jesse bit his lip and sighed. "Look, forget what I said earlier. It's crazy for you to haul your computer and speaker around on trains and in an FBI car. I'll just work from your apartment until the dispatched officers come. Once they've documented everything, I'll call in someone to fix your window and won't leave till it's done."

"You would do that for me?" I asked, genuinely moved.

"Yeah. I'm not in the mood to deal with the police, but I'm always in the mood to help you."

I walked over to him and gently pushed his chest so that he leaned against the back of the chair. Leaning down, I gave him a deep kiss and buried my hands in his mussed hair.

"Thank you, Jesse. So much."

He grabbed my hips and pulled me down onto his lap. "How thankful are you, Sofija?"

Blood rushed to my cheeks and my skin tingled. "Very. But I'll have to show you tonight. I'm going to be late."

Jesse gave a reluctant grunt. He kissed me on the nose then pushed me to my feet.

"I'll try to get off early, if I can," I assured him.

"Not without me, you won't," he teased.

I rolled my eyes but smiled as I walked over to the doormat where I kept my plain white canvas shoes. "I meant 'get off' as in 'get off work,' but you knew that, didn't you?"

He didn't answer. After I laced up my shoes, I said, "Okay, I'm headed out. Thanks again Jesse, you're the best." Silence. I looked over and saw that he was texting furiously.

Jesse always walked me to the door whenever I left earlier than him. Maybe it was a silly ritual, but it was ours, and I didn't want to break it. I came over to stand in front of him, but he was oblivious to my presence.

"Jesse?" I asked tentatively.

His head snapped up and he shoved his phone into his pocket. "Sorry, babe. Work stuff. You know how everything is a crisis in a startup. Here, let me walk you out."

When we got to the door, I turned to him. Rocking up on my tiptoes, I pressed a kiss to his chin. He chuckled and bent down to press his lips against mine.

"Your height is perfect," he murmured.

"Not for dating a tall Adonis like you, it's not," I protested. "I can't reach you half the time."

"But it's kinda cute, watching you struggle," he countered, pinching my side. I squealed and gave him one more kiss before taking off.

"See you tonight?" he called after me.

Without breaking my pace, I glanced over my shoulder and hollered, "You better."

****

The walk to the police station was an easy one, just a flat mile and a half. It wasn't even 8:30 yet, so I had plenty of time to make it there and be the first one in line when doors opened at nine. Then it was an easy ride on the train over to Worcester.

Usually, I put on music during my runs or walks. Today, though, the sounds of the world waking up were too invigorating to tune out. The chirping birds, the gentle breeze, the occasional babbling creek that ran under the road whenever it turned into a bridge—they made me feel more genuinely relaxed than I had for days.

About fifteen minutes later, though, things started to feel wrong. A prickling, eerie sensation coursed up and down my back. My heart beat faster and faster.

Stay calm, Sofija. You're just frazzled. It's been a crazy couple of days.

I tried to ignore it, but the disquieting feeling grew with every step. It was the same apprehension I would feel when men walked behind me for too many blocks in a row at night.

While I wracked my brain for what to do, I strolled along as if nothing was wrong. I knew if I were too obvious and stopped to look around, it would tip off whoever was tailing me. If I were lucky, the person would back off. If I weren't, he or she might try to attack me—and I was still at least a half mile from the police station.

Calling 911 wouldn't do me any good, because there was nowhere I could barricade myself in and wait for someone to arrive. It was me, the open road, and the woods. The dense, lonely woods that would hide my rotting corpse if my stalker decided to clean things up before the cops arrived. Or, if the stalker fled, the police might think I was hysterical. Then they might not take my report about the brick and the threatening note seriously.

A small, reckless part of me wanted to investigate. Maybe it was inspired by my interactions with the FBI over the last few days. Maybe I just wanted to feel some sort of control over what was happening to me again. Either way, I felt a powerful urge to do some sleuthing.

I needed to figure out how to see what was behind me without turning too obviously. It had to appear natural, like I had no idea someone was following me. At the same time, I had to make it clear to my stalker that if he or she tried anything, it would be caught on camera.

Think, Sofija.

When the idea came to me, it was so simple I almost laughed. I unlocked my phone and video called my best friend, Keiko, flipping the camera so that it was in selfie mode. I knew it would be too early for Keiko to pick up, but I let the call go, the ringing in my earbuds stopping after no answer. I pretended she had picked up.

"Good morning, Ko!" I chirruped. "Sorry, I know it's early," I said loudly, feigning conversation. "But it was just such a pretty morning, and I'm having a perfect hair day for once." I held my phone up higher and rotated it, as if I was giving Keiko a view of my hair from all angles. As I did so, I snapped a series of screenshots and immediately emailed them to myself, writing STALKED ON THE WAY TO THE POLICE in the subject line.

If I got abducted or harmed, at least someone could use the photos as clues.

In the meantime, I kept up my fake conversation with Keiko. "So, tell me more about this guy you're seeing! You said you met him on that dating app, right?"

As I babbled on for several minutes, the feeling of being watched subsided and then disappeared. Before I knew it, I was at the police station.

I collapsed on the steps leading up to the building entrance and checked the time on my phone. The doors wouldn't open for another seven minutes, but there were already some officers inside—I could tell by the cars parked out front. I sighed in relief, knowing that nobody would be stupid enough to attack me here.

While I waited, I scrolled through the screenshots I had taken. There wasn't much: trees, the road, a mountain of my curls, more trees, more road...and then there it was.

In the first and second screenshots was something that was a little blurry but unmistakably human. A tall, dark-haired figure dressed in jeans and a black jacket was darting off onto a dirt side road obscured by trees. His profile was pixelated, but it was clear that he was pale.

I couldn't help but think that it looked a little like Adam Armitage.

But he's in San Francisco, I reminded myself. *Besides, millions of people are tall and pale with dark hair.*

In any case, I decided to show the screenshots to the police when I filed the report about the brick.

Maybe I would share the images with Velasquez too. They might help clear my name.

And maybe he would be impressed by my quick thinking—though that wasn't why I would do it, showing him.

It really wasn't.

Chapter 10

Mateo

While I certainly never binged telenovelas or the Spanish-dubbed Turkish soap operas, I had grown up around them. My uncle Luis was an especially big fan. Whenever the family gathered at his house on Sundays, he and his wife prepared food in the kitchen while my cousins and I played in the living room, next to the TV. Luis took small breaks from shredding the *barbacoa* to steal glances at whatever was unfolding on the screen. Whenever there was an especially tense moment, Luis ran into the living room and shouted encouragement or rebukes at the characters. He looked ridiculous, grease-covered hands held up and away from his apron, careful not to touch the furniture.

For years, I never understood what was so compelling about series like that. I would glance over at whatever had caught my uncle's attention, become bored within a matter of seconds, and go back to playing with my cousins. I was too young to be interested in adults' relationship drama.

As I got older, though, I became intrigued by the passionate kissing and grasping, by the clandestine, desperate encounters. But by then, I was also old enough to recognize that the plotlines were ridiculous—especially those revolving around instant, soul-deep connections between strangers.

That wasn't just improbable; it was impossible.

Of course, it was normal to be physically drawn to someone at first sight, and it was normal for that initial attraction to ignite a desire to know more, to see if there could be something deeper. I knew now that I wasn't immune to the feeling. No more than a few minutes after meeting Sofija, I had wanted to discover if there was something equally appealing beneath the enticing exterior—even though I would probably never have the chance to do so.

That's normal. It's a normal impulse to have and it's nothing more than that, my pragmatic side insisted.

But I *did* know a little more about Sofija than just the color of her eyes and the length of her beautiful, riotous curls. Based on our admittedly limited conversations, I had realized that we both knew what it was like to grow up in a loving but high-expectations immigrant households. In that sense, I felt like I could understand her.

Plus, I could discern little things about her character. I knew she was smart, given what she had told us about her academic history. Her occasional attempts at little jokes indicated that she was funny—or at least tried to be. She wasn't afraid to stand up for herself and it sounded like she'd been through a lot, so she was strong and resilient. On two different occasions, she had teared up at the thought of Sandra. If it wasn't an act, if the emotions were genuine, then Sofija must also be an incredibly loving person.

I exhaled slowly and reminded myself that not only was all of this moot, but that I had only gotten glimpses into Sofija. It wasn't the same as knowing someone for a long time, through their highs and lows.

But you're seeing Sofija at her low, and you still want to know more about her.

I leaned back against the bland concrete wall of the FBI building and massaged my temples, frustrated by my intrusive, errant thoughts. It didn't matter. I wouldn't let it affect how I approached the case. I would treat Sofija with the respect I showed to everyone. No more, no less.

To take my mind off of her while I waited for Cantrell, I caught up on dozens of messages from my extended family's texting group. I was almost done reading through the debate about whether my little cousin Aleja should accept a spot in a JD or MBA program when Cantrell pulled into the parking space in front of me.

He poked his head out of the window and said, "Bright and early, I see. Eager?"

In truth, I was both eager and full of dread about seeing Sofija again, but Cantrell didn't need to know that. I opened the passenger door and sat down. "I'm always early, but yes, I am eager to get this day over with. I'm not thrilled about driving down to Worcester and back."

Cantrell chuckled. "Can't say I blame you. Waste of gas. At least we get to expense it."

At first, we rode in silence. I was highlighting and marking up the notes I had taken over the course of the last two days when Cantrel finally spoke.

"Nervous, Velasquez?"

I turned to look at him. His strong jaw and buzzed haircut made for an intimidating profile.

"What gave you that impression?" I asked.

The corner of Cantrell's mouth twitched. "You

haven't stopped bouncing your leg since you sat down in my car."

Looking down, I realized he was right. I uncrossed my legs and planted my feet firmly on the floor of the car.

I hemmed and said, "I guess I'm concerned that we won't be able to get the information from Sofija that we need. The inside of a car, it's a pretty non-traditional setting for questioning, isn't it?"

"That all?" Cantrell prodded. I could hear the challenge in his voice.

I wanted to be finished with Cantrell's mini-interrogation, so I tried to think of a convincing response. Nothing, I realized, would be more convincing than the truth—even if it was only a partial one.

I sighed. "All right. I *am* a little anxious. You gave me the chance to conduct interviews on my own for the first time, and I'm not confident that I'm doing such a great job. Adam Armitage jetted off to California before I could ask him anything. Jesse ran off in the middle of questioning. The maid who quit right after Mrs. Armitage died—I still haven't been able to track her down. So I feel some pressure to get high utility information from Sofija today, especially since you'll be watching."

With bated breath, I watched as Cantrell processed this. He seemed to buy it, because he eventually nodded and said, "I can see why you'd feel that way, but don't sweat it, Velasquez. Those other things aren't your fault. We'll get to Adam once he's back, we'll make Jesse talk to us again, and somehow, we'll find that maid. What was her name?"

I flipped through my notes until I found what I

wanted. "Frannie McDonnell told me her name is Talia Portnoy. I gave her a call last night and left a message."

Cantrell harrumphed. "If she hasn't returned your call by EOD, we need to do a house visit ASAP."

"I completely agree," I said, suppressing a smile. Cantrell's characteristic overuse of acronyms amused me. I couldn't tell if it was a remnant of his military days, or if he simply didn't believe in wasting precious oxygen and effort on unnecessary verbiage.

For the remainder of the ride, we didn't talk. Cantrell put on Boston's debut album, and I let the progressive rock push out all other thoughts from my head. By the time we pulled up to Rosegrove Residences, I felt relatively calm.

"You can go get her," Cantrell said, giving me a piercing look.

"Why don't you want to come?" I asked. I had the distinct feeling that I was being tested.

"I'm comfortable here, and it doesn't take two grown men to retrieve an unarmed, five-foot-nothing slip of a girl. Does it?"

"I guess not," I forced out.

"Give me your case notes and I'll brush up on them while you get her," he said.

"All right," I grudgingly agreed. I handed over the notes. "They're organized by person, and I have a color code for themes. Blue highlighting denotes when someone was talking about the relationship between Sandra and her sons. Orange is—"

"Velasquez, I appreciate attention to detail as much as the next agent, but you've got to tone it down."

I bit my lip and nodded. "Sure, I'll work on that. I'll be back."

I opened the door and stepped out. Taking a deep breath, I unlocked my phone and dialed Sofija's number. She picked up after a few rings.

"Morning, Agent Velasquez! Are you almost here?"

Any semblance of calm that I had managed to achieve on the ride over was gone. Pulse thrumming, I did my best to channel the distant affability of a pilot over the inflight intercom as I replied, "Good morning, Sofija. We're out front, in the parking lot. Where are you?"

She sounded overwhelmed as she said, "Listen, I'll be there as soon as I can, but my patient doesn't want to leave. It might take me a little longer to get him comfortable and back inside."

"Back inside? Where are you?" I asked, confused.

"We're in the park behind the residences. You can come over and start your questions while you wait."

"Won't that be a bit awkward? With your patient right there?"

There was a sadness to Sofija's voice as she replied, "This patient—I can't tell you his name without a warrant, privacy rules and all—he doesn't remember how to speak English anymore. He forgot. All he understands is his mother tongue. So he won't understand what you're asking me."

"All right," I said uncertainly. "Give me a second." I pressed mute and tapped on the driver's side window. Cantrell rolled it down and I leaned toward him.

"Still here?" he asked.

I explained the situation and asked if he thought I should go to the park and start questioning Sofija.

"Don't see why not. The more questions we can get in, the better. Just confirm that the patient can't speak

English."

Nodding, I straightened up and walked a few paces away from the car. Unmuting my phone, I said, "I'll be there in a second."

"Okay—we're on the benches to the left of the entrance."

As I walked toward the park, the trees lining the sidewalk seemed to sigh. I felt like I was on the precipice of something.

Soon, a bench came into sight, upon which sat an old man and a tiny woman with curly hair who I immediately recognized as Sofija. The bench and their bodies were angled such that the old man could clearly see who entered the park, but Sofija would only have a peripheral view.

That was good. I didn't want Sofija to notice me approaching. I wanted to observe how she was with a patient.

Her attention seemed to be completely focused on the old man next to her, whose thick, hoary hair stuck out in every direction. There was a glazed-over look in his eyes, and if he saw me approach, he didn't give any indication.

When I was a few feet away, I paused and watched Sofija. She was giving the old man's forearm small, soothing pats while murmuring in a language I couldn't understand. It sounded pharyngeal and powerful, even spoken so gently.

So she was telling the truth about the patient not speaking English.

The man slowly craned his neck up until he was looking at Sofija. Tears slipped down his face. He shook his head with an impressive amount of force for someone who looked so frail.

Sofija produced a cloth from her bag and gently dabbed the wetness from his face and murmured more of the foreign language. Slowly, he nodded. A dazzling smile broke over her face and she clapped her hands together. The old man offered her a dazed smile of his own.

Sofija's happiness was contagious. I couldn't help but smile, because I'd just seen evidence—though not concrete proof—of something that I'd been hoping, deep down, to be true.

Clearing my throat loudly to announce my presence, I waited for Sofija's reaction. I wanted to gauge if she had been aware that she had an audience.

She jumped at the noise and spun around so fast that her curls flew into her eyes. "Jesus, you scared me, Agent Velasquez! How long have you been standing there?"

"Not more than a minute," I quickly replied.

"Is this a strategy? Spying on the people you're investigating?" Her face was flushed and her chest was rising and falling rapidly.

Frowning slightly, I said, "I wasn't spying on you. I was observing."

Sofija snorted lightly. "Semantics." She paused and looked like she was considering something. "Maybe I overreacted. I'm extra jumpy right now. You're not the first person who has crept up on me from behind today."

My eyes widened. "Explain," I urged.

"Okay. Let me just get my friend here back to his place."

I watched as she murmured something to the old man, again in that language I couldn't place. She assisted him as he struggled to stand up and grip his walker.

"Can I help?" I offered.

Sofija shook her head. "Thanks, but I don't think it would be appropriate for you to touch him unless it were an emergency. He's strong. He can do it with just my help." She turned to the man and said something that sounded encouraging. He nodded and gave her a watery smile as she looped a hand under his arm.

"See? Follow us, Agent Velasquez."

We walked slowly to the back end of the residences to accommodate the elderly man's pace. It gave me plenty of time for questions.

"What did you mean when you said someone crept up on you earlier today?"

Grimacing, Sofija replied, "Last night, someone threw a really menacing note attached to a brick through my window. I was too tired and stressed last night to report it, so I put it off till this morning."

I was about to protest, and she must have sensed it, because she cut me off. "I know, stupid of me. But I figured it was just some neighborhood kid who read the story about me and wanted to be a troll. Plus, I wasn't alone at my apartment last night, so I didn't feel like I was in any real danger."

At this, my stomach soured, though I knew I had no right to feel jealous. "Were you with Jesse Armitage? He got a call from you while I was questioning him and then left right after," I added by way of explanation.

"Yes, he was with me," Sofija said, blushing a little. "Anyways, this morning, when I walked to the police station to make a report, I got the sense someone was following behind me. I pretended to video call a friend and took screenshots so I could see if I was right. I was."

"What did the person look like?"

"Tall, pale, dark hair, probably male. I'll show you and Cantrell in the car. Kind of hard for me to reach my phone right now," she said, nodding her head to where her hand was still supporting the old man's arm. "Anyways, I shared the photos with the police too."

"And what did they say?"

"They agreed that it seemed like a man was following me, but that the resolution on the picture wasn't good enough to do anything more. They also told me to call my insurance about the window and get a second lock for my door," she said wryly. "Speaking of doors, we're here, so give me a couple minutes."

"Of course."

Sofija reached for a retractable badge holder attached to one of her jean loops. She swiped it on the card reader and pulled open the door, never removing her hand from her patient.

She smiled at him and said something. He mumbled a response, and she patted him gently and guided him over the threshold. The door clicked shut behind them.

While I stood there waiting for her to return, I mulled over what she had said. It was certainly plausible that an immature teen was trolling her with the brick and menacing note, but the stalking? That seemed a bridge too far.

The whole case was turning out to be more complicated than I anticipated.

Just then, the door opened and Sofija reemerged. She rocked back and forth on her feet and said, "He's set. I'm all yours."

I wish you were, but you never will be.

Pushing aside the effect of Sofija's phrasing, I

asked, "What was that language you were speaking with that patient? Are you allowed to tell me that?"

Grinning, she replied, "I sure am. It was Arabic!"

I blinked. "Arabic? Didn't you say your family was from Malta?"

"Yes, but *Teta*—my grandmother on my dad's side—was actually from Lebanon. She spoke Maltese well enough, but it wasn't her default. As Teta got older, I wanted to hear about her early life. Bond with her before it was too late, you know? And I really believe that people express themselves best in their primary language. So I learned Arabic for her. It's not so different from Maltese."

"It isn't?" I asked, genuinely intrigued.

"I mean, they're not mutually intelligible, but they're both Semitic languages. Anyways, Teta loved that I learned Arabic for her, so I made a point not to lose it. It keeps me connected to her. Plus, it's come in handy several times throughout my career," she said proudly. "As you saw, that patient only remembers Arabic."

"Does that happen a lot? The elderly forgetting things they learned later in life?"

Sofija looked sad as she nodded. "It does. Sometimes, my patients can't remember anything but their youth, language included. It's like their memory is an onion and dementia strips off the layers, you know? Obviously, that's not physiologically what's going on, but it can seem like it."

"It must be terrifying to feel yourself go through that," I remarked somberly. My thoughts flitted to my aging grandparents. I was lucky that their memories were still intact, but I felt a new sense of fear about it.

"I bet it is. And so lonely too, especially for

immigrants who forget the language of their adopted country. They feel the world collapse in on them and they don't even have the words to convey how scared they are to people around them. It's why I'm so glad whenever I can connect with them in their mother tongue."

There was that tightening in my chest again. Seeing Sofija in action, hearing how much she seemingly loved her grandmother and cared for her patients' wellbeing...it was getting harder to convince myself that everything I was feeling about her was just a physical reaction and nothing more substantive.

I swallowed and said, "I'm sure they appreciate it."

"I think they do," she agreed. "I'm actually trying to learn Spanish right now, since so many of my patients speak it. It's going a little slower than I want, to be honest."

"Three months with me and I could turn someone like you into a *hispanohablante*, no question," I confidently proclaimed.

Then the implication of what I had just said hit me. *Fuck!* I panicked.

For a moment, I was overwhelmed by a fog of angry doubt. Thoughts rushed at me faster than I could process them. *Did she make the comment about Spanish because she can sense how I feel? Is she playing me? Am I making myself a useful idiot?*

But then I looked at Sofija, and her expression washed away my doubts. Shock painted her features; she clearly hadn't expected me to offer to teach her Spanish.

Damage control time, Mateo.

Clearing my throat, I said, "What I meant by that is, since I am a native speaker, by conversing with me and with other Spanish speakers around you, I'm sure you'd pick it up quickly. Immersion is best, they say, and from what you've told me, you have a knack for languages."

For a few more seconds, Sofija stared at me with the same surprised expression. Then, she did something that threw me off.

She gave a nearly imperceptible smirk.

I bit down on the inside of my cheek so hard that I could almost taste blood.

"I think I get what you meant, Agent Velasquez."

"Good. Good," was all I could manage.

We stood there for a few more seconds before she said, "As fun as it is to talk about language, I've got a patient waiting for me. So how about we get going and I answer whatever other questions you have in the car, like we planned?"

"Yes, of course. We're out front. After you," I rushed out.

As I followed Sofija, I cursed Cantrell for pushing me to interact with her alone. By now, I was convinced that he was testing me, making me prove that I could maintain boundaries and compartmentalize. It was insulting. I was thirty-three years old, and just because I was one of the fresher FBI agents didn't mean that I was some untried novice in the professional world. Prior to joining the FBI, I had been a very successful prosecutor. I didn't need these little tests to remind me to toe the line.

Or did I?

Maybe a part of me was mad at Cantrell because I was afraid he was right. When it came to Sofija, I wanted to get carried away. Some primordial force was tugging at me as I stood on a ledge, slowly leaning further toward the inviting water below. Balance faltering, only the balls of my feet kept me connected to solid land. It would feel good to leap, or even to let gravity do the work for me. To stop resisting and fall into exactly where I wanted to be.

It was pure fantasy—indulgent and pointless. Surrendering to my impulses and telling Sofija what I felt would be nothing short of a disaster for my FBI career. It probably wouldn't do her any favors either, given that she was already being investigated.

Thankfully, I didn't have time to stew, because we reached the car.

"Hello, Agent Cantrell," Sofija greeted.

"Ms. Zammit," he acknowledged.

"Sir, I want to politely remind you that I prefer to be called Sofija. You can even say 'Ms. Sofija' if you want."

"Ms. Sofija, would you like to ride shotgun or in the back?" Cantrell said, clearly making no effort to conceal his annoyance.

"Backseat," she coolly replied.

Once we had all buckled in, Sofija shared the address of her destination and we were off.

Cantrell and I asked her a series of questions based on what I had learned from the previous day's interviews. Her accounts more or less matched everything the others had said.

Then we transitioned into questions that probed her relationships with the three Armitages. According to Sofija, she and Sandra had developed a close, pseudo-mother daughter relationship over the past three years. Adam had never given Sofija a second thought, though he had never been unkind. And Jesse had flitted in and out of the picture for brief periods in the first two years, during which time her crush on him had grown. During the past year, when he had appeared more frequently at the Armitage estate due to his mother's worsening health, Jesse and Sofija had grown closer. He had flirted overtly and eventually asked her out for coffee. Things had progressed from there.

After we exhausted our list of topics, we sat in uncomfortable silence. Sofija looked lost in thought, and Cantrell was clearly percolating over her account of things.

Thankfully, my phone rang, breaking the silence. I looked down; it was Frannie. "Hello, Frannie," I answered.

"You on a first name basis with all the suspects?" Cantrell muttered.

Ignoring him, I pressed the phone closer to my ear. "Is everything all right?"

"Not really," came her agitated reply. "Remember the other maid I told you about, Talia Portnoy?"

"Yes. I tried calling her last night, but I have yet to hear back."

"Well, don't hold your breath. She's dead."

"She's dead?" I repeated. Out of the corner of my eye, I could see Cantrell tense up.

"Very much so. We just learned that her body was found in her apartment. Seems like she died after going into a coma. I don't know any more than that."

"Thank you for calling to inform me," I said perfunctorily, still stunned by the news. "We'll look into this. Keep close to your phone in case we need to reach you."

"Will do. It's nasty business, isn't it? You be sure to take care. Who knows who people are, anymore. It's madness." With that, Frannie hung up.

"Who was that?" Cantrell demanded the minute I lowered my phone.

"Frannie McDonnell."

"What did she want?" Sofija asked.

"That's none of your concern," Cantrell scolded. He shot a glance at me before refocusing on the road. "But what did she want?" he asked.

"She called to let us know that the other maid, Talia Portnoy, is dead."

A gasp escaped Sofija. Cantrell's grip on the wheel tightened. "Foul play?" he asked.

"Unclear. Frannie said it looked like she fell into a coma before she died."

"But Talia was perfectly healthy, and I'm almost positive she didn't have a drug problem!" Sofija cried. "It doesn't make sense!"

"You wanna tell us how you know she didn't use drugs, Ms. Sofija?" Cantrell asked sharply.

I glanced in the rear-view mirror and saw Sofija cross her arms and glare. "I make it a point to get to know my colleagues. Also, I'm a nurse. A good one. I probably would have noticed the signs."

"Do you keep close tabs on all the people at the Armitage estate?" Cantrell pressed.

Sofija let out an exasperated sigh. "Agent Cantrell, I can see what you're getting at. But even if I were the elder-abusing monster you clearly think I am, why would I kill Talia?"

"Maybe she knew something about you and Mrs. Armitage that you'd rather keep hidden, so you silenced her forever," Cantrell replied.

Sofija was glowering. She opened and closed her

mouth several times, as if she wanted to say something but was too furious to form words.

I didn't want to derail Cantrell's questioning, but he seemed hellbent on insulting Sofija as much as possible. After all she'd been through in the last forty-eight hours, I felt a powerful urge to defend her. While I couldn't do that, I could at least share information with Cantrell that, while not exonerating, did provide important context.

Any good agent would do that. It's about being thorough, I reassured myself.

"Cantrell," I began. "Back at Rosegrove Residences, Sofija informed me that last night, her house was vandalized and she received a threatening note. This morning, she was stalked on her way to the police station. It seems likely that she's being targeted and victimized too."

The scowl on Cantrell's face deepened. "She could be setting that up, doing that to herself to divert suspicion. And you're awful eager to defend the girl, Velasquez," he snapped. "Wanna enlighten me as to why that is?"

At this, I winced and bit my tongue. If I kept going, I would get in trouble. I didn't want the situation to devolve into an argument that should be kept private, if it took place at all.

"So what about it, Ms. Sofija?" Cantrell resumed, his attention having reverted back to her. "What other insights do you have about the people around Mrs. Armitage?"

Sofija gave him a spiteful look. "Why don't I just hand you my phone and the keys to my apartment so you can look through everything I own? It'll save us both time," she hissed. "And you know what? If you're coming at this so eager to find me guilty, then I'm going to do my own investigating. You can let me out here— I'll take a bus the rest of the way."

"Sofija," I began urgently. "I strongly advise against that. If you investigate on your own, there's no telling what kind of danger you'll expose yourself too. Leave it to us."

Her expression softened a little. "I wish I had the luxury to kick back and wait for you or someone else to resolve this. But think about it from my perspective," she pleaded. "I'm an active suspect in elder abuse and now murder. If I don't clear this cloud of suspicion hanging over my head, it's going to impact my professional and academic future. I don't want that. I don't *deserve* that."

I was thinking about how to reply when Cantrell said something that surprised me.

"We understand that your situation is stressful, Ms. Sofija. But in the fact-finding stage of a case, we have to treat every suspect as if he or she might be guilty. Rest assured that if you're innocent, we'll confirm that and make it known."

It wasn't exactly reassuring, but it was a shade gentler than I'd heard from Cantrell at any point during this investigation. Maybe he had a better understanding of people's breaking points than I gave him credit for.

"Thanks, I guess," Sofija said, sounding halfway placated.

"So you won't go off investigating on your own?" I asked hopefully.

Sofija met my eyes in the mirror and gave me a glum smile as she shook her head. "I can't promise that any more than you can promise to find me innocent."

Dammit. The thought of her putting herself in

harm's way made me extremely anxious.

"It's my reputation, my good name. It's my family's name too, you know? Even if people have mocked me for it, it's still my name, it's still our name. I have to try to save it."

As much as I wanted to argue, I deeply understood and respected that. The three of us spent the rest of the ride without talking.

Chapter 11

Sofija

I walked through the door to my apartment and wanted to collapse. Being stalked on the way to the police department, caring for two patients, submitting to another round of FBI questioning, learning of Talia's death, sitting cramped on the long train ride home—it had been a lot.

Jesse was waiting for me with a hot plate of food. It was the first time all day that someone had really taken care of me. A warm happiness spread through my sore, tired body. I kissed him, grabbed the plate, and sunk onto the couch with a contented sigh.

"It's going to be one of those nights, huh?" Jesse asked.

Covering my mouth with my hand, I asked mid-chew, "What do you mean?"

"A night where you're too tired to eat at the table—one where we just melt into the couch until we fall asleep."

I took a swig of water from my bottle. "Afraid so. Is that okay? I'm-I'm sorry. I know you like going out and doing things."

"Sofi, there's nothing I'd rather do than curl up with you until you fall asleep. It's after ten anyways." He wedged himself between me and the couch and began massaging my shoulders.

"You're the best, Jesse. Don't you want something to eat though?"

"I'm actually doing a juice cleanse for a week. I've been feeling pretty negative since mom died, and I need a reset."

Rolling my eyes, I bit my tongue. More than once, I had tried to explain to Jesse that juicing removed the good fiber in food. Healthy kidneys would do all the detoxing he needed. He didn't listen, insisting that his friends swore by it and that mainstream medicine would catch up eventually.

I just didn't have it in me to argue with him, so I said, "Well, feel free to help yourself to whatever you want if you change your mind."

"Okay," Jesse whispered against my neck. I leaned back into him and looked up to meet his eyes.

"Hi," I said with a small smile. "Wanna come down here, closer to me?"

"You don't have to ask me twice," he replied, sliding down to spoon me. "So, what was stressful about today? Was it the ride with those FBI agents?"

"That definitely didn't help," I muttered. News of Talia's possible murder, combined with Cantrell's aggressive questioning, had thrown me off. But it was Velasquez's possible Freudian slip when we were talking about me learning Spanish that had rocked my emotional stability the most. It had fanned the flames of a ridiculous crush. I felt guilty that it had made me a little happy, and I didn't want to be reminded of it. Especially not while Jesse was right here.

Realizing that Jesse was waiting for me to elaborate, I said, "But the other thing is, halfway through the ride slash interrogation, Agent Velasquez got a call from Frannie. She said that Talia died."

Behind me, Jesse tensed. "I'm sorry, what? Talia is *dead*?"

"Yeah. They found her dead in her apartment."

"How did she die? Do they know?" Jesse asked.

"Seems like she went into a coma. Frannie didn't know more than that."

Jesse exhaled. "Damn. We make it so hard for sick people to get preventative healthcare in this country. Maybe that's what my next business should be—connected, affordable healthcare with smart devices."

Pushing myself up and twisting to face him, I said, "But Talia wasn't sick."

Jesse raised his eyebrows. "She wasn't?"

I shook my head. "Super healthy. She biked like ten miles a day and ate well, from what I could see. We talked about our families' health too. There was no history of strokes or anything like that on either side of her family. I would be surprised if she died naturally."

Jesse's jaw dropped as the full implication of my words hit him. "You mean—you think she was—" he faltered.

"Murdered, yeah. Maybe," I said gloomily. "Agent Cantrell seems to think so too. He interrogated the hell out of me in the car. I think it's safe to say that he considers me a suspect."

Jesse gave me a pitiful look. "*Fuck*, Sofi. I'm so sorry. I know it must be awful, having all that suspicion piled up on you."

"It's heavy," I agreed.

He reached out to cup my face and smoothed his thumb along my cheekbone. "Baby," he began. "I know you probably don't want to hear this right now, but I'm going to say it because I care about you. This is just another reason for you to hurry up and execute my mom's will—"

"Jesse, I don't want to talk about this right now," I pleaded. I knew where he was going. If I let him start, he might actually wear me down this time—I was feeling incredibly vulnerable. I didn't want my life to be a cycle of people telling me to ignore my feelings and do the correct thing until I caved because I was in a tight spot.

"Just hear me out, Sofi—I'm trying to help you! If the FBI really decides that you're a suspect in Talia's murder, it could complicate your eligibility to inherit what my mom left you. Sign the papers and settle things now. It's much harder for the law to take away what's already in your bank account than it is for them to stop it from being deposited in the first place."

"And if I take the money while the FBI still suspects me, there goes whatever's left of my reputation! We've been over this before, Jesse. I'm not going to actively try to lose my patients and throw away my chance at nurse practitioner school!"

"With the kind of money my mom left you, you could afford to lose a few patients. Hell, you wouldn't even have to work as a nurse anymore. Go do something that doesn't leave you feeling so tired and unappreciated!"

There was a weed in my mind, one that I had starved by refusing to give it air or sunlight. Now, I could feel the weed unfurling, its tendrils creeping toward the forefront of my consciousness. I couldn't ignore it anymore.

"Jesse," I began cautiously. "Are you afraid that if

I'm not able to access your mother's inheritance, you'll be left high and dry? Because if that somehow happens—if the money doesn't go to me for whatever reason—my share would probably go to Sandra's descendants. That's you and Adam. I'm not an expert, but I feel like even if he took you to court over it and you two had to battle it out, there's a good chance the judge would give you half of what would have been my seventy five percent. Unless Adam could prove that you'd been a horrible son, which he couldn't, because you weren't."

For the briefest second, I thought I saw something flicker in Jesse's eyes. I couldn't tell if it was hurt, relief, worry, anger, or something else.

His response, though, wasn't ambiguous at all.

"No!" he said emphatically. "That's not it. I'm worried about you, Sofi. Not about the money. I've got stocks and investments. I'm not going to be, you know, destitute either way. But you need to have something, especially because you might need to hire a good lawyer soon."

Groaning, I let my head fall back against his chest. "Oh, for God's sake, I don't want to even *think* about that! I barely have enough energy to workout, grocery shop, and sleep with everything that's happening. I so do not want to spend time researching lawyers."

Jesse nuzzled my neck. "You won't have to, baby. I have lots of friends at big New York law firms. They're not cheap, but they'll do the job. You won't spend a second more than you have to in a courtroom."

Trying to lighten the mood, I teased, "As long as they do a better job than the contractors you hired to fix up the estate, I'm fine with footing a big bill."

Jesse's head snapped up. He looked somewhere between panicked and angry.

"Why the hell would you bring that up now, Sofija?!" he fumed. "I'm trying to make you feel better and give you honest advice, and all you can do is rub my past failures in my face."

I felt a sickening mixture of guilt and unease at his reaction. "I'm sorry, Jesse, I didn't mean anything by it," I apologized.

Pushing away from me, Jesse said, "I find that hard to believe. Probably Agent Velasquez planting stuff in your head, right? Trying to make me seem like a spoiled, privileged idiot."

"No, he hasn't done anything like that. Jesse, calm down," I pleaded.

It was no use. Jesse's temper was a train without breaks. As if he hadn't heard me, he snarled, "Well, he's *going* to try to turn you against me, because newsflash, Sofija, the man wants to bang you."

Jesse's words sparked such a jumble of feelings that I couldn't disentangle one from the other. I was sad that Jesse was clearly hurting. I was angry that he had spoken to me so crudely. I was unsettled by the strength of his reaction—it seemed weirdly disproportionate. And, though I felt ashamed about it, I was a little thrilled that Velasquez was attracted to me.

There was no way I could come up with an articulate response, mixed up in my own emotions as I was. Instead, I crossed my arms and petulantly insisted, "He does *not*."

Jesse gave a cynical laugh and leaned toward me.

"You're either willfully blind or naïve, Sofija. When Agent Velasquez was questioning me at the estate yesterday, he practically had an aneurysm when I told him what you're like in bed."

"JESSE!" I cried. "Why would you talk about our sex life with law enforcement? What the fuck?!"

"Because the nosy bastard had it coming!" Jesse bellowed. "Thought he could waltz in and take what's mine! I don't give a damn if he's from the FBI. He can shove his badge right up his ass."

Jesse's possessive outburst both thrilled me and repulsed me. A small part of me was happy that after months of hiding our relationship from his family, Jesse was finally broadcasting it loud and clear.

A larger, louder part of me hated the way the whole thing sounded. I wasn't a thing that belonged to one man as long as he could guard me from being snatched away by another.

In the calmest voice I could manage, I said, "Jesse, I appreciate that you're dealing with some difficult feelings right now. I don't love how what you said sounded, but as long as you don't make a habit of divulging our sex life to investigators, I'm not going to stay mad about it. But my emotions are pretty frayed after today, and I need an hour or so to cool off. Then we'll cuddle. We can do more than that, if you want."

Jesse rubbed a hand over his face and nodded. "No problem, Sofi. I completely understand. I'm sorry for being an ass." He moved to get up.

"Where are you going?" I asked.

"I'm going to get you some kombucha and hang out in your room. Just call me back in when you're ready okay?" he said, planting a kiss on my forehead before heading for the fridge.

"Thanks, Jesse. I don't deserve you."

He came back with a fizzing glass full of my raspberry-peach brew. After he set it down, he gave me a strange, almost contemplative look and said, "I guarantee you, it's the other way around."

Once he had closed the door to my bedroom, I propped myself up on the couch arm and sipped my drink, surveying my apartment.

When my eyes landed on a shard of glass from my broken window that had slid under the rug, I grimaced. My windows were one of the only things I truly liked about my apartment. They were bay ones that let in plenty of sunlight. I loved the little ledges beneath them, which I had covered in cushions and tiny pillows so that I could curl up on them and read in my rare moments of spare time.

I looked up from the rug to the window to remind myself of how bad the damage was. Instead of jagged glass and haphazard tape, I saw only a shining new pane. Suddenly, I remembered that Jesse had volunteered to stay in my apartment during the day until a repairman could come, so that I wouldn't have to lug my laptop and speaker around with me.

It sent a pang of guilt through me. Jesse was so sweet to have done that. He could be so considerate—and I had just told him to leave me alone.

Really, I was the asshole. Maybe that's why I reacted so strongly—because I knew that I was in the wrong. Jesse had touched on a subject too close to the secret I had been trying but failing to guard even from myself: I was attracted to Velasquez. Worse, it wasn't just because of his appearance, though that certainly didn't hurt.

I liked how fastidious he was, with his perfect,

smudgeless notes and sharp appearance.

I liked that he seemed to care about propriety. I thought back to his obvious mortification when he realized that he had practically offered to teach me Spanish. His clumsy attempt to course correct had been cute.

I liked how easy it was to have conversations with him, at least when he let his guard down. He had seemed interested in what I had to say about language learning. He had asked me things about my job and patients that had no bearing on the investigation.

I liked that he listened to what I said. He had remembered that I was Maltese—though I guess it was his job to recall details about suspects. Still. It made me feel so seen. Most people could barely remember that I wasn't Italian.

I liked that he understood my experience as a first-generation American in a way that none of my previous boyfriends—or current one—understood.

I liked that he had stuck out his neck to deflect some of the heat when Cantrell got too harsh in the car. It felt good to be worth defending, even if he still considered me a suspect.

I liked his hands and forearms. They were veiny and powerful in a good way. More than once, I had imagined them pinning my small wrists together while he kissed down the column of my throat, lower until—

A knock on the door interrupted my thoughts.

"Coming," I hollered as I slipped my feet into my flip flops and padded over.

Nobody was there when I opened the door, but something bright caught my eye. On my doormat lay an envelope with the words GREEDY BITCH scrawled across it in red.

I heard the door to my bedroom open. "Who is it, babe?" came Jesse's voice.

Quickly, I snapped a photo of the envelope before pocketing my phone and running down to the sidewalk, whipping my head from side to side to see if someone was fleeing on foot or in a car.

All I saw was the back wheel of a bike spinning around the corner—along with a swish of long, black hair.

"Sofi?" Jesse shouted.

"Out here," I called, turning back to face my apartment.

Jesse started to step outside, his foot on a trajectory to land on the envelope.

"Jesse!" I screamed in warning. "Watch your step!"

Looking down, he jumped back. "Oh shit!"

I charged up the path to my apartment and ran right past Jesse and into my bedroom where I flung off my pajama shorts and flip flops. I fished around in my drawers for a shirt, jean shorts, and pair of socks. "Call the police. Tell them what happened," I yelled back at Jesse. Clothing in hand, I ran back to the front door, slipped into my shirt and shorts, and jammed my feet into my socks.

"Okay, but where are you going?" Jesse asked worriedly.

As I laced up my sneakers, I explained, "I just saw someone riding like a bat out of hell on their bike. I'm going to follow them."

"That is a horrible idea, Sofi!" Jesse exclaimed.

Ignoring him, I stood and grabbed my helmet, fastening it snug around my chin. Jesse reached out as if to stop me, but I swatted his hand away and retrieved my phone arm band and mace keychain from a little shelf next to the door.

"Sofi, please," he protested.

While I slipped my phone into my arm band and attached the mace keychain to a belt loop, I said, "I'm not unarmed. Just call the police, Jesse. Then call me and keep me on the phone while I ride. I've got my wireless earphones." I pushed them into my ears and pointed to them.

Without waiting for a response, I grabbed my bike and ran out the door. When I hit the concrete, I hopped on and began pedaling furiously as I rode in the direction that I had seen the biker go.

Luckily, it was a straight shot for at least a half mile. There was nothing but residences in a long line, no branching side streets or massive parking lots to worry about.

Less than two minutes later, my earphones rang. I hit accept on my phone and said, "Jesse?"

"Police are on the way. Where are you, Sofija?"

"On Calhoun Street—shit Jesse, I think I see him!" I squealed, pumping harder. My muscles screamed in protest, but I ignored them, too full of adrenaline. The dark speck in front of me was bobbing up and down on the road.

"For fuck's sake, Sofija, you could get hurt!"

Just as I was about to assure him that I would be fine, my wheels caught on something and spun out. I went flying. When I connected with the road, I skidded for at least three feet.

I felt and heard my helmet scratch against the pavement. Thankfully, my head was well-protected.

The same couldn't be said about my limbs. Searing pain licked up and down them, and there was an excruciating stinging that went beyond road rash. When I looked down, I gasped.

My arms and legs were torn up, with little black chunks of something hard sticking in the cuts. I looked around and saw the same rubble everywhere around me. It was as if someone—maybe the fugitive biker—had poured out a big bag of the stuff when he sensed me gaining on him.

With great effort, I picked up one of the black pieces and brought it closer to examine it. It looked like crushed asphalt, the kind used in paving.

A sickening thought came to me.

I had already suspected Adam a little—he was tall, pale, and had dark hair. He was also a biking enthusiast.

But now, as I stared down at the scattered asphalt grindings, it occurred to me that Jesse knew people who worked in paving. He had hired one of them for the botched driveway job at the estate—and they had used crushed asphalt that looked just like this.

Were the Armitage brothers working together? What if they wanted me out of the way, so that what I was set to inherit would be split between them instead? Were they trying to scare me so badly that I'd renounce any claim?

But that didn't make sense. Jesse kept insisting that I hurry up and execute the will. Was that just an act to throw suspicion off him and Adam? Or was Jesse hoping to scare me into finalizing everything so that I would move into the safe, gated Armitage estate, where I could hide from the world and share the money with him? He *had* pointed out to me that it would be more secure than living in my apartment. Would that mean that Jesse was playing me *and* double-crossing Adam?

The more I thought about it all, the less sense any of it made. I shook my head and tried to push it out of my mind. Adam was curmudgeonly, but not a bad person. Jesse was pampered, but with a heart of gold, and—

And he was calling me. I groaned in pain as I lifted my hand to where my phone was still fastened to the arm band. I swiped to accept the call.

"Sofija, where are you?" came Jesse's panicked voice.

"Crashed," I said weakly. "I'm still on Calhoun. Literally on it—my bike spun out. Ran over some rubble."

"You're not making sense, but the police are here now and I'm going to have them pick you up. We're coming now. Get out of the middle of the road if you're still there, okay?"

"Thanks, Jesse," I croaked, wincing as I sat up and pushed myself off to the side of the road.

"See you in a second," he said before hanging up.

When I saw the police car approaching, I glanced down at my arm band. Wincing, I reached up and removed the phone from it.

It was nearly midnight. Velasquez would probably be sleeping. But he would see my text in the morning.

I texted him the picture of the envelope that I had snapped before the bike chase, along with the words, "Delivered to my doorstep."

As soon as the message read 'Delivered,' I deleted the chat between us and shoved the phone into my pocket. I didn't want to be paranoid, but after Jesse's outburst tonight, I wanted to erase evidence of my correspondence with Velasquez outside of what he initiated as part of his investigation.

I heard the police car park and the door open. Jesse disembarked and sprinted toward me.

For the most part, I was relieved to see him. Still, as he and an officer looped their arms under me and gently placed me in the shotgun seat, something nagged at me. So, as we drove back to my apartment, I made two resolutions.

One: I would try to find out if Adam was really in San Francisco.

Two: I would get my hands on the receipts for the maintenance jobs that Jesse had overseen for the Armitage estate—particularly the one for the company that paved the driveway. I would check his phone too.

I hadn't yet worked out how I would do it, or what exactly I expected to find. I hoped that I wouldn't discover anything damning. But as my wounds throbbed and I brushed the crushed asphalt out of them, I knew that I needed to check. Just for my own peace of mind. Just to chase away the nagging feeling that I couldn't seem to escape, even as Jesse sat in the police car behind me and tenderly brushed the pebbles and twigs from my hair.

Chapter 12

Mateo

After my workout and shower, I settled into my nightly routine. I prepared a salad and microwaved the red *pozole* that my mother had sent back with me after my most recent visit. Arranging the food on the table in front of me, I lounged on the couch and flicked on Streamii.

For whatever reason, none of my go-to shows appealed to me. Sighing resignedly, I threw on an episode of a popular sitcom and ate my dinner. Belly full, drowsy, and my usual guards down, I allowed myself to indulge. I opened my phone, searched for Sofija Zammit, and aimlessly scrolled through the results as I half watched the episode. Gradually, I felt myself start to drift off.

The sound of rapid knocking at the door reached me, muffled as if it were traveling through water instead of air. Groggily, I rubbed my eyes and slunk over to the door. I peered out through the peephole.

Standing on my porch was a panicked-looking Sofija, shivering in a light jacket.

My throat constricted as I considered my options. Every impulse was screaming at me to let her in, to warm her up, to take care of her. But that warred with a voice that screamed, "Professional boundaries!"

What Sofija said next decided the matter. She quavered, "Agent Velasquez? I'm so sorry to come here. I know it's not appropriate—but I think someone is trying to hurt me, and I'm scared."

The cold wind whooshed through the door as Sofija tentatively stepped inside. I did a quick visual sweep of the street. Nothing.

Hurriedly, I shut and locked the door. Sofija stood just inside, looking at me uncertainly.

"Come in," I said, gesturing toward the living room.

"Ah—ok, thanks. Should I take off my shoes? They're wet."

"Yes, please."

She slipped off her running shoes and I turned to walk toward the couch. I could hear her following behind me.

"Please, make yourself comfortable," I said, pointing to the other side of the couch.

"Thanks," she mumbled. The blush of her cheeks, presumably already rosy from the cold, deepened.

"Don't be shy, it's fine," I reassured her.

Sinking down on the couch, she began crying.

Normally, if a family member or a friend was crying, I would comfort them, rub their back or at least pat them on it. I couldn't do that with Sofija. "Can I get you something warm to drink?" I offered instead.

"I'd love that," she warbled through tears.

I scooped up the dishes from my dinner and headed to the kitchen. I deposited them in the sink and turned on the electric kettle.

On my way back to the couch, I grabbed a blanket and offered it to Sofija. Immediately, she accepted it and wrapped it around herself. She looked almost comical, a frightened face peeking out from under a huge pile of curls, protruding from a blanket cocoon.

"Tell me what happened while we wait for the water to heat up."

As I waited for Sofija to start talking, I took in her appearance, her demeanor, her presence. Something was off. The faint whiff of lavender that usually clung to her was completely absent. But it was more than that—there was something fundamentally *different* about her, but I couldn't put my finger on it.

Finally, Sofija drew in a deep breath and began to speak.

"I borrowed my dad's car to do some grocery shopping for him. I came out of the store and was walking back to the car, but I had parked pretty far away from the entrance because the lot was packed. I noticed a man in a mustard yellow baseball hat walking between the cars two rows over, parallel to me. It seemed a little...off. But I tried to ignore it."

She paused and pushed a hand up from the wrap of blankets to wipe at her tears. "Well, as I started driving off, I could have sworn that a red jalopy was following me. It was at that weird distance, right? A few cars behind me, but I was on a main road, so it could have been a coincidence. Eventually, though, the cars between us had all turned off, and the jalopy was still behind me. At a red light, I looked back in the rearview mirror at the driver. I didn't have a perfect view, but I could tell it was a man wearing a mustard yellow baseball hat. He must have seen me looking, because he gave me this *super* creepy grin." She shuddered as she finished.

I pursed my lips and nodded thoughtfully. "It does sound like he was following you. But how did you end up here?"

At this, Sofija blushed. "I was scared that the man would run me off the road, or that he'd attack me once I got out of my car. And I didn't want to lead him back to my dad's house. But also, I didn't want to go to the police in case I'm just being paranoid. I figured I would be safe with you."

"Right, but how did you know where I lived?"

Sofija looked down at her hands and gulped. Her answer came out in a rush. "I—I searched you and Agent Cantrell online. It's creepy, I know. I'm really, really sorry. The day after you and Agent Cantrell came to visit me, I looked you both up online and read everything I could find. I got a few results when I searched for your name plus Massachusetts. Anyways, one of the hits was this article from a couple years ago about the Porchfest in your neighborhood. The author had done interviews with the homeowners who allowed musicians to play on their porches, and you were one of them. You were quoted, by name. It's cool that you play guitar, by the way," she said with a tentative smile.

I worked to keep my expression unchanged. Sofija's smile fell and she quickly resumed.

"Anyways, they took a picture of you and the musicians playing on your porch, and your house is on the corner, right? So I could see the street signs at your intersection and your house number from the mailbox. Put them together and...voila. Address," she finished awkwardly.

I sat in stunned silence for what must have been a full minute before I said, "I've got to get that article taken down somehow. You'd make a decent open-source analyst."

"Thanks," she said shyly.

"So that's the how. Now, let me ask: *why* did you look me and Cantrell up after you met us?"

"Seriously? It can't surprise you that I wanted to know everything about the two men who hold the fate of my career and reputation in their hands!" Immediately, she shook her head and said in a remorseful tone, "I'm sorry. That was uncalled for. You've been—you're being—so fair and kind. But I just—okay, to be honest, I wanted to know as much as possible about you both so that I could figure out how to seem trustworthy and innocent to you."

Holding her gaze, I pressed, "That's not the only reason, though. Is it, Sofija?"

"I don't know what you mean," she said, looking away. Her exposed skin, from her neck down to where a hint of cleavage poked out from her shirt, grew increasingly flushed. The effect was intoxicating.

In that moment, it struck me with painful clarity that I was always eating myself alive around Sofija, forcing one part of myself to subsume the other. I was starting to believe that it might be worth leaving the FBI and going back to practicing law if it meant even one day with her, one night inside her—hopefully more. So, when she turned back to look at me again with pupils so dilated that her limpid green irises were nothing but thin rings, I abandoned my precious control.

Lowering my voice seductively, I said, "Oh, I really think you do know."

Rolling her eyes, Sofija admitted, "Fine. I thought you were hot and had a few fleeting thoughts about what it would be like to meet you when you weren't investigating me."

Triumphantly, I leaned back and regarded her. "And what did you fleetingly envision us doing?"

Sofija shook her head fiercely. "No. Come on, Agent Velasquez. Please don't make me spell it out."

"I think I'd like you to, though. Unless you'd prefer to show me," I added, seized by a sudden boldness.

Her mouth dropped open almost comically fast.

The electric kettle whistled, but neither of us moved.

"The kettle," Sofija said.

"Do you still want a drink?" I asked.

"Not really," she breathed.

"And Jesse?" I forced myself to ask.

"We're on a break."

No sooner had the words left Sofija's mouth than I leaned closer to her, closer to the edge of something from which there was no turning back. "Then let me try to convince you to make it permanent," I murmured. Her breath caught and her eyes widened.

It hardly felt real, what was happening, but then the sound of her chattering teeth snapped me out of my trance.

Even with the blanket, Sofija was trembling—from the cold, fear, nerves, or all of the above, I couldn't tell. I curled my arm around her shoulders and rubbed up and down to warm her.

A satisfied little sound escaped her and she scooted even closer. She tilted her face up to mine and our eyes locked. I felt my world narrow down to the space between us, like a black hole that was becoming infinitely dense, pulling us inexorably together.

Tentatively, she pressed her mouth against mine, then parted her lips to dart her tongue along the edge of my upper lip.

It was all the encouragement I needed. I kissed her everywhere I could, along her jawline, throat, collarbone, and, after I shifted her beneath me, down her stomach until I reached the waistband of her leggings. Craning my head up, I managed to rasp out, "Can I?"

"Mmmhmm," she hummed enthusiastically. *"Please."*

Heart hammering so fast that I was almost dizzy, I rolled down the band of Sofija's leggings and dragged my nose and lips along the velvety, tawny flesh of her thighs. She let out a breathy gasp and trembled as I nosed upward, tortuously slowly, building her up until she was whimpering. Finally, I pressed a kiss to where I knew she'd be most sensitive, our flesh separated by nothing more than her flimsy cotton thong. The slightly musky scent drove me wild, and I shoved the thin strip of cloth aside and took a long, relishing lick.

Sofija cried out and clamped her thighs around my head while she tangled a hand in my hair and gently pushed down, urging me on. The tightness I felt in my pants became unbearable. Unable to ignore my own need to move, I started thrusting against the couch, moaning while I continued to delve into her.

****

Almost immediately, I woke up with a start, panting. Pulses were radiating from my lower abdomen and the base of my spine, through my groin to my upper thighs. I felt an almost painful tension, an overwhelming urge to follow the feeling that had been building in my dream before the ruined crescendo.

My phone was poking out from under my couch cushion. I swung my arm up and grabbed it.

Once I had unlocked the screen, it was staring at me,

the impetus for the dream I had been having. Before I had fallen asleep, I had been scrolling through the image search results for Sofija Zammit and had clicked on a selfie linked to her PixABoo account.

There was nothing particularly salacious about the picture. Only the faintest outlines of her breasts were visible under a well-fitted navy T-shirt. It was her eyes, so vivacious, so playful, that did me in. I recalled how they had lit up, electric in their defiance, when she had defended herself on the day Cantrell and I had first questioned her. I remembered how I had seen them soften into something tender and loving when she had been caring for her patient.

Groaning, I debated what to do. Sleep didn't seem to be on the horizon if I took no action.

Should I work out again? It was very late. I had to wake up for work in a few hours. Should I run by the pharmacy and get some melatonin? The wind outside screamed at me not to. Should I find release? The picture of Sofija shone up at me from my phone, tempting me, taunting me.

Not to the subject of an investigation, Mateo!

Reluctantly, I pushed myself up from the couch and balled my hands into fists. I trudged off the bathroom and took a tepid shower. It worked well enough, if not perfectly.

But even though I was no longer throbbing in discomfort, I still wasn't tired—not even after I made myself a glass of warm milk with honey and cinnamon and put on soothing ocean sounds.

Might as well be productive.

I opened up my work phone and began scrolling through my to-do list, then my emails. I was devising a new, more granular email classification scheme, which I always found soothing, when a thought occurred to me. Frannie McDonnell had said that she would email me the receipts for the contractors that Jesse had hired to do maintenance around the Armitage estate. So far, I hadn't received anything—but it had been awhile since I had checked my spam folder.

I opened it, and sure enough, there was an email from an FMcDonnell10 sitting in spam. I dragged it back to the main folder and then opened it.

There were at least five different big ticket jobs documented by the receipts, none of them costing less than $40,000, some of them as much as $250,000. In total, the jobs had taken place over the course of about a year and a half, the last one dated to a few months before Sandra fell very ill.

I wrote down the names of each company and searched their addresses. The search returned no results.

I frowned. What kind of pavement business without a website was prominent enough to charge $40,000 for what should have been a $5000 job? The pattern repeated for every receipt. It made no sense.

As I tried to deduce what was going on, sleep finally overtook me. With my last conscious thought, I glanced at the time on my computer screen's upper right corner. It was 11:23 p.m.

Finally, I thought as I slipped into unconsciousness.

I dreamed that I was trapped in a sealed room. Next to me sat a blank sheet of paper. There was nothing with which to write, which was unfortunate because I had a powerful premonition that there was something crucial I would need to remember at some point in the future.

But there was no pen: only a small pocketknife.

Reluctantly, I opened the knife and studied it. It looked clean, spotless. Taking a deep breath, I pricked my finger until a small stream of blood flowed down. I used it to write something in smudgy red letters on the paper. A sense of relief washed over me.

When I awoke the next morning, I couldn't for the life of me remember what I'd written.

My head was pounding when I stood. A poor night's sleep caught up to me fast.

This is going to be a two coffees kind of day.

Trudging over to the kitchen, I started the coffee machine and opened my phone. Right in the middle of the screen was a notification for a text from Sofija.

I cracked the knuckles of my free hand while I opened the text. It was a photo of an envelope with the words GREEDY BITCH scrawled across it in deep red.

The words that accompanied it sent cold, biting electricity down my spine: "Delivered to my doorstep."

Chapter 13

Sofija

Despite the exhortations from the urgent care staff who treated me, I didn't go to the hospital for an x-ray or CT scan.

I knew I hadn't broken any bones and that my helmet had saved me from a concussion. I just wanted to go home, take some Ibuprofen, curl up in my bed, and be lost to the world for a little while. I didn't think I could stand having doctors poke and prod at me.

So after they dressed my wounds and gave me an oral antibiotic, I insisted that Jesse take me home. He agreed, and even used his car instead of using TripHitcher. I was grateful. I couldn't handle interacting with a stranger right now.

Though in all honesty, Jesse was starting to feel a little like a stranger to me. For the first time, I wasn't sure about him. I wanted so badly to believe that he was who I thought he was when I had fallen for him. But I was starting to realize that it would be unforgivably stupid of me not to look into the looming question marks that hung over him.

I couldn't let Jesse know what I was thinking, but I also didn't have the energy to pretend that everything was normal. So, I leaned my head to the side against the headrest and closed my eyes. Nobody would question my behavior, because of course I would be exhausted and traumatized after my ordeal.

When we made it to my place, Jesse scooped me up and placed me gently into my bed, then curled up behind me.

"Sleep, baby. I'm so glad you're okay."

Too tired to respond or to even register fear or gratitude, I slipped into a dreamless slumber.

****

When I woke up, I felt Jesse's arm flung over me. I squirmed out of his embrace and stood, watching as he readjusted by pulling a pillow closer in place of me. He really was so affectionate.

Please don't let me find out anything bad about him.

I slipped out of my bedroom and walked up to the front door. There was a pile of letters and flyers that had been slipped through the mail slot. Gingerly, I bent down. My fresh cuts burned as my skin stretched taut and my bruised muscles clenched in protest.

Hobbling over to the couch, I leafed through the mail. There were the usual magazines from companies I had bought from in the past and hadn't managed to unsubscribe from; a postcard from Keiko, who was hiking around Peru and Colombia right now; and the usual utility bills.

When I got to my internet bill, I noticed something strange about the envelope. It was crumpled, as if it had been opened and resealed. Carefully, I ran my nail under the edge, popped it open, and took out the month's statement.

Except it wasn't a bill. It was a photo of a bird I instantly recognized—a blue rock thrush, the national bird of Malta. Its eyes had been gouged out, as if a pen had ground into the sockets until it pierced through to the surface underneath, leaving a jagged, inky ring in its wake. A thick, dripped red line had been painted across the thrush's throat. No words accompanied the photo.

Everything had been building up, and for some reason, this was the last straw. I let the picture drift down to the table as I cradled my head in my hands and sobbed.

"Sofi?" came Jesse's voice from behind me. I didn't even turn around. I just pointed a shaky finger at the picture.

I heard Jesse's sharp intake of breath. "We're calling the police and then you're going to come stay at the estate. It's mostly yours anyways—or it will be once you sign the papers for the inheritance and make it yours. No need for you to stay in this place a day longer."

Why does he have to use every opportunity to bring up the inheritance? I thought angrily. The question reminded me of my purpose, and I steeled my resolve.

"You're right Jesse—I have to get out of here. For a day or two, at least. Help me pack a bag? We can drop this letter off at the police station on the way."

Jesse beamed at me triumphantly. "Glad you see things my way. Let me pack your things for you. Just sit there and relax."

He disappeared into my bedroom. I took the opportunity to snap a picture of the latest mailed threat and immediately sent it off to Velasquez. Like last time, I deleted the chat between us once the message was delivered.

Jesse re-emerged from my bedroom holding a stuffed bag. "I packed a few day's worth of clothes. Though I'm hoping you'll see reason and stay longer."

I gave Jesse my best grateful smile, which wasn't

entirely disingenuous. He was being helpful. Maybe all of this was nothing.

But it was time to find out definitively, so I put the first step of my plan into action.

"Thanks, Jesse. Just give me one second." I walked over to the fridge and pulled out a few of my homemade kombucha bottles. I packed them into a cloth grocery bag. Turning, I gave Jesse a nod. "Now I'm totally ready."

Jesse rolled his eyes playfully and said, "You and your home brews. Let's go."

****

The ride to the Armitage estate was uneventful. When we made it through the door, I pulled out one of my kombuchas.

Step two.

I flipped open the top of the bottle and lifted it to my lips. Then, I pretended to stumble, making sure that the opening was pointed at Jesse. The drink spilled all over the front of his shirt.

"Sofija! Dammit!" he shouted.

Pretending to be horrified, I slapped my hand on my forehead and said, "Oh Jesse, I'm so sorry! I tripped—I'm such a klutz, I know. Sorry!"

Jesse sniffed his shirt. His nose wrinkled and his mouth curled in distaste. "It's fine, Sofi, I'm sorry for yelling. I just…I don't love your homemade stuff."

"You've never tried it!" I protested.

"I know, it's just…it smells too strong, you know? I'm not a fan," he said apologetically. "Are you okay to wait in my bedroom while I shower this off?"

"Of course, Jesse. I'm just going to pop into the kitchen and put the rest of these into the fridge, okay?"

He gently lifted my chin and kissed my forehead. "Of course, baby. Meet you upstairs."

"It's a date," I joked as I slowly walked toward the kitchen, making sure to exaggerate the limp in the leg I had landed on during the bike crash.

Once I saw that he had made it up the stairs and through the hallway that led toward his room, I picked up my pace. I had to move fast if I was going to execute step three of my plan. Luckily, Jesse was the type to take long, indulgent showers, complete with several types of exfoliation.

I thought it would hurt to move so quickly, but the adrenaline must have muted the pain, because I barely felt anything as I breezed into the kitchen. It was past lunch but well before dinner, so Roland was nowhere to be found. I hauled over to the fridge and deposited my kombucha bottles inside. If Jesse checked, my story would be consistent with what I'd told him.

Then I scooted off toward the room Frannie used for administrative purposes. It was common knowledge that she kept all of the finance and property documents here. Peering in, I scanned the room to make sure nobody was there. Once I had confirmed that it was empty, I slid inside and began frantically searching through the binders lining the shelves on the wall opposite the computer desk.

Faster than I had hoped, I found one labeled "Upkeep Expenses." I opened it and flipped through the receipts until I came to those for maintenance jobs completed during the past five years. After I double checked that my phone was on silent, I took a series of rapid pictures of each of the receipts, then snapped the binder shut and replaced it. I ran out of the room and didn't stop until I made it to the elevator that had been installed when Sandra got too sick to walk up the stairs. I dashed inside and pressed the button for the third floor.

The doors sealed shut. I felt as if a protective, mechanical cocoon had closed around me. I was no longer out in the open. When the elevator reached the third floor where Jesse's room was, I didn't immediately step off it. Instead, I pressed the button to keep the doors closed and emailed each of the pictures of the receipts to myself. Every time the whooshing sound effect let me know that my mail had been sent off into the ether, I felt a deeper sense of relief.

After I sent each image, I examined the names of the companies. It didn't take long to find what I was looking for: Smooth Streets, LLC. Hired a little over a year ago to pave the driveway.

Quickly, I scanned my inbox to make sure that all of the pictures had been received. They had. Satisfied, I deleted all of the photos from my phone's album.

I checked the time. It had been ten minutes since Jesse had gone to shower. That meant that I had about two minutes before Jesse would be done with his whole routine.

Dashing off the elevator, I silently thanked God for Jesse's vanity and elaborate grooming rituals. I skidded to a stop outside of his bedroom.

Just as I opened the door, Jesse emerged from the bathroom. Steam enveloped him, and he had nothing but a towel slung low around his waist.

I swallowed nervously, afraid he would ask me where I had been.

Jesse must have interpreted my gulp differently, because he smirked and asked, "See something you like?"

Nodding vigorously, I said, "Yes. You look like an advertisement for a sauna or something."

He laughed, but then his smile turned into a confused frown. "Why are you out of breath? And where have you been?"

"Stairs," I improvised. "I tried to take the stairs, but with my injuries it was harder than it should have been. I slipped a couple of times. It's not easy to put weight on the right leg." I grimaced for added effect.

Jesse seemed to buy it, because he gave me a sympathetic look and guided me to the bed.

"Don't move then. Let's just relax here."

"Oh, you know what might be fun?" I exclaimed, as if the idea had just occurred to me. "What if we have wine and popcorn and watch a movie? I think I need some good, simple fun to take my mind off the accident."

Jesse grinned. "I like the way you think. Red or white?"

Pretending to mull over the decision, I titled my head. "Been awhile since I've had red, so maybe we could have a merlot. But I *do* love a good cabernet, especially one from California..."

"Why not both? Desperate times, you know," Jesse said with a wink as he hopped off the bed. "I'll be right back."

Time for step four.

I snatched up my phone, went on the Massachusetts Secretary of State site, and looked up Smooth Streets, LLC. There were only two employees listed. One of them, Danya Monroe, was listed as both the CEO and COO.

Danya Monroe. Danya Monroe, I silently repeated

to make sure I wouldn't forget it.

To be extra safe, I cleared my search and browser history from the last hour. Not a second after I set my phone on the nightstand nearest to me and leaned back against the pillow, Jesse appeared with a big tray. It was loaded with a bowl of popcorn, a platter of fruit and cheese, wine glasses, and two bottles of red.

The red that I was depending on to knock Jesse out for hours, as it had in the past.

"I could get used to you spoiling me," I said, half meaning it. The spread looked decadent. I felt like Jesse really *was* taking good care of me.

"You deserve it, Sofi, with everything you've been through. And just because you're you," he said as he set the tray down on the nightstand next to his side.

Part of me melted. It was confusing, feeling so much affection for and attraction to someone who might be a criminal.

Maybe that's how Velasquez feels about you.

I shook my head at the unwelcome thought. Now more than ever, I had to stay focused.

"You okay?" Jesse asked. "You were shaking your head."

"Ah—I just have a little headache from the crash. Nothing serious," I said.

Jesse gave me a reproachful look. "I still think you should have gotten a CT scan."

"If mild symptoms persist or worsen, I'll get one," I automatically replied.

Jessed knee-walked across the bed toward me, a wine glass clasped in each hand. "You know it gets me so hot when you use nurse-speak like that," he said, handing me a glass and kissing the scratches on my collarbone.

There was no need to pretend; I was genuinely getting turned on. I took a large swig of my wine and set the half empty glass on the nightstand, then leaned up to kiss him.

He quickly downed his own drink and latched onto my mouth, letting the empty glass fall on the covers.

"What if that stains?" I murmured between kisses.

"Then it will get cleaned. Don't be too worried about making a mess—I'm not," he whispered.

Must be a nice feeling, I thought enviously.

Jesse gripped my upper arms, causing one of the deeper cuts to throb. I sucked in my breath, and he paused and looked at me. "You're probably too hurt to do much, aren't you?"

"Yes, but I wish I weren't," I said truthfully. "Maybe the wine will dull the pain?"

He looked at me disapprovingly. "Sofi, we're not going to numb you up just so you can tolerate sex."

The way he said it, authoritative but caring at the same time, made me feel warm and fuzzy. *See, he does care for you!*

"You're probably right," I reluctantly conceded. "Let's just stream something. But you better be ready to make up for tonight's lack of 'and chill' the minute I'm better."

"Don't threaten me with a good time," Jesse murmured, grinding slowly against my leg so that I could feel every hard, taut muscle on his body.

I plucked up my wine glass and polished off what was left. I extended the empty glass toward him and tapped it with my pointer finger. "Until then?"

Jesse smirked and refilled my glass and his. "Until

then, cheers babe."

I took a big sip but held it in my mouth, the acidity tingling the back of my tongue. When Jesse tilted his head to knock back his own glass, I grabbed my empty flip top water bottle and quietly spit the wine into it. I snapped the top closed so that the wine's fragrant bouquet wouldn't escape.

"Are you double fisting it?" Jesse teasingly asked.

Tensing up, I gave him a quizzical look. "Huh?"

He nodded toward the water bottle. "Got something special in there?"

For a second, I panicked, searching for what to say. If I told him it was water and he asked for some, my trick would be revealed.

Then it came to me.

"Sort of—it's half water, half my homemade kombucha. I wasn't sure how long I would be here, so I wanted to stretch out what I brought for as long as possible. Voila, watered down kombucha." As an afterthought, I added, "It's from my ginger apple brew."

Jesse wrinkled his nose. "Ugh. Can't stand ginger. Doesn't that ruin the taste of the wine?"

"Nope. I'm going to use popcorn as a palate cleanser anyways," I said cheerily, stuffing a too big handful into my mouth. A couple of kernels fell down onto my lap and I could practically feel my lips glisten with butter.

Jesse chuckled. "Glad to see you're taking to heart my advice to make a mess." He took another gulp of his wine and said, "So what are we watching for this chill-free streaming?"

I took a small sip of wine and swallowed it for real this time. While Jesse did the same, I scooted closer, until I was snug against him. "Whatever you want. I picked the food and drinks, so you pick the movie."

"Hmm…how about something lighthearted? A comedy?"

"That would be perfect," I said with a smile. I meant it. If I didn't have an ulterior motive, this night would be perfect. It made me a special kind of sad that it wasn't.

"The Producers?" he suggested.

"Yes! I'll toast to that," I said, purposely slurring my words just a little. We clinked glasses, finished our second pour, and started on our third.

Throughout the film, I made sure to alternate between swallowing the wine and spitting some of it out into the water bottle. When the credits rolled, one bottle was empty, the other half full. I was certainly tipsy, but not drunk. In total, I'd only swallowed about two and a half full cups. Jesse had gone through four and then fallen asleep with half an hour left in the movie.

His gentle snore, combined with how completely peaceful he looked, twisted something in my heart. I wanted so badly to brush the hair out of his face and kiss him.

I'm sorry Jesse, but it's time for step five.

Carefully, I slipped my small hand into the pocket of his joggers and extracted his phone. I pressed the button to open it and then held it in front of his face to unlock it.

Once in, I navigated to his messages and searched for "Danya" and "Monroe." There were no results, so I scrolled through his apps until I found what I was looking for: an encrypted messaging app called Sine. This time, the same search pulled up a conversation.

I started at the beginning of the conversation and worked my way down.

There were no texts from earlier than this past April—a full year after Jesse had hired Smooth Streets, LLC to redo the driveway. Or, if there had been texts, they had either been auto deleted by the app or manually deleted. I couldn't tell.

Since then, there were a few exchanges, mostly about live music. It was the standard, "We're playing at this venue at this time," and "How many tickets do you want?" It seemed like Danya was in a band. There was nothing too suspicious about that, though I did find it a little strange that Jesse had never invited me to one of the band's performances. Then again, we were still a pretty new couple.

The second most recent exchange, dated to a few days ago, wasn't about music. It wasn't exactly damning, but it definitely didn't assuage my fears.

Jesse—*I might need your services soon, I think. The road up to the house is rougher than expected—*

Danya—*No problem. I've got plenty of supplies. Give me a call tomorrow and we can hammer out the details. I'm free after 6—*

Jesse—*Knew I could count on you. thanks—*

Danya—*Meet at High Tide Bar and Grill soon to catch up? June 5th work for you? We're kicking off a great set starting at 7. We can talk after—*

Jesse—*I'm down. It's been too long since I've had an authentic dive bar experience—*

Danya—*"Authentic dive bar experience." If I used emojis, I'd send you the eyeroll one, you prep school snob—*

Jesse—*I am who I am* ¯_(ツ)_/¯ —

Danya—*What the hell is that?—*

Jesse—*It's like a proto-emoji. It's me shrugging*

160

unapologetically—

Danya—*That's my cue to dip. I'll talk to you tomorrow–*

It was all innocuous enough, if a little cringy.

I scrolled down to the last message. When I saw the time stamp, my heart began pounding erratically. My arms and hands felt like they belonged to a stranger, like I wasn't controlling them, as I opened my own phone's call log to cross compare.

It was the same time. Jesse's last text to Danya had been sent at the same time that he was on the phone with me while I chased down the man on my bike.

Jesse—*All right, let's commit to that repaving.—*

Danya—*Consider it done. I've got my best man with our best product on it. I'll let him know ASAP—*

That was it. It wasn't proof—certainly not enough to convict—but it was enough to feed that ugly suspicion of Jesse that I had been trying to starve.

A tear slid down my cheek as I took a picture of the texts between Jesse and Danya, emailed them to myself, and then deleted them from my photo album. I exited out of the Sine app on Jesse's phone and carefully slid it back into his pocket. He shifted a little, but didn't wake.

My legs felt like lead, but I swung them out of bed and stood. Quietly, I picked up my water bottle and walked over to the bathroom, where I emptied the contents down the sink. I filled it with real water, trudged back to bed, and lay down.

As I stared at Jesse, I started sobbing, trying my best not to make a sound. The heartbreak hurt worse than any of my injuries. I felt myself making excuses, saying it was a coincidence, that the texts didn't prove anything.

I grabbed the half empty wine bottle and took a deep

pull, no longer caring if I got drunk. Maybe it would finally put me to sleep. Anything to silence my mind.

When I finally felt drowsy, I nuzzled my nose into Jesse and inhaled. His scent was the last thing I consciously registered before I fell asleep.

****

A chime from my phone woke me. Still a little woozy, I cracked an eye open to see who was texting me.

But it wasn't a text. It was an email from one of the admissions officers at a nurse practitioner program to which I had submitted an early decision application. Holding my breath, I opened it.

Dear Ms. Zammit,

In light of recent allegations made against you regarding the treatment of your patients, we encourage you to apply again to our program after the matter is resolved.

While I cannot definitively say that an application made during this application cycle would be unsuccessful, personal character and a demonstration of regard for medical ethics are essential criteria that our admissions committee takes under consideration.

We are well aware that in the law of the land, you are innocent until proven guilty. That said, the standards for admission differ from those needed to prove guilt in court. This communication should not be read as the committee's or any one member's opinion on your innocence or guilt; rather, it is out of an abundance of caution that we scrutinize the professional record of all potential students.

Your candidate profile is otherwise strong, and so once this matter is cleared up, we encourage you to reapply. However, should you wish for us to evaluate your application now, we will do so.

Sincerely,

Norma Battelle

I stared at the screen and then closed my eyes. When I opened them, the email was still there.

This wasn't a wine-fueled nightmare.

This was my life.

One of my grade school science teachers made us watch a documentary on the La Brea Tar Pits in Los Angeles. I felt like one of those prehistoric rabbits that had gotten caught in the oily, bubbling pits. I was thrashing around helplessly as the tar swallowed me up until I couldn't breathe or see the sunlight. Nobody would dare help me—they'd be too scared to be dragged down into the muck alongside me.

Dear Ms. Zammit.

Something about that sent me into a rage. It wasn't just me, Sofija, who was being drawn into this. It was Zammit.

I may have spent my young life resenting the way my last name had been used to mock me, but I was still proud of it. At least, I was proud enough to refuse to let it get sullied on my account.

I'd be damned if I let that happen.

Jesse stirred next to me and pushed himself into a sitting position. He must have noticed the grim set of my face, because he rubbed my back and asked, "What's wrong, Sofi?"

Wordlessly, I handed him my phone, the email still pulled up. I watched as his eyes scanned line after line.

After a moment, Jesse handed it back to me and wrapped me in a hug. His cologne smelled nice, familiar. "Oh, baby, I'm so sorry," he whispered, planting a kiss

163

on the side of my forehead. "I'm sure as soon as this whole thing dies down and some time passes, you'll have better luck. If you still even want to go by then."

I leaned back against him, feeling the irresistible pull of blanking out.

"And even if it doesn't happen for you, it won't matter. With the kind of money you'll have, you won't need to work ever again. Throw half of it into an index fund and have fun with the rest. You've already paid off your house," he joked, gesturing around us.

Incensed, I pushed away. "Jesse! It's not about the money. I want to practice my profession! I want to take care of people! Not sit around all day and rot away like some trust fund baby."

Jesse's jaw twitched. "That's what you think I would be, if my mom had left me the money, don't you? Or maybe that's what you think I'll be once you split the money with me. Maybe that's why you haven't done it yet—you're just waiting for an excuse to back out of our agreement."

Twisting to face him, I protested, "NO Jesse, that is not what I think of you! You're an entrepreneur!"

I meant to sound sincere, but Jesse must have taken it otherwise, because he sneered. "Save the sarcasm for someone who appreciates it, Sofija." He got off the bed and started dressing. "I'm leaving."

"Wait, Jesse!" I cried out. "I really didn't mean it like that!"

He didn't respond as he walked toward the dresser and fastened his $10,000 watch around his wrist. It was clear he was leaving and that there was nothing I could do about it.

I knew I shouldn't care, now that I strongly

suspected that Jesse was behind my recent harassment. Still, I didn't want to end things before I had definitive proof. I still needed to determine why he was doing this, and that would be difficult to do at a distance.

Plus, a small, irrational part of me still clung to hope. Hope that this was a misunderstanding, or that Jesse had a good, if misguided, reason for what he was doing.

"You stay, Jesse. I'll—I'll take the train home," I offered.

He gave me a cold look, devoid of the affection that was always there. "It's your house," he said bitterly. "Or at least it will be if you do what's good for you. But I'm tired of trying to help you to help yourself, Sofija. Only you can do that."

"What-what does this mean? Are we breaking up?" I asked, tearing up.

You sound pathetic, Sofija.

"I don't know. Probably not. Probably I just need time to cool down. But I want space, okay?"

Jesse's request stung. I looked down at my hands as I played with the edge of the oversized long sleeve shirt I had slept in. Jesse's shirt.

"Okay," I whispered. My vision was blurred with tears, my mind too numb to register that Jesse had sat down next to me until he kissed the top of my head.

"Sorry. I just need to work through some things. I'll text you."

He didn't say anything else. Sniffling, I watched him walk down the stairs. I felt as though I was seeing something irretrievable disappear, like the last summer of college before it was time to enter the working world.

Very little in my life was certain anymore—but one thing was. I most certainly would not be splitting any money with Jesse until I got to the bottom of this.

That meant that I needed to learn more about Jesse's connection to Danya.

I checked my email for the picture I had sent of her and Jesse's text exchange.

Danya—*Meet at High Tide Bar and Grill soon to catch up? June 5th work for you? We're kicking off a great set starting at 7. We can talk after—*

For several minutes, I debated telling Velasquez and Cantrell. Ultimately, I decided against it. If I was wrong about Danya, then I would be casting suspicion on an innocent woman. It would be better for me to watch her and Jesse's interactions before I told the FBI about my hunch.

Decision made, I started thinking about what I had in my closet that would be dive-bar appropriate, because in two weeks, I would be visiting one for the first time.

High Tide Bar and Grill. Sounds like a place where sex-starved deep sea fishermen go for a drink and a quick lay. I wrinkled my nose at the thought, though the sneaking around undercover was a little thrilling.

Slowly, I hauled myself up from the bed and took a shower. I considered leaving the room as it was, but I realized that would mean extra work for Marly, and I didn't want that. I gathered up the empty bottle of wine, recorked the half full one, and placed them on the tray along with the popcorn bowl, platter, and wine glasses. Carefully, I balanced the tray in one hand and my overnight bag in the other and headed to the elevator.

When it reached the ground floor, I stepped out. I set my bag on the floor next to the front door and walked toward the kitchen with the tray.

I was about to step inside when I heard Frannie and

Roland's voices. They seemed agitated. I paused outside to eavesdrop.

"Awful what happened to Talia," Frannie fretted.

"Sure is. Never could have seen any of this coming. She seemed far too healthy and young."

"Exactly!" Frannie agreed emphatically.

"Didn't know her well, but seemed like a nice enough girl."

"She was, although I myself thought she was the one who got the FBI involved in all of this. Turns out it was Adam."

"Why would you suspect Talia? Didn't seem like the type to snitch to me," Roland said.

Frannie sounded defensive as she replied, "Well, you know, she was newer here. And because last week, I saw her rummaging through the room where I keep all the financial and legal documents related to the estate. She had pulled out the binder where I keep all the utility bills and the one where I keep the estate maintenance receipts. It just seemed suspicious to me. Why would she care about that? Wasn't her job."

Whatever Roland said in reply, I didn't hear. There was a buzzing sound in my head and it took everything in my power not to drop the tray.

Talia had been looking at the receipts?

The only person who had a reason to be sensitive about that would be Jesse, since he was the one who hired the contractors.

What if Jesse had seen or gotten wind of what Talia was doing? Worse still, what if Talia had confronted Jesse about it?

Jesse would never murder someone, Sofija. Get a grip.

Still, there was a bad feeling in my stomach, like all the popcorn from last night was churning in a vat of acid, partially digested, little solids bumping into the inflamed lining.

I tuned back into Frannie and Roland's conversation.

"Take the reins for a second, Frannie? I've got to use the bathroom," Roland said.

"Again? You went five minutes ago! You've got yourself a stomach bug, don't you? My son knows a great GI. She helped set him right after his summer in the DR had him living on the toilet."

"No, Frannie, it's not that. I—well, to be frank, the last few weeks, I've got to piss all the time. Like a pregnant woman. Hell, I've even been feeling tired like one, and God knows I've got the belly."

"Oh stop that, Roland. You look fine. And the peeing thing, it's just aging. My husband got like that when he turned fifty-five. Couldn't take a road trip without stopping every hundred miles for him to—"

"Frannie!" Roland cried desperately.

"Sorry, Roland! Go on, use the restroom. I'll stir the sauce and make sure it doesn't burn."

"Thanks. Let me just get my apron off."

Fuck. He's coming out here.

As gently but as quickly as I could, I set the tray down outside the door frame, just far enough away from it that nobody would trip over it. I snatched up the half empty bottle of wine.

Going to need some liquid courage over the next few days.

I managed to make it back to my overnight bag before Roland emerged from the kitchen. Without bothering to untie them, I slipped on my shoes and scurried out the door.

Once I was safely outside, I walked to the edge of the porch and sat down, away from the windows and behind one of the hydrangeas. Even though I knew I was out of anybody's line of sight, my heart was pounding as I laced up my shoes and stowed the bottle of wine in my bag.

Ready to run, I hopped off the porch and dashed through the back of the estate, past the pond. Scaling the fence at the edge of the property wasn't difficult. It was a small, white picket fence—more for aesthetics than to keep people out. There wasn't much need for security, given the area's near zero crime rate. It was a safe place.

At least, I had thought it was. Now, I was wondering if a killer lived on the premises—a killer I had thought I loved.

Maybe it was even worse than that. Maybe there were *two* murderous people hiding in plain sight within the walls of the estate. I couldn't shake the image of the tall, pale, dark haired man following me to the police station, of him riding away from me on his bike into the night. The more I thought about it, the more I realized that with all the wealth he had at his disposal, Adam could easily afford to fly back from San Francisco on a private plane for a little game of scare-little-Sofija. Maybe he had never been in San Francisco at all.

The thoughts flew at me as I sprinted toward the road and checked my phone, muttering a prayer of gratitude when I saw that I had strong service.

Fingers trembling, I ordered a ride on TripHitcher and sank down in relief when a driver accepted.

After I gained control of my breathing, I considered

my next move.

I needed to do some digging into Danya on my own before I shared my hypothesis about her with the FBI. The last thing I wanted to do was throw an innocent female entrepreneur under the bus for no reason. She might not know who Jesse really was.

Hell, I didn't know, and I had dated him for months. Coincidences were piling up around him, but they were circumstantial. Part of me hoped that's all they were, and that we could pick up our relationship where we left off once this whole ordeal was over.

But I couldn't ignore the information about Talia that I had overheard today. She deserved for someone to turn over every stone until her killer, assuming there was one, faced justice.

The fact that Talia had been looking into the maintenance receipts was something I knew I had to share with the FBI. I couldn't just text Velasquez about it, though. It was too sensitive. I wanted to make a formal, in-person report to the FBI to make sure that I wasn't misunderstood.

The thought of seeing Velasquez again thrilled me, but the excitement immediately soured.

It wouldn't be right.

Our last interaction, when he had offered to teach me Spanish only to clumsily backtrack when he had realized what he had said, made me suspect that he felt something for me. So did what Jesse said during his angry outburst.

Maybe it was just physical attraction on Velasquez's part, but it was something more for me. If I were being honest, since the night I met him, my curiosity had been about more than what he was hiding under his fitted FBI suit. When he had told me how he understood what that special mix of love and pressure from immigrant parents felt like, I had felt a connection. Throughout our interactions, it had grown into a full-blown crush. I might as well call it what it was.

There was something so appealing about his restraint and how flustered he got when it slipped. I was willing to bet that underneath all that control was so much bottled up passion and an urge to give—and I wanted to *take*. I wanted to take everything and give it back just as good.

I wanted it way too much.

You shouldn't be around him at his workplace, Sofija. You're too transparent. What if someone sees your reaction to him and gets the wrong idea? Cantrell already seems to think he has a soft spot for you. He could get in trouble. He could lose his job.

The thought sobered me. Sometimes, I hated my conscience—but I knew I had to listen to it. I couldn't be around Velasquez for more than a minute before I was blushing.

Grudgingly, I promised myself that I would share the information about Talia with Cantrell. The prospect filled me with dread, so when the TripHitcher ride pulled up, I was sitting on the damp earth and scowling. I dragged myself up and confirmed my identity to the driver, ignoring the concerned looks he was shooting me in the mirror.

Mateo. In my head, I'm going to call him Mateo. If I can't have him and let him have me, I'm going to give myself this.

It was a stupid, pointless thing, but the small act of rebellion that only I would know about was enough to improve my mood. I drifted off to sleep for the rest of the ride.

Chapter 14

Mateo

I came into work right at 9 a.m., which, for me, was late. I hadn't slept very well the last few nights, preoccupied as I was by the escalating threats against Sofija that had most recently culminated in her ill-fated bike chase. Every time I saw a text from her, my insides seized up with worry over what had happened this time.

Consulting with the FBI Laboratory's handwriting analysts had yielded little. Since they had nothing against which to compare the writing on the envelope that had been delivered to Sofija's doorstep, they couldn't tell me anything about who might have written it. Sofija had given the first letter that had been attached to a brick, along with the envelope, to her local police station. When their examinations had hit a dead end, they had forwarded the items to the FBI for analysis. Whoever had created the letter and envelope had been meticulous, because there wasn't a trace of usable DNA.

The only potentially useful piece of information we had been able to glean from our analysis was that the writing on the envelope was wax based, almost as if the perpetrator had used an artists' crayon or a lumber crayon. Still, it was essentially nothing to go on.

As I walked toward my desk, the conference room door to my right opened and Cantrell stepped out—

followed by Sofija.

"Thanks for sharing this information, Ms. Sofija. You know to report anything else that you think may be of interest," Cantrell's voice boomed.

"Will do, Agent Cantre—" Sofija cut off when she saw me, her eyes widening. "Agent Velasquez! I was just—well, I found out something useful, and-and—"

"And I'll update you about it in ten minutes, Velasquez. I'll come by your cubicle after I escort her out," Cantrell finished for her.

I knew I must have looked hurt, because Sofija glanced up at me and then quickly averted her eyes as she said, "Well, I hope you're doing well, Agent Velasquez. I've got to head off to work."

"Nice to see you," I said stiffly.

Nodding while she edged away from me, she said, "You too. Take care, both of you!" She scurried off to the elevator and Cantrell followed. They were exchanging words, but I didn't care to stand there and attempt to lip read, so I stalked off to my desk.

Had Sofija gone to Cantrell because she didn't think I would be able to do anything valuable with the information? Did she think I was incompetent, since I hadn't yet produced any leads about whoever was responsible for the threatening notes she'd received?

The thought was a blow to my self-esteem. As I sat in my chair, sullenly scrolling through the lab's report one more time, Cantrell appeared beside me.

"No use looking into that. We've gotten all there is to get from it," he said matter-of-factly.

"Then I'll move on to the receipts that Frannie showed me." My voice sounded listless, even as I tried to seem like my usual self.

"Get to that later. You and I are going to follow up on a lead Sofija just gave us. You're the one with the silver tongue, so I'm going to need your help on this one."

"And what lead was that?" I asked, my mood improved a little by Cantrell's vote of confidence.

"Sofija claims to have listened in on a very interesting conversation between Frannie and Roland. Frannie apparently said that Talia Portnoy was looking through documents in the room of the Armitage estate where all the financial and legal documents are kept."

"The same room where the receipts are," I mused aloud.

"That's right. Talia had pulled out that binder specifically, along with the one with all the utility bills. Seems like a strange thing for a maid to do."

Pieces of the puzzle were slowly coming together. "What did the coroner say about Talia when you saw him?" I asked.

"Said the coma was caused by hypoglycemia—but the girl wasn't diabetic. It's too early to know for sure, but he thinks she was injected with insulin."

I furrowed my brow in thought. "You don't happen to have a copy of the police report, do you?"

"Sure do," Cantrell replied. "I can email it to you, but I had them print me two copies. You can have one." He turned and ruffled through a few papers on his desk. The way he organized his files was beyond me—it looked like an unmitigated mess. But he always found what he needed when he needed it, so maybe there was a method behind his madness.

"Here," he said, thrusting a file folder at me.

I opened it and flipped through the pages inside,

quickly skimming their contents. I would go over them more thoroughly on the ride to wherever today's destination was.

"Talia had two chicken breasts marinating in the fridge? And two containers of fresh berries?" I asked.

Cantrell grunted in the affirmative. "That's what the file says."

I looked up from the pages. "That doesn't seem like the kind of thing someone who was intent on killing herself would do," I remarked.

"No, it does not," he agreed. I got the feeling he was waiting on me to continue, so I did.

"She wasn't a diabetic—her medical records show that. She didn't live with anybody, diabetic or not, and she didn't work in healthcare. So, she had no reason to come into contact with insulin. An accident doesn't seem plausible."

"Correct."

"It's almost certainly foul play," I concluded.

"That it is. You prepared to follow this thread no matter where it leads, Velasquez?" Cantrell asked. He was observing me closely.

I swallowed and gave a monosyllabic, "Yes."

"Good. Then meet me at the car. We're paying a visit to Springfield."

****

On the ride over to Talia's apartment, I poured over the coroner's notes, as well as those Cantrell had taken while speaking with Sofija earlier that morning.

"Ms. Sofija claims that Talia picked the area because she liked the sense of tight-knit community," Cantrell said once I'd closed the file folder.

"If that's true, then most likely she would have been

known to her neighbors and local business people. Restaurant and café owners, the doctor, the dentist, the hair stylist, that kind of thing," I speculated.

"Good assumption, Velasquez. We should talk to them and try to paint a picture of who she was, who she hung around."

"She was twenty-seven, according to her file. So let's start at the hipper bars and cafés."

Cantrell gave one of his trademark bark laughs. "Not too many of those around Springfield, Velasquez. It'll be quick work."

"Better for us, then," I said. "Let's drive to her apartment and then work our way downtown. We can stop at every place that fits the profile of somewhere she'd go. That way, we'll hit the closest ones first."

Cantrell gave a nod and continued driving until we arrived.

Talia's apartment complex was fairly upscale and sleepy. All of the cars looked no more than ten years old, and most were parked under fancy gazebo-style shelters. Two ponds were tucked into the surrounding landscape, part of which seemed to be a golf course. It was hardly the type of place I would expect a murder to occur.

We parked in the visitor's spot and Cantrell walked into the reception to alert the employee on duty of our presence. I stepped out of the car and leaned back against it, one leg bent so that my foot was propped up on the wheel behind me. With every fiber of my being, I tried not to think about the disappointing turn of events from the morning, instead directing my energy to scheming the best way to approach the Springfield locals we were about to talk to.

The air wasn't quite warm yet, and a strange mist

wove around the trees and buildings. It was eerie, but had I been there for a different reason, it might have seemed quaint.

A quick scan of the apartment revealed nothing new, so we set off on foot toward downtown.

We learned very little of value from our first few stops—two cafés, a grocery store, a bookstore, and a laundromat—though the people we spoke to were pleasant enough. By the time we were done with the baristas in the second café, all we had was a supersaturation of caffeine in our bloodstream.

Nobody had noticed anything suspicious in the last few weeks. Talia had been a creature of habit, rarely deviating from her weekday routine of stopping by Anne's Pastry Depot for a croissant and coffee before taking off for work. Most Fridays, she reportedly frequented Harry's Jazz Lounge or Nick's Tavern, sometimes alone, sometimes with a companion. Without fail, on Sunday mornings, she would brunch with a regular group of girlfriends at The Pearl Shell.

"The Pearl Shell isn't too far from here—just a couple of blocks up. Let's speak with people there," I suggested.

Cantrell harrumphed. "Agreed, but I'm not buying anymore coffee. If you want to support local businesses, you go ahead. I need food to soak up some of this caffeine."

I chuckled. "I'm on the verge of overdoing it with coffee too. I'll stick with orange juice from here on out."

We stopped in front of a cozy, off-white house that looked like it had been recently renovated. Out front, a light ecru sign hung from a post. In swoopy, millennial pink letters, it read, "The Pearl Shell."

"What do you think the chances are that this place serves some normal breakfast? Just eggs, bacon, plain white toast, or hash browns?" Cantrell asked.

I gave him a sympathetic smile and laughed. "You might be able to convince them to hold the garlic aioli."

Cantrell gave me a frown and sighed. "Don't know why people your age can't just call mayonnaise what it is. Let's get this over with."

I followed him inside. Tables made of reclaimed planks, benches fashioned from cut and sanded driftwood, wicker chairs, ceramic plates, and tea lights strung along the upper walls made for a fresh, beachy feel.

A perky looking young waitress practically skipped up to us and greeted, "Welcome to *The Pearl Shell*! We've got a number of specials, including fresh Pemaquid oysters just in from Maine and our massaged kale, watermelon, feta, and pumpkin seed salad. It's also happy hour, so our bottomless mimosa option is half off."

I thought I heard Cantrell mutter, "Starving today it is," under his breath before he jerked his head in my direction and then at the waitress.

Clearing my throat, I said, "Sounds delicious. We'd actually like to sit at the bar, if that's possible."

"Absolutely!' she replied. "Frees up more tables for late brunch parties. Come with me, please." She spun on her tennis shoes and walked quickly toward the bar. As she placed two sets of silverware wrapped in linen napkins on the dark wood countertop, she called out, "Mark, we've got two for you at the bar. Can you get them waters and menus?"

"Sure thing," the man at the cash register said. He

snatched up two menus, filled up two glasses of water, grabbed two coasters, and arranged it all in front of us with impressive alacrity.

"Like Emily said, I'm Mark. I think she's already been over the specials with you, but if you have questions about them or about anything else on the menu, let me know."

I turned to Cantrell and gave him a small smile. "What do you think? Bottomless mimosas?"

Cantrell glared at me but I saw the corner of his mouth twitch before he turned to Mark. "I'll have a glass of orange juice and two eggs sunny side up. White toast and bacon, if you have it."

Mark cocked his head slightly and looked at Cantrell as if he were really seeing him for the first time. "No problem with the eggs, but we only have peameal bacon and wheat toast or brioche."

Cantrell's nostrils flared a little but he replied, "All right. I'll try the piecemeal bacon and—" he turned to me. "You're the food expert, Velasquez. Will I like brioche?"

"You won't like the way it looks, but you'll like how it tastes," I answered honestly.

Cantrell threw up his hands. "All right. Why not? The brioche."

Mark scribbled on a pad of paper and said, "Got it. And you?" he asked, turning to me.

"I'll have orange juice and *migas*. What kind of hot sauces do you have?"

"No brands—we have a red, a green, and an orange, all made in house," Mark listed.

"Red, then. Thank you," I said.

"You got it," Mark replied as he walked off to the

order interface. When he came back to us with our orange juices, I casually observed, "This place is nice. Pretty different from the other restaurants around here, though. Skews a little to a younger clientele, no?"

"You're not wrong," Mark agreed. "There aren't as many young people here as in Boston or Amherst. But lately there's been an influx of thirty-something yuppie types who work remotely and only commute into the big cities once or twice a week, so they moved out here. Get more bang for their buck and can afford houses. Our owner saw the opportunity that came with that and took a gamble. It was popular with the new folks pretty quickly. Then older locals noticed and decided to give it a try. We're doing well," he finished.

"You definitely are, if you can afford to bring in oysters from Maine," I said encouragingly. "So would you say people who work in Springfield pretty much know everyone who lives here?"

Mark paused thoughtfully and then answered, "I'd say so. I definitely know everyone who is a regular customer here. But that could also be because I've been working double shifts to pay for grad school next year. I'm here so often, they've got a cot with my name on it in the back," he joked.

Jackpot, I thought elatedly. I could tell Cantrell was pleased too as I sensed him perk up beside me.

"If that's the case, you might be able to help us out," I said. "We're with the FBI and are working with local police to investigate the death of Talia Portnoy, along with some possibly related matters. Did you know Talia?"

Mark looked down and swallowed. "Yeah. I don't want to hide anything from you, so I may as well come out and say that we were hooking up on and off."

"Did you stop doing that prior to her death?" Cantrell asked.

"No, but it was pretty irregular. Talia wanted it that way."

"Why? Was she seeing other people? Were you mad that she kept you at a distance?" Cantrell badgered.

Shrugging, Mark said a little defensively, "She told me that she didn't want to hook up too frequently or else she'd get attached, and she didn't want that since I'd be off at grad school soon. We never explicitly talked about it, but she never seemed interested in a long-distance relationship. So we were on really good terms, but we didn't...get physical all the time. It was an occasional thing."

"You two were just scratching an itch, huh?" Cantrell asked.

Mark crossed his arms and narrowed his eyes at Cantrell. "Before I answer anything else, how about you clarify something for me. Is this related to that nurse who's suspected of ripping off her elderly patients? That's why you're here, isn't it? Because Talia worked for that old lady Armitage. What, you think Talia was in on the scheme with the nurse too? Because if that's what you think, you're wrong. Talia wasn't like that," he said emphatically.

I could tell that Mark was on the verge of clamming up, so I did my best to redirect the conversation. "We're definitely interested in Talia's work life and how she felt about her employers and coworkers, but today, our primary goal is to piece together the events that led to her death. Mark, you must have gone to Talia's place a few times, right?"

"Right," he said, still sounding suspicious. At least he uncrossed his arms, which I took as a good sign.

"Did you see any insulin around her place? Or any evidence that she was diabetic?"

Mark shook his head. "Absolutely not. And she would come here pretty much every Sunday and eat and drink whatever she felt like with her girlfriends. Never saw her take a shot and she didn't use a patch. She was very healthy."

"Right," I said. "That's what we've been given to understand."

"You think Talia was murdered, don't you?" Mark asked, agitation creeping back into his voice. "Is this you questioning me as a suspect? Do I need a lawyer?"

"No, no," I reassured. "We're mostly just trying to get a sense of who might have done this. Did Talia seem off or even just different in the last few weeks?"

Mark poured himself a glass of water and gulped it down before responding. "I've worked back to back double shifts several times over the last couple weeks, so I didn't see her enough to know for sure. Maybe she was a little quieter and drank a little more wine than usual the last time we had dinner together. But that might just be my perception now because you're asking me about it. Like, I don't know if I would have said that if you'd asked me at the time."

There was a ding from the kitchen window. "Your food is up. I'll be right back," Mark said before retrieving our dishes and setting them in front of us.

Cantrell looked at the brioche with a nonplussed expression. "What is this, a fancy hamburger bun?"

I made sure he couldn't see me as I rolled my eyes. Mark caught me, though, and gave me a surreptitious smile.

"Just slice it in half and put some butter on it," I instructed.

Cantrell slathered butter on one half and bit down. After a few chews, he gave a grunt of pleasure. "You weren't wrong. It's good. Shaped kinda funny, but it tastes great."

"I'm glad you like it," I said. Turning back to Mark, I asked, "Did Talia seem to like her job?"

"As far as I can tell. She said it paid well and gave her a pretty good work life balance."

"What about her colleagues? Did she talk about them?".

"Not much, to be honest," Mark answered. "Sorry I can't be more help. We didn't have super in-depth conversations about work. I mostly talked about my grad program and she talked about the house she was saving up to buy and renovate."

"She wanted to renovate a house?"

Mark smiled wistfully. "Yeah. She would light up talking about it. It's just down the street from her place. She'd done the research on contractors and everything."

Cantrell and I exchanged significant glances.

"Did she mention who she was researching or considering?" I knew it was a stretch, but I had to ask.

Mark shook his head and looked confused. "No, she never discussed anything that specific with me. I think she said she wanted to ask around, talk to people she knew to see if they had recommendations. Why? Do you think a contractor is the one who killed her?" he asked, eyes widening.

"We can't discuss that," Cantrell replied curtly. Mark flinched a little.

"Mark," I said gently, trying to put him back at ease. "Can you think of anyone who would have wanted to hurt Talia?"

He shook his head sadly. "I wish I could help you there. I really do. If Talia was murdered, I want the guilty asshole behind bars. But there's just nothing coming to mind for me. People here thought she was nice, if a little reserved. She was well-liked."

Suddenly, something dawned on his face. "Although, there was this one creep. Definitely not a local. It was about a week ago, two weeks ago, I don't know. The last couple of weeks are blurring together for me. Anyways, this guy came in around the time Talia had brunch with her friends. He just installed himself at a table where Talia was right in his line of sight. For two whole hours, he just stared at her really intensely."

"Could he have been a customer who came in and leered at her because he thought she was pretty?" Cantrell asked.

Mark shook his head. "The guy didn't act like a customer. Over the course of two hours, he only ordered coffee and a salad. That's it. And he wasn't leering at Talia—it didn't seem sexual, I mean. It almost looked like he was trying to listen to what she was saying, or read her lips or something. I can't really describe it better than that," he finished apologetically.

I turned the information over in my head before I asked, "What did the man look like?"

"That's the other strange thing. He wore a hat the entire time, and those super thick lensed glasses that make people look bug-eyed. I mean, we get people who dress all kinds of ways. But it was strange because everything else about his outfit was trendy and super nice. Like one of those young venture capitalists or big law millionaires or something."

"Could you discern anything else about his physical appearance?" I pressed. "Height? Weight? Skin color? Hair color?"

Mark considered this for a minute. "He was tall, thin but not skinny, really pale, and had dark hair that went to about his chin," Mark replied. "Prominent nose. Can't remember his eye color, though. The glasses were too distracting."

Again, Cantrell and I exchanged glances.

Sounds like Adam in a bad disguise.

"Before you ask, he paid in cash, so I have no idea what his name was," Mark added. "A minute or two after Talia left, he put bills on the table and left. If he did something to her, it wasn't that night, though, because she sent me a text the next afternoon. Asked if we were still on for dinner in a week."

Wrapping his knuckles on the table, Cantrell said, "Well, thanks for this. Velasquez, got any more questions?"

"Just one more, if that's okay," I said.

"Sure," Mark agreed.

"Do you have any idea why Talia quit her job?"

Mark picked up our empty plates and set them in the bus bin behind the bar. "Talia said she wasn't sure that there would be a job for her there much longer, what with Mrs. Armitage being gone. Again, we didn't talk too much about work things, but I do remember her saying that the older son didn't need anything from the estate. Guy is loaded, apparently. The younger son annoyed her. And she had no idea what the nurse was planning to do. Said the whole situation gave her a weird feeling. In any case, Talia had enough saved up to buy that house she had been planning to renovate. Some extra financial cushion would have been nice, but she didn't need it," Mark concluded.

I nodded. "Did Talia say what about the situation gave her a weird feeling?"

"Nope. But it doesn't take a genius to guess, does it? The nurse gets most of the money instead of the old woman's own sons. That's just strange. It doesn't seem right. Not to me, at least, and not to Talia."

By now, the tables around us had completely filled up with customers, and Emily the waitress had started to direct new arrivals to the bar. Mark glanced around and said, "It's starting to pick up. Not to be rude, but if you have any more questions, could you make them quick?"

"That's all for now. We'll let you get back to your job," I said as Cantrell put down the money we owed.

"Keep the change," he said.

Mark looked bemused for a moment before he nodded. "Thanks. Been awhile since someone has paid in cash," he said.

Cantrell's mouth twitched in what I assumed was disdain. He gave the table a perfunctory slap. "Let's go, Velasquez."

"Thank you for your time," I said, sliding an extra five onto the table.

"No problem. I'll be here for the rest of the summer if you've got any more questions. Hope you catch whoever did this."

"We do too," I said.

When we made it out to the porch, Cantrell leaned over the railing and started working over a toothpick. "Saw you slip the guy a five. Why? I tipped."

"You tipped him fifteen percent," I said.

"And? That's standard."

Be delicate, I cautioned myself. I settled on saying, "I think the new norm is twenty percent, for good service."

Snorting, Cantrell asked, "When did *that* happen?"

"Not sure," I replied lightly.

Cantrell shook his head and plucked the toothpick from between his lips. "All right. I'll do that next time. Things change faster and faster, these days."

I hid my smile by angling my face toward the town. "Should we press on?" I suggested.

"Yeah, though I have a bad feeling that the guy we just talked to was as informative as they're gonna get," Cantrell predicted as he walked past me toward the stairs.

"Let's hope not. He wasn't incredibly helpful."

"He wasn't, was he? We knew the girl wasn't diabetic. Only useful piece of information was about that man who was sitting at the table watching her."

"Right," I concurred. "And it was a pretty vague description. Although…"

"You're going to say it sounds like Adam Armitage, aren't you?" Cantrell guessed.

"I was."

"I've only seen the pictures of Adam that are in the files or online, but I agree, there's a generic resemblance. Lots of men match that description though."

"Lots of men do," I echoed, lost in thought. "Still, it wouldn't hurt to confirm his whereabouts during that period of time."

"It's a good idea," Cantrell agreed.

I allowed myself to get lost in thought as we strolled to the next stop.

****

The day had been frustrating, to put it mildly. Hours of driving and questioning had yielded almost no new insights into the identity of Talia's presumed killer. All we had was Mark's nebulous description of a potential suspect, confirmed by the hostess at Harry's Jazz Lounge. She recounted seeing a similar looking man observing Talia and a friend two nights before the incident Mark reported.

None of that was actionable information. The day was essentially a wash—yet another thing that had me questioning my competence. I was still annoyed with myself for having found zero leads as to who was harassing and threatening Sofija.

Sofija. I finally admitted to myself that, though it shouldn't, her opinion really mattered to me. It made the fact that she didn't seem to think too highly of my investigative abilities sting all the more. She'd given me a chance. She'd sent me pictures of the harassment that she had received. I hadn't been able to do anything with it, so she'd confided to Cantrell and not me about what she'd overhead between Frannie and Roland.

Cracking my knuckles, I stared out the window at the approaching dusk. Just a few more days and it would be Friday. I'd take the train to the city to do my favorite run, the one along the Charles River Esplanade, and watch the sun set. That view never failed to impress upon me how insignificant my setbacks were in the grand scheme of things. I hoped it would work just as well this time.

Chapter 15

Sofija

Friday at 4 p.m., Keiko burst through my door with her usual exuberance and sidled right up behind me before I could tear myself away from my computer screen.

"Intro to Vypyr? I go on vacation for a couple of weeks and when I come back, you're planning a career change? Or are you facing competition from robot nurses?" she teased as she leaned over my shoulder to examine the screen.

I swiveled to face her. By now, she knew what was going on, so I answered honestly. "Because, Keiko, Casa Sofija runs on pretty slim margins. If even a few of my patients drop me—and this week, two already have— I've eventually got to make up the money somehow. Programming can be pretty anonymous. I can make a profile on GigMeNow or something and take on freelance jobs. Nobody has to know that I'm the nurse with the terrible reputation," I said with a shrug. "And most of the jobs are remote, so I wouldn't even have to look at my colleagues in their judgy faces."

Keiko frowned. "That doesn't sound like your kind of thing, Sofi. You love people."

"I do, but lately they don't seem to love me," I lamented.

Keiko gave me a kiss on the cheek and pulled me up from the chair. "That's why I'm here—to show you that's not the case. Come on, let's go."

"Go where? I thought we were going to do a low key girls' night here."

"I said that so you'd let me come over. We're going to Boston—as in, we're going out, okay? Gonna take your mind off things."

"I'm starting to regret telling you about the mess I'm in," I groaned.

Keiko waved away my comment. "As if I wouldn't have figured out that the FBI is investigating my best friend. Word spreads, Sofi."

"Gee, thanks," I deadpanned.

Keiko gave me a knowing look and said, "That—sarcasm—it's not going to work on me. I know how much you love dancing. We're doing this."

"I don't want to spend money," I protested.

"And you won't have to. Tonight is on me, okay?"

"Ko," I started. "I can't ask you to do that."

"Oh my God, Sofi, please. It's no big deal. If it makes you feel better, if you do end up getting that old lady's money, you can take me on a vacation. Vietnam. I want to go to Vietnam. I hear they have a wicked coffee scene."

"And if I don't? If somehow I'm found guilty and I don't get a single cent?"

"Then you can room with me while you finish your Vypyr and B courses or whatever coding language it is you're learning. When you become a rich techbro—techsis, whatever, you can take me on a more modest vacation. I'm thinking Phoenix or Savannah. Deal?"

In spite of myself, I smiled.

"Deal," I said.

Keiko's face split into a triumphant grin. "And since you're not with Jesse—"

"I didn't say that, not exactly" I interrupted. "I said he needed space, but he thinks we're probably still together."

Rolling her eyes, Keiko said, "This from the man who wouldn't tell his mother about you. Has he texted you since?"

"No," I admitted.

"So, it seems to me that gives you license to have fun tonight." Before I could protest, she held up a hand. "You don't have to hook up with someone. But you should change into something that makes you feel sexy. And you should dance exactly how you want, with as many guys as you want."

Keiko's energy was infectious. Nobody was better at pulling the Sofija I liked to be, the real Sofija, out from the suffocating spirals of worry I occasionally got caught in. I felt a sudden surge of confidence.

"You're so right. I *deserve* to have fun."

"There's my girl!" Keiko said, grabbing my shoulders and steering me into my bedroom.

"So, what's your look for where we're going?" I asked.

"Glad you asked," Keiko said, unbuttoning her long coat and revealing what was underneath with a dramatic flourish.

"Oh my gosh, Keiko, did someone sew that onto you? It fits perfectly," I exclaimed. Keiko's small frame was adorned in a tight-fitting, sequined romper with a V-shaped neckline that plunged to just above her belly button.

"Well, that's the idea. Since I'm wearing this," she said, twirling around, "I'm thinking that you should be equally bold."

I pursed my lips and nodded. My closet wasn't large, but I hadn't had a reason to wear the dress I had in mind for years, so it took some fishing around before I found it.

"Thoughts?" I asked Keiko as I held it flush against my body. It was a short, satin slip mini dress trimmed with lace in strategic places. I had always thought that the faded periwinkle looked especially nice against my olive skin.

Keiko gave me a conspiratorial grin. "You're gonna make it hard for people in the club to focus on much else, dressed in that. Pair it with your ankle strap stiletto heels."

"Yes, ma'am," I eagerly agreed. I was starting to feel genuinely excited to leave the house for something other than work or investigating.

"Let's slap some makeup on and get out of here. I brought my car," Keiko said, dragging me into the bathroom.

I looked at us both in the mirror as we got ready together for a night out, just like we had done since we were freshmen in college. The thought overwhelmed me; I knew that I would never truly be alone. I gave her a hug that she immediately returned. "Thanks, Keiko. I love you. You know what I need more than I do."

"And you're smart enough to listen," she said, squeezing me tight. "Get all your soft girl feelings out now, though, because you can't cry with the makeup I'm going to put on you."

"Actually, I was thinking. Your outfit screams bold,

what with all the sequins. But mine is muted, kind of natural. So I'm going to try to go for a natural makeup look."

"Ooooh, like a nymph," Keiko said. "I love it."

"Yeah. I think I love it too," I said with a smile.

We put on the final touches and then hurried off to her car.

****

"I hate driving in Boston," Keiko grumbled as we slowly made our way down Storrow Drive. "And it's mostly because of this fucking road."

"No, it's mostly because of drivers who don't read the damn sign," I corrected, jabbing my thumb at the clearance warning sign.

"Tomato, tomahto," Keiko replied. "Since this street is a parking lot right now, why don't you tell me more about Agent Velasquez?"

"Wha—why?!" I fumbled.

Keiko shot me an unimpressed look before her eyes returned to the centipede of cars crawling down the drive in front of us. "You know why."

"Am I that transparent?" I moaned, leaning back against the headrest.

"He's handsome, he's nice, he understands what it's like to be first-generation, he's easy to talk to," Keiko mimicked. "Yeah. Clear as polished glass, Sofi."

I stared out the window at the Esplanade. Joggers and bikers wound their way along the smooth pavement, framed by the Charles River. Right now, the water was reflecting the last minutes of today's blue sky. It looked like a river of heaven flowing right through the city. Finally, I turned back to Keiko.

"I *am* attracted to Mateo," I admitted.

"Mateo?"

Blushing, I kicked myself. "I think of him that way in my head now. But I call him Agent Velasquez to his face."

"And maybe you still will, if you hook up someday. You know, if he brings his handcuffs into play."

"KEIKO!" I exclaimed. "Come on, I shouldn't even think that way."

"But you clearly have," Keiko observed smugly. "Had any fun dreams about him?"

"I—yes," I confessed. "Pretty vivid ones. And frequent. I don't know what to do about it."

"You march straight over to his place after this case is resolved and you ask him out. That's what you do about it," Keiko pronounced.

Something between a snort and a guffaw escaped me. "Right. This is all a moot point. Jesse and I might make up."

Keiko suddenly swerved to the right. "Sorry, we're taking a shortcut," she said as we exited Storrow. "Based on our last two conversations, I know you're hiding something about Jesse from me, and I won't pry, since you clearly don't want to tell me. But it seems like the kind of thing that could be a dealbreaker. And honestly, I've never been a huge fan of the guy. So while you're on a break, maybe it would be a good idea to at least consider other options."

"And you think I should start with the FBI agent who is investigating me. Stellar advice, Ko," I muttered.

"Well, at least he seems like the kind who would introduce you to his mom right away."

"Yeah, yeah. Where are we going anyways? I thought you said this place was a short walk from Back

Bay?"

"It is. I just don't want to deal with traffic anymore, so we're going to use my friend's guest parking pass and leave the car in Fenway."

"Sounds good. You'll have to walk in these heels, though."

We were silent for a moment before Keiko said, "You know, my grandmother was really fond of pufferfish. Fugu, in Japanese."

"I see," I said, nonplussed. "Is it good?"

"I have no idea. It's extremely difficult to find places in the U.S. where it's served, because it can be poisonous."

"What?! Why would anyone eat that?"

Keiko continued, "Its flesh is apparently delicious, and if it's sliced just right, you get a pleasant numb feeling in your lips when you eat it. But if the chef preparing it makes just one error, nicks the wrong thing with a tiny slip of the knife, it can poison and kill you. But mistakes like that are very rare."

I squinted at her. "Ko, are you getting at something? Is this night going to end with us trying fugu?"

Keiko shook her head. "No. It's a super expensive delicacy, because the chef has to have trained for years. We're not about to rack up a tab like that when it's my night to treat you," she said with a wink. "I mention it because there's a really famous saying about fugu."

"Oh?" I was increasingly confused.

"*Fugu wa kuitashi inochi wa oshishi.*"

I blinked and said, "Ko, that's really pretty, but it means nothing to me. How does it translate?"

"Literally, something like 'I want to eat fugu but I don't want to die.' But I guess an equivalent saying would be, 'Honey is sweet but the bee stings.' Do you get what I'm saying?"

I thought about it for a moment before I hazarded a guess. "Big risk, big reward?"

"Exactly. So do what you're doing. Get your name cleared. But once all the legal stuff is over, if you and Jesse end up splitting for good, don't stop yourself from trying something with Mateo if you think there's real potential there—which it sounds like there is."

We were at a red light, so I looked Keiko directly in the eyes. "Okay, Ko. I promise that if everything goes exactly as you just described, I'll go ask Mateo for coffee."

Keiko nodded with a satisfied smile. "And don't take him somewhere awful, okay? Take him to Ammo's or Kaiyo Koffee."

"I'll take him to Caffe Isabella or nothing," I said with a grin. "I'll need to be close to places that serve real food before a date like that. I already feel like a jittery mess around him. I don't need caffeine on an empty stomach to make it worse."

"Love to see you think ahead," Keiko said as she parked the car. "Gimme a sec—I'm just going to grab the guest parking pass from my friend."

In a flash of sequins and hair, she was out the door and pressing the buzzer on one of the brownstones.

When her friend came down, they started to chat, so I settled into the passenger seat and closed my eyes.

Some people loved moments of quiet nothingness.

I hated them.

They were the perfect opportunity for intrusive thoughts to creep through the cracks until they took up all of my brain's real estate. It happened no matter how hard I tried to push them away.

I was one of those people who had to stay busy. Maybe it was because I'd never really learned how to be alone as a child. On any given day after school, I'd either been prepping dinner with my mom, helping my dad repair things around our house, babysitting my brother, or visiting with people from our community's raucous group of family and friends. There was never a dull moment, but I didn't know how to really just sit and *be*. Maybe that was my problem.

Whatever the reason, whenever I didn't have enough work to occupy my mind, I spiraled until all I could imagine were worst-case scenarios. This week had been rough for that reason. With two fewer patients, I'd had way too much free time.

I could feel the vicious cycle of worry start up again as I sat in the car. Just as I was about to pull out my phone, Keiko rapped on the window.

"Ready to let off some steam?" she asked cheerily.

Am I ever.

Without waiting, I launched myself out of the car and shouted, "To the T! To the green line!"

"The screamin' green," Keiko said with a giggle.

I suddenly felt euphoric, almost manic. I was either going to beat these accusations and be home free, or I was going to be ruined by them and have to start over somewhere fresh. Either outcome was a powerful argument for letting loose tonight.

Tomorrow, I knew the anxiety would return, and I'd have to keep working to clear my name. But tonight wasn't yet tomorrow.

"I'm going to have fun tonight. Maybe too much," I announced, grasping both of Keiko's hands.

"That's the point. I'll take care of you, and my friend said we can crash at her place if we need to. This is our night."

"Ko and So, here we go," I sang as the train squealed up to our stop.

Keiko groaned. "How can I convince you to *not* make that the motto of the evening?"

"My brand is cheese, Keiko," I said as I stepped onto the train. "You know that. But I'll keep it to myself."

"Great, because the goal tonight is to score."

"We'll see about that. But I'm definitely getting drunk," I giggled, looping my arm underneath hers.

We rode for two stops before we hopped off. Keiko guided us through Back Bay, past the towering testaments to Boston's old money. We stopped in front of a small red door underneath an intricate latticed metal awning.

The bouncer glanced lazily between us and our IDs before letting us in. We walked up to the bar and placed our orders.

In a couple of gulps, I downed a glass of sparkling wine and ordered another. Keiko kept pace with me as we talked and laughed. A few men and one woman approached us, and soon we were all sipping negronis. The drink tasted extremely strong. The bartender had been generous.

Before we knew it, we were being led onto the dance floor. I gulped down the last of my drink and let Keiko pull me in tow.

The music penetrated my skin down to the bone. I moved without caring, not knowing how seductive or ridiculous I looked. Keiko was having fun, I was having fun, and that was enough.

Gradually, the crowd on the dance floor thickened. The whole building seemed to thrum and lurch as bodies closed in on us.

The music changed from upbeat techno to something deep and electric. It seemed to pound more loudly too. I could feel every pulse of the base throb through the veins in my head. Combined with the alcohol, which was really starting to kick in, it was all too much.

I needed to get out.

Pushing my way through the crowd until I was nearly nose to nose with Keiko, I said as loudly as I could, "Ko, I need some fresh air."

"I'm coming with you," she said immediately, disentangling herself from the arms of the handsome man she had been dancing with all night. He looked devastated.

She really is a great friend, I thought appreciatively.

"That's sweet, Ko, but I'm fine. Really. Just need some fresh air and a little walk. I might go get a smoothie or something on Newbury Street."

"I don't think you should be walking alone," Keiko insisted.

I gave Keiko's arm a reassuring squeeze and said, "I have my phone on me, and you have yours on you. Just make sure it's on vibrate so you can feel it if I call. But I'll be fine. We're in the middle of Boston."

Keiko studied me skeptically for a few seconds before she slid back against her dance partner. "Check in with me every half hour."

Rolling my eyes, I leaned in and gave her a kiss. "Okay, *mom*." I shot a stern look up at her dance partner. "Take care of my friend," I said, winking at the end to soften the words.

"I'll do whatever your friend wants," he said eagerly, looking down at Keiko like he couldn't believe his luck.

I smirked to myself and pushed my way out of the club.

The air was still balmy, but not oppressively hot or humid. Boston rarely was, though. It was surprisingly light out too. Checking my phone, I realized it wasn't even 9 p.m. yet.

I didn't make it more than half a block until walking in my stilettos became too painful. I could feel twin blisters being rubbed into existence on my ankles with every step.

Thanking God and the municipal employees that Boston had impressively clean streets for a city, I leaned against a tree and removed my shoes. I clasped them in my right hand as I crossed the street and made it to Commonwealth Avenue Mall. The tender grass caressed the soles of my feet, such a sharp contrast to the harsh straps on my stilettos. I ambled toward the statue of Leif Erikson and plopped down onto a tree-shaded bench to people-watch.

Often, when I came to this strip of green with Keiko or my brother, we would spend hours observing the dog walkers, joggers, couples on dates, and readers, making up ridiculous backstories for them. But right now, the two flutes of Prosecco and the negroni were doing their worst. Sitting still made me feel like my brain was sloshing around in a fish tank. I instinctively knew that I needed to keep moving, counter-intuitive as it was.

It was silly, but I felt a powerful pull toward the water, like a siren song. I left my perch on the bench and walked in the direction of Harvard Bridge. Along the way, I stopped at a convenience store to use the restroom and buy a glass bottle of fizzy water. I figured I would need something fizzy sooner rather than later.

By the time I had meandered down toward the waterfront, the bottoms of my feet had little twigs and pebbles pressed into them. It didn't bother me. I had a fuzzy idea that I would sit on one of the docks and dunk my legs, up to my knees, in the water. I'd let the Charles clean off all the dirt and grime that had accumulated on me.

I was about to step onto the little paved street of the Esplanade when a familiar voice called out, "Sofija?"

I started with a yelp and dropped the bottle. It shattered on the pavement, all around my bare feet. If it cut me, I didn't feel it.

Mateo came into view next to me and I heard him suck in his breath. "You're barefoot. Can I—can I pick you up?" he asked hesitantly.

For a second, I debated, but then I nodded. "Yes."

Gently, Mateo hooked one toned arm around my back and the other under the crook of my knees. Slowly, he lifted me and walked over to a nearby bench. He set me down gingerly.

I was overwhelmed and confused, my head spinning. I couldn't think of anything to say. Crouching down in front of me, Mateo examined my feet, brushing away the dirt and plucking off small shards of glass. Sweat dripped down his forehead and soaked his shirt. He was so close I could smell it. There was something deeply appealing about the scent. Something intensely masculine. My body started to respond to it, and I silently prayed that he would hurry up and finish his inspection of my feet before he could sense it too. My short wisp of a dress and bikini cut underwear didn't provide much of a barrier between me and the air he was breathing.

"Good, no deep cuts," he muttered before straightening back up and taking a step back. My mind felt relief, but my traitorous body felt disappointment.

"What are you doing here, Sofija, walking around without shoes?" he asked.

It was a reasonable question, but I was still shocked by his presence. Instead of answering, I blustered, "What am *I* doing here? What are *you* doing here? Did you follow me here?" The rush of feelings coursing through me was completely overwhelming. I was angry, flustered, worried, thrilled, aroused, and embarrassed.

Mateo cleared his throat. "I'm running. I live in Chelsea because it's close to work. But I love running here on the Esplanade. I try to do it once a week, at least. I didn't follow you here."

"Still seems like a pretty big coincidence," I tipsily insisted.

With a shrug, he said, "I'm sure it does. I'm as surprised to see you as you are to see me. But this is Boston, not New York. It's small. And it's not like there are a lot of other cities nearby that are good for clubbing," he finished, gesturing toward my outfit. "So I guess given that I live nearby, it's not that improbable."

Makes sense, I thought. Still, I wanted to make sure.

"Maybe…but maybe you were following me because you think I'm meeting up with one of my fellow criminals," I said sarcastically.

Mateo dragged a hand over his face and said, "Sofija, I can't comment on the case, but I can say this: you seem to think that I have a bad opinion of you as a person. You shouldn't think that."

He sounded sincere. "Thanks, Agent Velasquez. That means more than you know."

"I'm glad it makes you feel better," he said, reaching up and wiping sweat from his brow. His arm muscles rippled as he did, and his shirt lifted enough for me to see the line of hair trailing down toward his waistband.

"Oh, wow," I breathed. Immediately, I clapped my hands over my mouth, silently cursing the way too much alcohol which made me filter-less.

"Wow?" Mateo asked.

"Wow the view! I mean, I'm just seeing it now. I understand why you run here—it's nice," I said hurriedly.

"It is nice," he echoed. I thought I detected a smug edge to his voice. But maybe I was just hearing what I wanted.

We remained frozen in silence until I decided to break it by elaborating. "S' gorgeous," I said, nodding toward the Charles. "Like two different rivers. During the day it's blue, like the sky. Last time I was here, I sat on that little island there, next to those willow trees and flowers. It looked like paradise. Now that the sun's setting, s' like liquid fire,'' I slurred a little as I finished.

Mateo chuckled.

"What? I said that pretty well considering I'm wasted," I defended.

This time, Mateo laughed a little louder. "It's not that. It's just that the easier explanation is that the sky changes, not the river. It's interesting that you framed it the other way around."

My heart started hammering wildly as Mateo sat down on the bench next to me. I didn't look at him, keeping my gaze focused on the river. "Well, both ways of saying it are wrong, I guess. The river and the sky don't change. Perspective does. You know, 'cause the Earth is always spinning and moving." I made a pointer hand and rotated it around several times to emphasize my point, since I wasn't sure how coherent I sounded.

"Perspective *is* very important," Mateo murmured. "It can change everything."

If he meant something deeper by that, I was too drunk to decipher it. He turned to face me and said, "Sorry about your water. Do you want some of mine?"

I looked at him, confused. "You don't have any."

Mateo gave me a proud grin and patted each side of his chest. "Hydration pack. I always come prepared."

I gave him a silly grin. "You're organized, like me. I'm organized! Normally. This—" I gestured up and down my body, "s' not me. I mean, I'm fun! I like fun! But I'm not messy like this. I'm organized. S' just been a bad time for me."

He gave me a sympathetic nod and reached for the mouthpiece attached to the small hose that emerged from his hydration pack. "I know. Here—just bite down and suck."

I obeyed, leaning forward and trapping the rubbery mouthpiece between my teeth and closing my lips around it. After a couple seconds of sucking, water hit my tongue and I let out a small moan of relief, closing my eyes in bliss. It was lukewarm, but it tasted amazing. I hadn't realized how thirsty I was.

When I opened my eyes, Mateo was staring at me, his pupils blown wide, breathing a little heavily even.

It was then that I realized how compromising the situation might look. Quickly, I released the mouthpiece, wiped my lips, and scooted to the other side of the bench.

"Thanks," I mumbled. "I didn't realize how thirsty I was."

"No problem," Mateo said, his voice sounding strained.

For a long time, we sat in silence until I couldn't take it anymore. Any inhibitions I had were demolished by alcohol and our proximity.

Trying my best to sound sober, I said, "Look, there's something I need to say."

"Go ahead," Mateo replied.

"I'm sorry I gave the information about Frannie and Roland's conversation to Cantrell instead of you. You've been nothing but fair to me. Sympathetic, even. It's just—okay, I'm going to be completely honest. I know you can't say anything in response, so don't. The last thing I want is to put your job in jeopardy. And I'm *not* saying this to get some kind of favor or to stop your investigation," I hastily added.

Before continuing, I looked over at Mateo's profile. He cracked his knuckles and swallowed deeply, his Adam's apple bobbing down and then up.

"The thing is, Agent Velasquez, I'm really attracted to you. I don't want to be. I'm not sure where I stand with Jesse, for one thing. But regardless of whether that gets fixed, I know you're, like, as off limits as it gets. I just—I can't help it."

Mateo was quiet, seemingly focused on some distant point on the Harvard Bridge. I followed his gaze before I continued.

"I feel like you understand me, like we have similar experiences. I love talking with you. You work hard at your job, like I do. You're sensitive to my feelings. And

I'm very…physically drawn to you."

I stood up and picked up my shoes before I continued. "That's why I didn't come to you—not because I think Agent Cantrell is better. As far as I can tell, you're a great agent. I just don't want to be around you while you're at work or near other FBI agents. I'm afraid my attraction would be too obvious, and I would hate for someone to get the wrong idea. What I mean is, you haven't led me on or been inappropriate. I don't want anybody thinking that."

Mateo's jaw visibly clenched, but he didn't say anything. I took my cue and turned in the direction of the little island. I wanted to sit there between the trees and decompress after my confession. Maybe make friends with some people and grab some fast food. Anything but staying on this bench sounded good.

I hadn't made it two steps before I felt fingertips graze my palm. "Sofija," he said.

Turning my head halfway, I looked back out of the corner of my right eye. Mateo was shifting nervously from foot to foot.

"You're correct about what I can and cannot discuss with a subject in an active investigation. But I wanted to say, thank you for explaining why you went to Cantrell instead of me. I really appreciate it. I'm a newer agent, so I second guess myself a lot. It was good for me to hear this."

My throat felt too thick to respond, but I managed to say, "Thank you for helping me avoid the glass." I turned and walked off toward the island.

Just as surely as I knew that tomorrow morning, the river would look blue like the sky again, I knew that Mateo's eyes were boring into me.

Once I reached the little bridge that connected the Esplanade to the island, I looked back. Mateo was still sitting on the bench, staring at me, brow furrowed in what looked like concern or distress. I couldn't tell.

When our eyes met, he gave me a slow nod. Then he stood up and jogged off in a smooth, controlled stride.

Chapter 16

Mateo

My phone rang, startling me out of the flow state I had been in while studying the receipts that Frannie had emailed me.

"This is Agent Velasquez speaking," I intoned.

"Hello, it's Adam—just wanted to let you know I was able to wrap up my business a couple days early. I'm flying into Boston this morning. I'm going to spend time alone with my husband today, but if you'd still like to talk, I'll be available from 7:15 p.m. to 9:00 p.m."

The man is precise, I'll give him that.

"Today at 7:15 is fine," I said.

"Okay. I'll be at 7252 Larksong Avenue. You'll see our mailbox and go down a long drive. Park anywhere in the circle in front of our house."

"Thanks. See you then, Mr. Armitage."

"Goodbye," he said and hung up abruptly.

I created an event on my phone and set an alert for two hours before. Then, I saved the address Adam had given me into my phone's map app. He was a tricky man to get a hold of, and I wasn't about to squander a chance for some face-to-face time with him.

I turned my attention back to the maintenance receipts that Frannie had emailed to me. Something about them didn't sit right with me, but I couldn't say what.

There were five companies that Jesse had hired over the years: Smooth Streets to pave the driveway; Muskbusters to treat the mold in the basement; Tree Docs Inc. to eliminate the maple tree fungus; Wirerify to rewire the house; and Roof Solid to redo the roof. All of them were LLCs.

Something bothered me about the names of the companies. Service providers were often named after families, but these companies all seemed to have extremely generic names. They almost sounded fake.

Even stranger, the Massachusetts Secretary of State site showed that each company had no more than three employees. It seemed bizarre to me that Jesse, with his mother's deep pockets at his disposal, had hired small, unproven companies to restore the family's ancestral estate. The only explanation I could come up with was that Jesse was friends with or owed the companies' owners.

I poked around on the website some more, which revealed that Smooth Streets, Muskbusters, Tree Docs Inc., Wirerify, and Roof Solid were all owned by a larger holding company: Montage Enterprises.

Montage. Strange name for it, I thought with a frown.

The CEO of Montage Enterprises was listed as one Danya Monroe.

Does Jesse know this woman?

It seemed far too large of a coincidence that he would hire only companies that fell under the greater auspices of Montage Enterprises if he *didn't* know Danya.

There was no way for me to learn anything more on

the state website, but I had an idea of what to do next. I logged in to Sharewall with another one of the FBI's dummy profiles and searched for Danya Monroe.

While the search generated no profile hits, it did bring up a result from the High Tide Bar and Grill. The post from the restaurant's page said:

Come in on the 5th of June for live music performed by Dan Bissell, Dante Ciccolo, and Danya Monroe of the Three Bad Dans! Set starts at 7 along with happy hour.

Twirling my pen in one hand like I did whenever I was zeroing in on something, I searched for Three Bad Dans on PixABoo. Sure enough, there was an account with a series of pictures. Almost all of them contained two burly, unshaven men—a singer and a drummer— and a female guitarist with long, platinum blond hair and tattooed arms. I tapped on the photo and the tags popped up. The singer was tagged to a PixABoo profile named BissedOff, the drummer to one named DanteChico, and the guitarist to one named DanYeah. The former two were public, while the latter was set to private. It didn't matter; it was enough to confirm that Danya Monroe was in a band that would be playing at a nearby bar in a matter of days.

I stood and strode over to Cantrell's desk.

"Got a second?" I asked.

"Sure," he said, spinning away from his screen to face me.

"I suspect that Jesse Armitage was colluding with a woman named Danya Monroe to steal money from his mother through botched, overpriced maintenance jobs. I know where Danya is going to be on the night of June 5th, so I'd like permission to tail her and observe her."

"Back up," Cantrell said, swinging forward so his

elbows were resting on his knees. "Tell me how you got there."

After I'd taken Cantrell through my processes step by step, he leaned back. Finally, he gave me a small smile and a curt nod. "You young agents really are savvy with all that social media. Mostly the stuff is a waste of time, if you ask me—but that was some good detective work, Velasquez."

"Thank you very much," I replied. "So can I tail and observe her?"

"Think you can fit in at a place like the High Tide?" he asked, giving me a skeptical once over.

I looked down at my impeccable clothing and clenched my teeth.

"I can be inconspicuous in a dive bar, if that's what you mean."

"That's exactly what I mean."

Suppressing a sigh, I said, "Leave the blending in to me. I'll borrow some of my brother-in-law's clothes and do something with my hair."

"Don't go overboard now. None of that eyeliner shit. Nobody actually looks like Johnny Depp in places like that," Cantrell said with a small smirk. I could tell he thought this was amusing.

"Would you like to come with me, so that you can verify that I'm dressed appropriately?" I asked.

Now Cantrell guffawed loudly. "Absolutely not. It's hard enough for one agent to stay under the radar. Two and you're asking to get caught. And I'm not coming over to your place just to watch you try on outfits. This isn't prom."

Cantrell having initiated the teasing, I felt confident that he was in a good enough mood for me to give as good as I got. "I can do a fit check and send you pictures instead so you can make sure I look convincing. You can work your phone well enough to open photos in a text, right?" I quipped.

Delighted amusement flashed across Cantrell's face. "Did you just make a joke at my expense, Velasquez?"

"I'm as surprised as you are," I said with a grin.

"Atta boy," Cantrell chortled, slapping me hard on the shoulder. "Do I want to know what the hell a 'fit check' is?"

"I'm going to guess no, you don't."

"Good man," he said. "All right then. You've got the go ahead from me to tail Danya Monroe at the bar. Do not interact with her directly, and get out of there the minute anyone starts looking at you funny. You got that?"

"Absolutely," I agreed.

"Good. I'm going to keep working through the Talia Portnoy business. Going to check with nearby pharmacists and hospitals to make sure there's no insulin inventory missing. Then I'll check with police jurisdictions around here to confirm there haven't been any reported thefts of the stuff. What's next for you?"

"I got a call from Adam Armitage earlier. He said he'd be back from San Francisco today, so I'm finally going to talk to him."

Cantrell grunted in approval. "About time. Something fishy about a man who skips town right after he files a report with the FBI. Right before we found Talia's body to boot. Doesn't feel right."

"I'm going to try to suss out if he knows about Talia's death, see if it's a shock to him. If it's not, I'll figure out how he learned about it."

"And if it's a surprise to him?"

"If it *is* a surprise, I'll make sure to watch how he reacts. Either way, it might give us an idea of whether we should press harder on that particular point."

Cantrell nodded and turned back to his computer. "Solid plan. I look forward to the debrief after you've questioned him."

I knew that was my cue to go back to my desk, so without another word, I walked back. For the next two hours, I organized and indexed my case notes until it was time to leave for the interview with Adam.

****

While I drove over to Adam's, I reflected on the past weekend. I had carried Sofija away from the shattered glass, holding her against me, close enough that I could smell the vermouth on her breath. With all my being, I had wanted to slide my tongue inside her mouth and taste it for myself.

I had examined the soles of her feet for cuts and scrapes, wishing all the while that I could massage them, could work my way up to the smooth-looking skin of her calf.

I had listened to her confess what I had simultaneously been dreading and hoping to hear. It had taken all my control to refrain from reciprocating.

Then I had allowed her to walk away, like I knew I had to.

And it had *burned*.

After the encounter, I had sublimated all that deep, pulsing need into energy that had propelled me on my run. I had skipped the train and ran miles home. When I made it to my door, panting, I was so drained that I had thought I was safe.

But lying down in bed later that night, my thoughts had flitted back to Sofija. Exhausted from the constant battle for control, I had finally permitted myself to fantasize, justifying it by telling myself that doing so was better than refusing all outlets until one day I snapped and acted on the impulse.

I had fantasized about a date with Sofija: how we would bond over similarities in our upbringing and learn about our cultural differences; talk about our personal and professional aspirations; find excuses to touch each other over the course of the evening, until it drove us to a fever pitch we couldn't ignore; barely make it through the door of my house before I hiked up her little satin dress, shoved aside her panties and tasted her. After she crested her peak, I would lay her on my bed and rock in and out of her, slowly and tenderly at first and then faster as I cupped her small, round breasts for purchase. I would kiss her to sleep, and we would wake in the morning and do it again before sipping coffee together.

Even though I wasn't touching myself, I knew that, in theory, I should feel guilty. I was allowing a suspect—albeit an unlikely one—to star in these scenarios. But for some reason, I didn't. Frustrated, yes. But guilty? Only a little. I couldn't understand why, given how prone I was to the emotion.

Maybe it was because Sofija had admitted that she was attracted to me, so it felt reciprocal. Lying in her cold apartment, she might be imagining the same things, or her own version of them.

Perhaps it was because I knew now, without a shadow of a doubt, that my feelings for Sofija weren't just rooted in lust, but in the very real connection we shared. Or, at least on the connection that I suspected we would have, were circumstances different.

Or maybe it was because I knew the futility of trying to flush Sofija out of my system through reading, exercise, and whatever other distractions had thus far failed.

I realized that it was probably some combination of all of the above.

Whatever the reason, I knew that if I found evidence of Sofija's guilt, I would report it to Cantrell and he would do what was necessary. It would pain me, but I wouldn't ignore the law.

This line of thought was interrupted by the smooth voice of the map app, which informed me that I had arrived. I parked in the circle out front, as I had been instructed to do.

Adam and Xiaoming Armitage-Chen lived in a beautiful but surprisingly humble home, given their combined wealth.

I strolled up to the house and rang the doorbell. The door opened almost immediately.

Xiaoming was a tall, handsome man who looked to be around Adam's age. He wore navy slacks and a fitted cashmere shirt that highlighted his perfectly sculpted muscles. His hair was much like mine: thick, black, and straight, though he wore his much shorter. A silver watch gleamed against his golden-tanned skin.

"Welcome, Agent Velasquez," he said with just the faintest trace of an accent. "Thank you for accommodating our schedules on such short notice."

"Not a problem," I replied. "I'll try to make this quick. I'm sure you want to spend time with your husband since he's been gone so long."

Xiaoming laughed lightly. "A little over a week isn't

long at all. Now, if you had asked me how I felt during the seed funding stages of the company, I would be singing an entirely different tune. That was a brutal period."

"Is that Agent Velasquez, Xiao?" came Adam's booming voice.

"It is."

"Bring him in. I've got the crudité and charcuterie board almost ready."

"This way, please," Xiaoming said.

I followed him through a hallway that was painted in a tasteful off-white with a light gray undertone. Hung along the wall in perfectly spaced intervals were paintings that reminded me of the sort I had seen in the houses of my former law firm's partners. I could tell they were expensive, but I didn't think they were evocative or even particularly fun to look at. Despite my tendency to keep my own life neat and ordered, I preferred art to be bold and bursting with color, like the kind of thing decorating my cousins' houses in Oaxaca.

The hallway opened to a kitchen that was equally trendy. A floor-to-ceiling shelf stood next to an extremely spacious, granite-topped island. Adam stood over it, slicing vegetables and arranging them on a wooden tray. Industrial pendant lights shone down from the ceiling, their gleam catching the knife as Adam moved it up and down in smooth motions.

"Agent Velasquez," Adam said, glancing up once and giving me a nod. "Thanks for coming by. Please have a seat and I'll bring over some food."

"What do you drink?" Xiaoming asked.

"Thank you, but I can't consume alcohol while on the job," I demurred. Xiaoming looked disappointed, so

I said, "But if you have any tea or coffee, I would love that."

Xiaoming frowned. "I'm not sure what tea goes with crudité and charcuterie. Let me think."

He walked over to a large cupboard and opened it to reveal rows of neatly arranged teas and dried roots. After picking up various canisters and examining the labels, he asked, "Does rose vanilla tea work for you?"

"I've never had it, but I'd be happy to try. Thank you."

"Of course. We want to serve you something you like. You're a guest."

That wasn't strictly true, but I thought that correcting him would do more harm than good. My offer to help was politely rejected, so I sat at the table. By now, Adam was setting down the food, along with small plates and navy colored cloth napkins.

"So, Agent Velasquez. What is it you would like to know?" he asked as he sat down in front of me. He folded his hands as if in prayer, then rested his chin on top of them.

I found his gaze unsettling, his eyes boring into me from a severe, pale face. I cracked my knuckles and mimicked his pose.

"How was your trip to San Francisco?" I inquired.

Adam looked taken aback, but quickly composed himself. "It went exactly like it always does. Schmoozing with potential clients, explaining to investors what direction we want to take the company in, that sort of thing. Tiring but necessary."

"At least you probably got some good meals out of it, right?" I said, attempting to be jovial.

Adam shrugged. "They were fine. Nothing that I

haven't had an equally good or better version of in New York or Paris."

I wasn't sure how to respond to such a statement, so I just nodded. "And you were in San Francisco the whole time? You didn't make any trips back here or somewhere else?"

Adam arched an eyebrow at me. "I wouldn't waste emissions jetting around when I have continuous business in a city."

"Of course not. All the same, if you could produce some witnesses for your time there, we would greatly appreciate it," I said, watching him closely.

Something dark flashed in his eyes. "I can and will, but I'm wondering to what end, Agent Velasquez."

"Just being thorough," I deflected.

Adam shook his head. "No, something clearly happened while I was gone and you want me to produce an alibi. What was it?"

He really is smart, I'll give him that.

"A person involved in this case has been the subject of harassment and threats. The person has reported seeing a tall, pale man with dark hair fleeing the scene of these threats on more than one occasion."

Adam laughed derisively. "And you think it was me?"

"We're only doing our due diligence."

Adam crossed his arms and looked at me, amused. "Agent Velasquez, if I wanted to intimidate someone, I wouldn't do it myself. I'm both too busy and too smart for that."

"Honey, be polite," Xiaoming scolded from the kitchen island where he was pouring hot water into a clay teapot.

Adam's expression softened as he turned to look at his husband. "You're right. I'm sorry." Then he cleared his throat and turned back to me. "No, Agent Velasquez, I didn't fly back from California to harass anybody. I'll get you the proof you need, though."

"Thank you," I replied. Then I turned to Xiaoming. "You were here the entire time that Adam was gone, correct?"

Xiaoming shook his head as he added a spoonful of honey into the teapot and stirred. "I was here the first two days he was gone, but I'm part of a racing group that trains and competes together. We went to a race in Atlanta, and then spent a few days in the city after. I just got back yesterday morning. I can get you receipts for meals and my race registration."

"That would be very helpful."

"And if you want proof of his participation, you can look online. He finished second in his age group, so there's a picture of him on the podium," Adam said with a subtle but unmistakable affection in his voice.

"Congratulations," I said earnestly.

Xiaoming walked over and gracefully set a beautiful blue and white teacup in front of me.

"*Jingdezhen* porcelain," he said as he poured aromatic liquid from the teapot. "It was a wedding gift from my sister."

"It's beautiful," I admired. "Your sister has excellent taste."

Xiaoming beamed. "Thank you. See, Adam, those are manners," he said, playfully swatting Adam's shoulder.

Adam gave a small but genuine grin. "Fine, Xiao, point taken. I'll be on my best behavior so you can play gracious host."

"Thank you," Xiaoming said before giving Adam a peck on his head. He topped off Adam's wine and poured himself a glass.

"So you've been on vacation?" I asked Xiaoming.

"No. Not exactly. I'm an endocrinologist, and two months ago I resigned from my previous practice and accepted a job at one closer to home. I negotiated the contract so that I don't start until July, though. I've been enjoying some much-needed free time."

An endocrinologist. He might have access to insulin.

My thoughts were interrupted by Adam asking, a little provocatively, "Well, it wasn't *exactly* free time, was it?"

"Oh honey, let's not go there," Xiao complained.

"Can you explain?" I asked.

Xiao sighed and took a small sip of wine. "My mother wanted to visit for the first two weeks I had off. She had her visa and was just so excited to finally have a chance to use it. She's a lovely woman, but, *you know*. It wasn't easy for her when I told her about Adam. His business was just a startup back then, and she had hoped I'd marry a fellow doctor."

"And a female," Adam added.

"That too," Xiaoming admitted. "She's gotten much better about it, but she's still extremely awkward around Adam."

"So it wasn't much of a vacation for either of us, the first two weeks," Adam added.

This seemed like a perfect segue into Adam's relationship with his mother, so I wasted no time capitalizing on it.

"Was it a similar situation with your mother,

Adam?" I asked nonchalantly.

Adam leaned forward, gaze piercing me. "Pretty good transition, Agent Velasquez. We've come to the part of the interrogation where we talk about my late mother, haven't we?"

Clearly, subterfuge was useless with someone as smart as Adam, so I replied honestly, "Yes. That's why you called me here, no?"

"It is," Adam agreed, settling back in his chair and crossing his arms. I had the distinct impression that I was an emissary from a distant land, kneeling in front of some great general or khan and asking for a favor. It wasn't the balance of power I wanted to project, so I straightened up and raised my chin, careful to keep my expression firm but non-confrontational.

After several seconds of posturing, Adam spoke. "To be perfectly frank with you, my mother and I had a very difficult relationship for about half a decade. When I brought Xiao home the first time, she completely ignored him and said some nearly unforgivable things to me later that night. For the next few years after that, I barely wished her a happy birthday."

"So you would describe your relationship with Mrs. Armitage as strained?" I asked.

"For a long time it was. Unquestionably. But about four years ago, she came around completely. She apologized to me and to Xiao and even threw us a belated wedding reception."

"More of a five-year wedding anniversary party at that point," Xiaoming chimed in. "But it's true. She was very kind to me, in the end."

"My mother and I fully reconciled," Adam resumed. "But by that point, my company was in the scaleup stage, so I was knee-deep in work. I simply didn't have as much time to spend with her.

"But he made sure to eat dinner with her once a week," Xiaoming pointed out. "That's more than anybody except for me can get from Adam, given his schedule."

"That's true. In any case, my mother and I were fine," Adam finished decisively.

"So you would say that her old biases had nothing to do with her leaving you only twenty five percent of her inheritance?" I asked, studying Adam's reaction.

A flicker of annoyance crossed Adam's face before he said, "I'm confident that my marriage to a man had nothing to do with my mother's decision. I think her falling under the thrall of Sofija Zammit is responsible for that little lapse in judgment. My mother had always wanted a daughter, and I think that Sofija was smart enough to see that. If you ask me, she molded herself into exactly what my mother was missing."

"To be fair, you have no proof of that," Xiaoming said gently, setting his arm on Adam's shoulder.

Adam reached up and gave his husband's hand a squeeze before crossing his arms again. "That is also true. But it seems a little too coincidental that this has happened twice for the girl."

I weighed a few options before I took a gamble and said, "You know, Sofija did not keep the money she inherited from the lady in Connecticut."

Adam sucked in his lips. "She didn't?"

I shook my head. "No. She gave it to the deceased's distant relatives."

Adam said nothing, but Xiaoming exclaimed, "Well, I guess that explains why she's still working as a nurse, doesn't it?"

"Do you have any evidence that Sofija manipulated your mother in an unlawful way?" I asked, looking directly at Adam.

For what seemed like minutes, he was silent. In my peripherals, I could see Xiaoming looking anxiously back and forth between us. Finally, Adam said, "I do not. Sofija seemed respectful and appropriate with my mother when I saw them together. I cannot vouch for how she acted when she was alone with my mother, or when it was her and Jesse and my mother."

I jotted down a paraphrase of what he said and then resumed my questioning. "On the subject of Jesse, do you have any idea why your mother would cut him out of the will entirely when she didn't do the same to you?"

Fists clenching, Adam swallowed and said, "My brother is an immature, chronically impulsive man. My mother spent years coddling and indulging him. If you add up all the money that she gave him for the boom and bust startups that he never took seriously, for the first class travel, for the flashy car, it probably equals the amount I'm inheriting now."

Bingo!

"So maybe your mother was justified in cutting him out," I said, playing on the emotions practically radiating from him.

Adam unclenched his fists and smoothed the napkin in front of him. In a controlled voice, he said, "If my mother had chosen to donate her assets to a charity or the public instead of Jesse, maybe. But she didn't. She gave most of what she had to a stranger. *That*, Agent Velasquez, is what bothers me."

"And how had your interactions with Sofija been,

prior to your mother's death?"

"They were limited to the brief periods in which I was at the estate at the same time as her, so mostly to dinner. She carried herself perfectly professional and was attentive. Again, though, I have no idea if she was normally like that with mother."

It was clear that pursuing this subject wouldn't yield anything new or useful, so I pivoted. "And how would you describe the relationship between your mother, Sofija, and Jesse with the rest of the staff?"

Adam shrugged. "I barely know Marly or—what's the other young one's name? Tania?"

"Talia, honey. Her name is Talia," Xiaoming supplied.

"Right. I don't know those two very well. They seem nice enough. Roland and Frannie have been around forever. Roland cooks well. To be honest, I don't think I've ever had a conversation with him that wasn't about food. I don't even know if he's married."

"And Frannie?" I prompted.

"Frannie talks a little too much—she's always roping me into long-winded conversations—but she's well meaning and runs a tight ship."

"She really does," Xiaoming agreed. "Frankly, your mother should have left the repairs to her. She would have found better contractors than Jesse—or she would have noticed much quicker if they were botching the jobs so badly and overcharging."

Adam chuckled dryly. "My brother gets these big ideas, whether it's for a company or a renovation and upgrade for the estate. The issue is, he does very little research before he jumps in. People play him and, at least historically, he's had enough of my mother's money to burn through to not care. So he never learns."

"And he's a bit nepotistic," Xiaoming added, clearly eager to contribute. "Adam, didn't you tell me he mostly hires his friends for c-level positions at his companies?"

"Yes, that's been a pretty consistent pattern with him," Adam said disdainfully.

"I don't think it's even just with his own companies," Xiaoming said. "Once, when I was walking through the woods in front of the estate, I saw Jesse with one of the contractors he had hired. They were standing behind a tree and seemed to be talking really intensely. Then they hugged. Jesse is charming, of course, but it seemed too familiar. He had supposedly just met the woman and he was her employer, right? But they acted more like old friends, or maybe even more. Although, it was a woman, and Jesse is…well he's—"

"A womanizer," Adam offered.

It occurred to me that the person Xiaoming was describing could have been Danya. "Xiaoming, do you happen to remember what the woman Jesse was hugging looked like?"

Wincing apologetically, Xiaoming replied, "Only vaguely. She was tall and had platinum blonde hair. Unfortunately, I didn't get a good look at her face, because she was wearing a baseball hat."

"Do you remember what was on the hat?" I fished.

"It had what looked like a sports team's logo on it. I mean, it wasn't just plain or just patterned. So my best guess is that it was a sports logo, or maybe even a destination logo. But I couldn't make it out very well."

Great. That narrows it down magnificently, I thought, frustrated. But I bit my tongue and asked, "Was there anything else distinctive about her? Scars, tattoos, that kind of thing?"

Xiaoming screwed his eyes shut. Finally, he shook his head and said, "I'm sorry, but I think she was wearing a long sleeve shirt and jeans. I wouldn't have seen anything on her arms or legs."

It was far less than I was hoping for, but Xiaoming's description was at least a high-level match with the woman I had identified as Danya in her social media posts. "Thank you, Xiaoming, that's very helpful."

"Is it?" Adam asked skeptically. Xiaoming nudged him none too subtly. "I mean, hopefully it's a useful lead," he grumbled.

Needing a minute to collect my thoughts, I took a sip of my tea. It was the perfect balance of sweet and floral. "This is delicious. Thank you," I said.

Xiaoming smiled warmly. "You're very welcome. The endocrinologist in me thinks that I should reduce the amount of honey I consume everyday in my tea, but I know it will always be my indulgence."

Endocrinologist. Here's my in.

"It's crazy how expensive insulin is these days, isn't it?" I said, ostensibly looking at Xiaoming but monitoring Adam out of the corner of my eye for his reaction. "I bet you see a lot of patients who struggle to treat their diabetes."

Xiaoming nodded solemnly. "It's a huge problem. I try to work with patients to make lifestyle choices that will reduce the amount of insulin they need, but at the end of the day, a diabetic needs insulin."

"There's a whole team in the FBI that deals with stolen prescription medications, and insulin is one of them. I don't even know how people go about stealing something like that," I remarked.

Sighing, Xiaoming said, "You know, people skim a little off of their own supply if they can get a doctor to prescribe the upper end of the dosage appropriate for them. They just take a little less every day, but enough to get by, and sell the rest. Maybe there are also inventory robberies. And as much as I hate to admit it, I'm sure there are some unethical healthcare workers and pharmacists out there."

Adam was staring, spaced out, on something behind me.

Time to go in for the kill.

"Did you hear, Adam, about Talia Portnoy?"

His eyes refocused on me. "Who?"

"The maid, honey," Xiaoming reminded him.

It was becoming increasingly clear that Adam truly had no idea what had happened to Talia, much less her name. That, or he was a master actor. I had to consider both possibilities, so I pressed on.

"She was murdered."

Adam frowned so deeply that his normally severe face looked downright intimidating. "What?" he asked, the final T of the word clipped.

"Talia Portnoy. She was murdered. Someone injected her with insulin and she went into a coma because she wasn't diabetic," I explained.

Fury came over Adam's face. "And you think me or my husband have something to do with that? Is that why you're discussing insulin theft with us?"

"Honey, he's just doing his job," Xiaoming soothed. He turned to look at me. "Agent Velasquez, I take the Hippocratic Oath very seriously. I would be more than happy to refer you to my previous practice. There is a record of every prescription I wrote. Of course, you'll have to obtain a warrant because of patient privacy laws. You can start by speaking with my colleagues though, who will vouch for my character."

Before I could respond, Adam cut in. "I'm curious, Agent Velasquez, as to your theory. Why would I call the FBI and invite them to probe my family's affairs if I planned to kill off a maid who I barely knew existed?"

"It's my job to be thorough. We are checking with every pharmacy, hospital, and police jurisdiction in a wide radius around your late mother's estate and Talia's residence."

"So you'll be checking with Sofija, presumably, since she obviously has access to her patients' insulin. Right?" Adam demanded, the challenge in his voice ringing through the room.

"Of course. It would be a huge oversight if we didn't," I answered smoothly. It wasn't a lie. I had planned on calling Sofija tomorrow to confirm when Cantrell and I could come to the estate and have her open Mrs. Armitage's locked medicine storage units. We needed to photograph the insulin inventory. The warrant had only come through earlier today.

"Good," was Adam's laconic reply.

I gulped down the rest of my tea and wrote down a list of every piece of information we had discussed. Then I tore it off from the notepad and pushed it across the table toward Adam.

"This is a list of the things I'll need to confirm— your time in San Francisco, your husband's time in Atlanta, references from his old practice, all of that. You can send it over to my work email, which I've written at the top," I said. "Other than that, I think we've covered everything we needed to. Thank you for making the time—and thank you for the tea," I tacked on at the end.

"Our pleasure," Xiaoming politely replied.

Adam nodded curtly and said, "You're welcome."

"You didn't touch the crudité or the charcuterie," Xiaoming said, sounding disappointed.

To appease him, I nibbled on a few slices of cucumber and some pecorino cheese on a cracker with fig spread on it.

"This jam is delicious," I said.

Xiaoming happily clapped his hands together. "It's great to hear that! I made it myself."

I brushed my hands together and wiped them with my napkin. "I should get going," I said. "Please call if you have any more information."

"Will do," Adam said as he stood abruptly. "I'll walk you to the door."

"It was nice to meet you," I said to Xiaoming.

"You too, Agent Velasquez."

As I headed toward the door, I could sense Adam's huge presence behind me. It felt almost menacing, but I made a conscious effort to act unaffected.

When I opened the door, my jaw dropped.

My car was lying almost flush with the ground. Every tire had been slashed, and every window smashed.

Chapter 17

Sofija

I spent the weekend with my dad. It passed simultaneously too quickly and too slowly. He was having one of his good periods, and for most of Saturday, we played backgammon while sipping Malta's "national soft drink," a carbonated beverage flavored with bitter orange and wormwood. I wasn't the biggest fan of it, but Mom used to say that it reminded her of Malta. I always drank it when I missed her, or when I was with my dad. It was our way of feeling her presence, and it never failed to bring a smile to his weathered face.

Sunday morning, we went to church together. Afterward, Dad sat with his friends in the parish meeting room for their weekly gossip session. I loitered in the parking lot, determined to avoid inquiries from well-intentioned old women about my love life, or worse, my career. I wasn't sure if my dad knew about the controversy surrounding me. If he didn't, though, I wanted to keep him in a blissful state of ignorance for as long as possible. That meant avoiding situations in which someone might ask me about Sandra in front of him.

Even though I had nearly reached my tolerance quota of listening to my dad worry about my health and if I was eating enough, I stayed with him Monday. I was too afraid that I would spiral if I went home and sat alone in my apartment. Now that a couple of patients had dropped me, their families citing the newspaper article, I had a lighter workload. Keiko had gone on a long weekend hiking trip to New Hampshire with the man she'd been dancing with at the bar. Four of my other close friends had gone to their parents' or significant others' homes for Memorial Day. I didn't have the liquid funds to fly out to California and visit my brother. And Jesse wouldn't be coming by anytime soon.

When Tuesday rolled around, I visited the single patient I had scheduled for that day and then forced myself to return to my apartment. It was only 10:30 a.m., which gave me a large, looming chunk of free time. As I meal prepped for the week, I started to ruminate on worst-case scenarios—and on my awkward, drunken encounter with Mateo.

I knew it was pointless to obsess over what had already happened, but I couldn't help replaying the night. Pretty soon, I was second guessing the wisdom of confessing my feelings to him.

At the time, it had seemed like the right thing to do. The hurt on Mateo's face when he realized that I had shared the information about Roland and Frannie's conversation with Cantrell and not him…well, it crushed me. And I could understand it. After all, Mateo had stuck out his neck for me. He had defended me to Cantrell. It had probably seemed like a knife in the back to Mateo, me skipping over him and going straight to his more senior partner.

But now I worried that telling Mateo how I felt might have been a little selfish. Confessing made *me* feel better, but he couldn't get similar relief. Not as long as the investigation dragged on.

Thinking about it was making me miserable, so I opened my laptop and dove into a couple hours of Vypyr. I didn't hate it—some things about it were almost fun, a lot like learning a language. Except programming lacked my favorite thing about language learning—talking to people and seeing new worlds through the windows that their mother tongues offered.

When I needed a break from programming, I put together the outfit I would wear to the High Tide Bar and Grill, where the planned rendezvous between Jesse and Danya would take place. Once I was satisfied with my choices, I searched for new ways to keep myself busy. Just when I had settled on going to Lake Lorraine State Park for a swim, my phone rang.

It was Mateo.

"Hi, Sofija. How are you?" he asked.

I smiled to myself. He always sounded like he genuinely wanted to know the answer to that question.

"I've been better, but I'm not as bad as I could be, which is something, I guess."

"Good. That's good. I'm glad to hear it." Mateo sounded strained, like he was holding something back.

I wanted to ask him how the rest of his run had been, but I told myself that bringing up that night was a bad idea.

"What's up?" I asked instead. "Any update on the case?"

"Potentially," he said after a pause. "That's what I'm calling about."

I knew that the investigation was the only reason that Mateo would ever call, but hearing it still made me feel disappointed.

"Oh? What happened?"

"We need to come over to the Armitage estate and check something with you present, at your earliest convenience."

"You can't tell me what?" I asked.

"I'm so sorry, Sofija, but I really can't," he answered apologetically.

I sighed and blurted without thinking, "Fine. I know that Jesse will be out of the estate at a music festival from four to eight today, so we can do then. He might be there tomorrow, though, so I'd really prefer to get it over with today."

"Why does it matter that Jesse isn't there?" Mateo asked.

Shit. I scolded myself for letting that slip. "Don't worry about it."

There was a stretch of silence, and Mateo said, "All right then. We're tied up until 5 p.m. but we can make 6:30 p.m. today work."

"Thanks for being accommodating. But-but I don't want to ruin your dinner…" I trailed off guiltily.

"Don't worry about that. We can grab something from the building's café."

"Or I can pour some kombucha and sauté up some kale and tofu for Cantrell," I said sarcastically.

Mateo snort-laughed on the other side of the phone and then quickly cleared his throat. "Sounds good. See you then. We'll text you when we're at the driveway entrance."

"See you," I said.

As soon as I hung up, I showered and dressed in something nice but not too nice. I grabbed a book and took the long train ride and bus to the Armitage estate.

Once I arrived, I quietly slipped inside and

squirreled myself away in the library. Even if Jesse happened to show up, I knew that he'd never come into the library.

For hours, I read my book, trying to lose myself in the world within its pages. Today, I just couldn't.

When I finally heard the chime of my phone, I scooped it up so quickly that I nearly dropped it.

Mateo Velasquez—*We're at the driveway entrance. See you shortly.*—

I rushed out of the library and stood at the front door. I couldn't tell if I was nervous because the FBI was once again questioning me, or because I was going to see Mateo. Probably both.

When the doorbell finally rang, I waited a few seconds and then opened it, trying to look a little bored.

"Hello. Come in," I said, ushering Mateo and Cantrell inside.

The three of us stood in the giant hallway not quite looking at each other. Eventually, I spoke.

"I mean this in the most respectful way possible; Why are you two here?"

Cantrell glanced at Mateo, who turned and finally looked me in the eye. "Sofija, we're here to photograph the place where Sandra Armitage stored her medicine. We understand that you and Sandra were the only two who knew the combination to the lock on it."

Tilting my head in confusion, I said, "That's true. But Sandra died of natural causes. I know that you know this. Are you saying you think I murdered her?" I asked incredulously.

"Not her," came Cantrell's terse reply. "The important thing is, we have a warrant, so you've got to do it." He fished out the piece of paper for me to inspect.

After I skimmed it, I looked back up and searched the agents' faces. I handed back the warrant and said, "Follow me."

I led them to a small, dingy room at the end of the corridor. It was barely bigger than a large closet, so it was a tight squeeze.

I pointed to the small fridge that stood against the wall, as well as a metal cabinet that was mounted above it. Both had a numerical keypad lock. "Here they are. One for her medications that have to stay cool, one for the other types."

"Great," Mateo said. "Now can you open them for us and show us what's inside?"

I frowned. "You've got a warrant, so of course I'll show you, but can't you tell me why? Why do you want to *photograph* Sandra's medicine?"

Mateo sighed and cracked his knuckles. "You know that Talia Portnoy went into a coma before she died."

"Yes," I said cautiously.

"Well, it was a hypoglycemic coma. She wasn't diabetic. The coroner confirmed that her levels of c-peptide were low and her insulin levels were high."

The implication of his words hit me, and suddenly it was alarmingly clear why they wanted to see Sandra's medications—especially her insulin.

"You're kidding," I murmured in horror.

Cantrell opened his mouth to respond when a phone call cut him off. He muttered, "Gotta take this—sorry." He held up the phone to his ear. "Hello," he answered in a disgruntled voice. "Uh-huh. Uh-huh. I know it's late, but Anna, this is not a good time." The woman on the other end was clearly agitated, her voice getting louder. Cantrell pinched the bridge of his nose. "You're sure it can't wait?" The voice hollered something and he said, "Fine. Coming now."

When he hung up, he looked at Mateo apologetically. "Sorry, Velasquez, but that was the wife. It's a family emergency. Can you take it from here?"

Mateo looked incredibly nervous, his eyes darting over to me and then back to Cantrell. "I guess I can," he said.

"Great. Good thing we took separate cars. We'll regroup tomorrow morning." He stood and looked at me. "Ms. Sofija," he said with a nod. I was impressed that he remembered not to call me Ms. Zammit.

"Bye, Agent Cantrell," I called after him as he hurried out.

Mateo and I stood alone in the room. The small space seemed to thrum with a frenzied energy. His presence saturated everything, and I knew that I needed to get out into somewhere more open. Somewhere I wouldn't fantasize about Mateo closing the door and shoving me up against the wall and—

"I'm feeling a little claustrophobic," I said. "Maybe you can get the photographs over with, and if you have any questions, we can discuss them somewhere else?"

"That should be fine."

"Do you, uh…do you have any idea of how long all of this will take?" I asked anxiously.

Mateo's eyebrows shot up. "I don't, not really. Why?"

I shifted from foot to foot while I considered how to phrase it. Finally, I opted for the truth. "Jesse and I are going through a bit of a rough patch. I really don't want to run into him here. Especially not with you."

Mateo cleared his throat delicately. "Especially not

with me?"

"You know, because you're the FBI. He'll think something's wrong," I hurriedly explained.

Surveying me with something that looked almost but not quite like hunger, Mateo nodded. "Right. I'll take the photos and then you can get out of here. Can you open these?" he asked, gesturing toward the locked fridge and cabinet.

"Yes." I turned around and punched in the code. "It's 487692 for both of them," I said.

Once they were open, Mateo snapped a series of photos. Then, he squatted and took close up photos of the vials of insulin.

I knelt down next to him. "They look normal to me," I said. "Right amount, right opacity, right color, caps screwed on correctly."

"This is strictly a formality. Just making sure we do our due diligence," he said.

Next, he dusted the vials for fingerprints.

"You should only find mine and Sandra's on there," I said as he carefully peeled the strips with the prints off of the vials. "Months ago, Frannie sometimes gave Sandra the injections too, but when I started seeing Sandra daily and spending some nights here, I was the only one. To the best of my knowledge, at least."

As Mateo straightened, he bumped into me and I lost my balance. He grabbed my shoulders to steady me.

My heart raced as I whispered, "Thanks."

"Thank *you* for being so helpful with the evidence," he replied.

Evidence. I crashed back into reality. "No problem," I said numbly.

For a few blissful seconds, I had been a woman

thanking her crush for catching her when she stumbled. But with one word, I went right back to being a suspect in a case, and he went back to being the FBI agent investigating me.

"Hey," Mateo said, squeezing my shoulders, which he hadn't yet released. As soon as he'd done it, he withdrew his hands, as if they'd been shocked by electricity. "It's just standard procedure. If Roland or Marly or Frannie had access to the medication, we'd be doing the same thing."

That did make me feel better, but only marginally. "I guess you're right. Listen, can we step out? I just—I can't be in an enclosed space right now."

At least, not with you, Mateo.

"Right. Of course. After you."

I exited the room first, and Mateo followed. I checked the time.

"It's quarter past seven already. Jesse will be here soon, so I should really get going. I hate riding the train by myself late at night anyways."

Worry flashed across Mateo's face. "Sofija, I don't want you to have to do that. Let me drive you back."

Bad idea. Really, monumentally bad idea.

"You really don't have to. I'll be fine," I assured him.

"It's your choice, but I'd feel much more comfortable if you'd let me. Especially since you've been on the receiving end of threats lately."

I considered this carefully before I said, "All right. I really appreciate it."

Mateo didn't say anything; he just gave me a gentle smile and nodded. I followed him out of the estate and sat in his car. We were quiet the whole ride. I wanted desperately to talk to him, but I got the feeling that I should avoid doing that when we were so near each other, with no outside eyes to keep us accountable.

When we arrived at my apartment, he parked and politely asked to use the restroom. "I've been on the road since 5:15 p.m.," he said apologetically.

"Sure thing. Come on in." As I turned the key and let him inside, I started freaking out. Mateo would probably think my bathroom was too girly, what with the flowery shower curtains and pastel bath bombs.

It is what it is, and it shouldn't matter, Sofija. It's not like he's thinking about moving in with you. It's not like he ever will, I thought bitterly to myself. I sat at my table, hunched tensely with my arms crossed.

When Mateo emerged from the bathroom, he started to say, "Thank you," but was cut off by a huge yawn.

"Can I get you something caffeinated to drink before you hit the road?" I offered.

He gave a small chuckle. "Caught me. I wake up around five this morning, so this is nearing my bedtime. I'll have some coffee, if it's not too much trouble."

"Not at all," I assured him. "I've already got some brewed, but do you want a fresh pot?"

"No, no. It's probably still better than the coffee at work."

I poured him a mugful and took a bottle of the bitter orange Maltese soft drink out of the fridge for myself. I was in the mood for something familiar.

"Do you want to drink this outside? I find that walking instead of sitting wakes me up," I said. It was true, but I had an ulterior motive. I couldn't stay indoors with Mateo. Not when it was just the two of us. Not when it was night.

He nodded and suppressed another yawn. I handed him the coffee and we walked outside. After I locked up, I cracked open my bottle. It was a warm, balmy night, and the coldness of the drink was especially appealing.

"What's that?" Mateo asked, sounding genuinely curious.

"It's unofficially the national soft drink of Malta," I said. "You want to try?"

Hesitating, he said, "Sure. Just a sip, if you don't mind."

"Go ahead," I said, thrusting the bottle at him.

He seemed to hesitate.

"I'm not sick," I reassured him.

"Neither am I," he said quickly. He pressed the rim of the bottle to his lips and took a swig. I watched him hold the liquid in his mouth for a few seconds, as if he were giving his taste buds ample time to register the flavor. Finally, he swallowed and handed me back the bottle. "Thank you," he said politely.

"What did you think?"

He gave me a sympathetic grimace. "It's honestly not my favorite. My guilty pleasure is super sweet drinks, like root beer."

I laughed delightedly. "I actually prefer things like that too. I only drink this when I want to feel Maltese or if I need something...I don't know, comforting. Familial."

Mateo nodded. "I completely understand. I'm like that with *horchata*."

I knew he'd get it, I thought happily. It was amazing how fast being around him improved my mood when I felt safe enough to just let go. When there were no FBI agents around who could see us and get the wrong idea.

As I put the bottle to my lips, I ran my tongue along the rim, as if I could pull traces of the taste of him off it. It was as close as I had ever gotten to kissing him. It was probably my imagination, but the sip tasted sweeter.

"Did you want to ask me anything else about Sandra's medicine?" I asked.

"You pretty much confirmed this, but none of her insulin has gone missing over the past few weeks, correct?"

"Not that I know of, no," I answered. "The levels in the vials were right where they should be and the solution itself looked normal. You can always test it, though."

"We very well might. Have you seen anybody at the estate coming in or out of that little room?"

I paused and searched my memory. "No. I haven't."

Mateo nodded thoughtfully. "Okay. I guess if none of it is missing, it's very unlikely that anybody was stealing—not from those vials, in any case."

"Right," I agreed, taking a deep swig of my drink.

I looked at the streetlamps ahead of us on either side of the road. There was something so enthralling about the light they cast and how it softly illuminated the tangle of trees and their leaves. Twilight was approaching, and I was walking through a suburban jungle with my crush. It was a high school dream, all the tension and burning hunger between us melting into the heady young summer air.

But there wouldn't be an explosive resolution. There wouldn't be any tension released by crashing into each other in the night until we couldn't tell where one ended and the other began. We would only implode within the too-small containers of ourselves.

It was unbelievably frustrating, but I tried to

appreciate it for what it was. Still, I was dying to know if Mateo felt it too, this intense ache.

I knew I couldn't ask him that—but that didn't mean I couldn't learn more about him. Harmless questions, I'd stick to those. Nothing more personal than a journalist doing a puff piece might ask.

I settled on an easy one. "Do you like being an FBI agent?"

Mateo looked a little startled, but quickly composed himself. "I do like it. It's challenging work and it allows me to use a fair bit of the skillset I had from my lawyer days."

"Like what?" I asked, genuinely curious.

"So, when I was a lawyer, I really enjoyed the discovery phase of litigation. It involved researching the specific details of a client's case, as well as relevant precedent and laws. That's a lot like the fact-finding phase of an FBI investigation. Then as a lawyer, you have to synthesize all of that together to build a case to argue in court. FBI agents do something similar when we piece together a story of what happened with the evidence we've gathered."

"It really sounds like you liked a lot about being a lawyer. And, I mean, it must have paid better, right? So why did you switch? If you don't mind my asking," I tacked on, worried that I had come across as too nosy.

"Not at all," Mateo replied. "I just didn't feel extremely fulfilled. I wasn't working in immigration or environmental law or anything like that."

"I've heard the pay in those sectors is terrible," I remarked.

"It typically isn't great. No better than what I make at the FBI, that's for sure. Especially when you account for the generous benefits and pension that come with federal employment."

"So you were in big law," I surmised.

"I was," Mateo confirmed. "I wanted to pay back my loans, which I did. Then I helped my parents with their mortgage. But maybe more than that, I wanted to prove to my parents that even though I didn't become a doctor or an engineer, I had still chosen a good career path."

We had paused under a streetlamp. I leaned back against it and stared at the sky. The faintest glimmers of starlight were becoming visible.

"There was a time when I worried that I wanted to work in healthcare just to please my mom and dad. Like, maybe I didn't have a real desire to do it, you know? I felt that way all throughout high school."

"And then?" Mateo asked, stepping closer.

A shiver ran through me, despite the heat. "When I started taking college-level science courses, and even more so after I started working as a nurse, I realized that I had picked the right thing. It just clicked, like, 'This is my calling,' you know? Some days, my job exhausts me, but it's really rare that I wake up and dread going to work. I mean, if I hated it, I wouldn't be actively trying to put myself through thousands of dollars and months worth of school to be better at my job."

"How's that going by the way? The nurse practitioner school applications?" Mateo asked, resting an arm on the light pole above my head. I didn't think he had any idea how romantic he looked, gazing down at me, framed by the light from the lamp and the stars.

"It's-it's not going," I stammered. "The early decision programs I applied to have let me know that they're aware of the accusations against me. One way or another, they've all said that even though I'm very qualified, they almost certainly won't admit me until everything is cleared up." Tears welled in my eyes.

"Hey, don't cry. You'll get to suffer through more studying and tests than you can stand," he said playfully, though his face was all concern.

"*Inshallah*," I muttered.

"What does that mean? *Inshalla*h?" he asked.

Despite my mood, I laughed. "My Lebanese grandmother used to say it all the time. It literally means 'God willing,' in Arabic, but it really depends on context. Sometimes it means hopefully, sometimes it means fat chance."

"How did you mean it now?" Mateo asked.

"I don't know," I confessed. "Just...*inshallah*."

He stared at me for a moment, and it felt like he leaned ever so slightly closer. Suddenly, his face lit up.

"Oh! You know what?" he exclaimed. "I bet we get *ojalá* from *inshallah*! It means 'hopefully,' in Spanish. We say, *'ojalá'* and then whatever we hope."

"Well then *ojalá que* I get accepted into nurse practitioner school," I joked.

He laughed at that. "Two words are better than none," he said.

"*Puedo hablar más, tu sabes. Yo sé más que dos palabras!*" I defended with a silly grin.

"That's not a *terrible* start," he teased, drawing out the word "terrible."

It felt like something was pulling us toward each other, like a hook just above my belly button. I wanted my world and his to collide and for something new to be remade from the shattered debris.

Mateo opened his mouth as if to say something, but

stopped. He pushed himself off of the light post and straightened up. "Let's keep walking?" he suggested, his voice tight.

"Yeah," I agreed lamely.

For several minutes, we strolled on the sidewalk in silence. Finally, Mateo broke it. "In the police report about your bike crash, you said the person you were chasing was tall, dark haired, and pale. It's the same description as the man who followed you to the police station. Do you have any guesses as to who it is?"

I was sorely tempted to tell Mateo that yes, I had suspicions. I wanted to say that the man shared a lot of features with Adam. I wanted to say that I suspected Jesse of colluding with Danya Monroe, the CEO of a shady company that may have provided the crushed asphalt used to cause my bike crash and to pave the Armitage estate's shitty driveway.

But the same problem remained: if I shared my suspicions and even one of the three were innocent, I wouldn't be able to live with the guilt. It was one thing to tell the FBI about the conversation between Frannie and Roland so that they could look into the question of Talia and the receipts for themselves. It was a totally different thing to come right out and name names.

If I overheard something that confirmed my fears when I went to the High Tide Bar and Grill to spy on Jesse and Danya, then I would inform the FBI. But not before that.

"As they say in those procedural TV shows, all I have is conjecture at this point. I'm not comfortable sharing that, in case I bias you against innocent people. I'm sorry," I said.

Mateo stopped walking and looked at me intently.

"That's very honorable, Sofija."

"What do you mean?" I asked, nonplussed.

He retrained his gaze on the sidewalk. We continued walking as he answered, "You have a large incentive to redirect our investigation away from you and onto someone else, but you're not willing to throw anyone under the bus to make that happen. Not even when you seem to suspect someone. That's honorable," he finished.

My heart was beating fast and my stomach was doing backflips. A gentle breeze wound through the trees. "Thanks," I whispered, my voice melting into the sound of rustling tree leaves.

"You're welcome," Mateo replied.

A quiet that was somehow intimate and comfortable stretched between us for a few minutes before I observed, "Massachusetts is funny, isn't it?"

Quirking a confused smile at me, Mateo replied, "I agree, but why do you say that?"

"The weather. It has this reputation for being cold and snowy. It does snow a lot, for sure. But nobody ever talks about how perfect the summers are. They're beautiful. Being outside in them gives me this kind of late-night adventure feeling. It's the same one I had when I would visit Malta and sit outside with my family, waiting for it to be late enough to go out to beach parties with my friends."

That must have piqued Mateo's interest, because he asked, "What's Malta like? Do you enjoy visiting?"

"I *love* visiting. I'm never there long enough," I said. "It's warm, the sea is never too far away, the people are super friendly, and the seafood is second to none. Do you like seafood?"

"I could eat it every single day," Mateo replied.

"Then you'd have a great time in Malta. I remember how my mom, my aunt, and my *Nanna* would take me down to this little seaside town, Marsaxlokk, so we could watch the fishermen haul in their daily catch. The buildings there are either orangish stone or painted some sort of sand color. A few of them have these brilliant blue windows, which is the same color as the small boats. It's so pretty."

"It sounds absolutely stunning," he said.

"We would sit at an outdoor café, drinking coffee— well, I guess they'd drink coffee, and I'd have orange juice, or even ice cream, if I were lucky. My mom and my aunt would point out which of the fishermen they thought were the most handsome, or they'd gossip about them. My Nanna would pretend to scold them at first, but then she'd join in. Afterward, we'd go to the fish market and buy something to cook for dinner. We'd pack it up in an ice-filled cooler and drive back home. Then my uncle would fry it or grill it while me and my mom made side dishes."

Mateo smiled. "That sounds magical. There's nothing like preparing and eating food with family."

"There really isn't," I agreed. "Unfortunately, the culinary gene skipped me. I mean, I manage, because I spent so much time practicing with them. It's a work in progress, though. I even had to ask Roland to teach me how to make something Maltese once."

"I'm impressed. Lots of people decide they can't cook and never try to improve."

"Well, I'm persistent," I said with a shrug.

"I've noticed," Mateo said admiringly.

Again, we paused, and I noticed for the first time

that we'd nearly looped the block twice.

"And what about Mexico?" I asked. "What do you miss about it and not miss about it from your childhood visits?"

"Well, it was more than just visits. Even though I was born here in the States, I spent a pretty good portion of my early childhood in Mexico. My mom wanted to move back for a while to be closer to one of her sisters, who was very sick at the time. I spent ages three to eleven in Mexico."

"In…Oaxaca, right?" I tried to sound uncertain, like I was really reaching back in my memory to pull up that information. In reality, I remembered everything. I clung to every personal detail about Mateo's life that he'd shared with me.

Mateo looked impressed. "Great memory! Yes, in Oaxaca. While we were there, we lived in Oaxaca City so that me and my siblings could go to a bigger school, but my mother's sister and some of our relatives still lived in our ancestral village. It's a little town called Santos Reyes Nopala. My mom's family is mostly Chatino, and that's where a lot of us are."

"Chatino…" I wracked my brain. "I've read about the Nahua, Maya, Apache, Mixtecs, Yaqui, and Zapotecs, but not Chatino," I confessed.

"Impressive," he said, sounding sincere. "That's six more than the average person outside of Mexico knows."

"Thanks," I said, blushing.

"Chatinos are a relatively smaller group, so it's not surprising that you haven't heard of us. The Chatino language is similar to Zapotec. There's a lot of shared culture too."

"Can you speak it?"

He shook his head sadly. "Regrettably, no. Not fluently. I can understand quite a few words, and I can string together some basic sentences. But my grandmother and mother spoke to us in a mixture of Chatino and Spanish, so I didn't have enough exposure to just Chatino."

"I'm sorry," I said. "So where is Santos Reyes Napo-Nalop—"

"Nopala," he said, chuckling. "Good try."

"Right. Where is that on a map?" I asked.

He pulled out his phone and typed the name into Trawlerr, then pressed images. "Right here," he pointed.

"Ah!" I exclaimed excitedly. "It's by the sea! Did you grow up eating a lot of seafood?"

Again, he chuckled gently. "I know it looks close to the sea, but it's actually a little over an hour away. The city is in a mountainous area. Chatino cuisine is more about chicken and eggs for protein. We also eat a lot of corn, beans, chilies, squash, and tomatoes."

"I bet you can make some great dishes from those ingredients," I mused. "But I could never live without seafood."

"At this point, me neither," Mateo agreed. "Boston's spoiled me. I'm a huge fan of oysters, mussels, lobsters…all of that good stuff."

"Did that taste carry over from your lawyer days?" I teased.

"Unfortunately," he admitted, grinning. "With the FBI, work lunches and dinners are less likely to involve fancy seafood, because we can't expense our meals."

"As a taxpayer, I'm kind of relieved to hear that we're not bankrolling your oyster and lobster habit. But for your sake, I'm sorry."

"The things we sacrifice for the sake of public service," he said with mock seriousness.

"Thanks for your selflessness," I shot back playfully. I lifted my hand and reached for his shoulder, planning to give it a playful nudge. Quickly, I realized what I was doing and pulled my hand away, pretending to stretch and yawn.

It would be too easy to fall into something with Mateo. Even keeping interactions outdoors didn't seem to be a foolproof safeguard.

"I'm feeling pretty tired," I said. "Did you have any other questions?"

"None that I can think of."

We wandered up to my door. It felt like he was walking me home at the end of the date.

"This is me," was all I could think to say.

Mateo opened his mouth to respond when his expression changed. "Get inside," he practically growled. He sprinted toward the corner of the building and disappeared around it.

"Hey!" I shouted, ignoring his command and running after him. "What are you doing?"

When I rounded the corner of the building, I saw Mateo spinning in a circle, searching frantically for something.

"What is it?" I panted, alarmed by his wild demeanor.

"Someone was watching us. Really intently," he said, still looking around. "He was gone before I could get a good look at him. Dammit," he spat, stomping his foot.

His cursing surprised me—it seemed like a rare occurrence for him. "Did you happen to notice anything about him?" I asked tentatively.

Mateo closed his eyes and scrunched up his face. "Tall, dark hair, pale."

"Sounds familiar," I muttered.

Mateo bit the inside of his lip and released it with a frustrated huff. "I know. I wish I had seen something else about his features. Nose, lips, chin, anything."

I chose my words carefully. "For what it's worth, I have a feeling there will be a break in the case soon."

"You can't know that," Mateo countered, running his hand over his face in almost palpable frustration.

"True, but I have a feeling, and my feelings are usually right."

He inhaled deeply and seemed to compose himself. "*Ojalá tengas razón*," he finally said.

I smiled encouragingly. "I know what that means, now, thanks to you."

It was enough to lift his mood a little. "Is there somewhere you can stay other than your place tonight?"

"I'm not driving to my dad's or to a friend's house tonight," I bristled. "I'm tired. I'm not letting this asshole mess up my sleep schedule."

Mateo looked like he was about to protest, but he seemed to change his mind. "Well then make sure you lock the door and use the bolt. Lock the door to your room too. Is your phone fully charged?"

"Yes."

"Good. I'm going to take my own phone off silent, so the minute you feel like there's something unusual going on, call the police and then call me immediately afterward, okay?"

"I think this is a little bit of overkill," I protested, despite the warm feeling that his display of protectiveness triggered in me.

"Please, Sofija," Mateo implored.

"Okay, okay," I agreed. "I promise."

For the second time that night, we were at my door.

"Goodnight, Sofija. Stay safe," Mateo said with a quiet urgency.

I didn't trust my own voice not to crack, so I simply nodded and slipped inside.

Chapter 18

Mateo

Since I had dropped off my car at the shop to have the sabotaged tires and windows fixed, I borrowed my older sister Carina's car to drive out to High Tide Bar and Grill.

A true testament to how old her car was, it had a CD player but no aux interface for connecting a smartphone. The radio was clinging to life, the signal barely good for more than a fuzzy rendition of whatever the station was playing.

Keeping my eyes on the road, I fished around in the CD holder above the passenger seat and grabbed the first disc I could get my hands on. When the light turned red, I glanced down. It just said, "Carina's College Mix #2."

Better than silence, I thought as I slid the CD in.

When the song began, I smirked at the reminder that my sister and I had wildly different tastes in so much, including music. With the exception of ska and grunge, I had never really gotten into popular American music, preferring the likes of Selena and Ritchie Valens. Carina, on the other hand, was very much a flavor-of-the-season, top-twenty-hits kind of girl. It had annoyed my parents to no end, but Carina had placated them with her deep appreciation of Mexican cinema, whereas I had disappointed them with my penchant for everything

David Lynch and Stanley Kubrick. But both Carina and I loved eating our mother's Oaxacan cooking and playing *fútbol* with our father in our small backyard. We were both fully Mexican and fully American.

A lot of people misunderstood that. They thought that it was impossible.

It was one of the reasons I felt such a connection with Sofija. From our talks, I knew she understood.

Enough. Tonight is not about Sofija.

I forced my thoughts back to the music as the first track faded and the second one came on. As the jaunty pop rock blared through the speakers, I realized that Carina must have made the CD during her incredibly obsessive Fall Out Boy and Panic! At the Disco phase.

I quickly recognized the song. The lyrics were practically dripping with longing. The singer had me convinced that all he wanted was for the girl to realize that he was the person for her, that he was the one who appreciated her for all she was—not the jerk she was currently seeing.

It hit too close to home.

I laughed to myself dryly. It wasn't clear to me if running into so many reminders of Sofija was a cosmic coincidence or if she was just so embedded into my thoughts that I was primed to relate everything back to her, no matter how tenuous the connection.

Thankfully, I arrived at my destination before any more angsty pop songs could play. That wasn't the mindset I needed to be in for this task.

After I pulled into a parking spot between a beat-up Lancer and a motorcycle, I switched off the engine and surveyed the building. It looked a bit like a harbor dock shack that had been converted into a bar and plastered with some neon signs. A few men were congregated on the porch, smoking and drinking from beer bottles.

I looked in the mirror to compare my appearance against theirs. Certainly, I didn't look exactly the same, but I was channeling the aesthetic closely enough. The denim sherpa trucker jacket I had borrowed from my friend Jackson was a good fit, if a touch snug in the arms. Instead of my usual derbies or running shoes, I wore combat boots—also borrowed. My hair, normally impeccably smoothed back, fell over my forehead and grazed my eyebrows. For good measure, I had grown out what little stubble I had as much as I could by not shaving for a week, though the scratchy feeling was driving me crazy.

I exited the car and walked up the wooden stairs to the bar. The group on the porch parted so I could get through, barely giving me a second glance. Relief flooded me—so far, I blended in well enough.

The feeling was quickly replaced by anxiety as I stepped through the doorway. I assumed that the band was warming up, because loud, clanging riffs came from the stage. On top of that, 70's rock blasted from the speakers. The entire floor was packed; most people stood around tall round tables with no chairs. Only a lucky few were seated at the bar, nursing their drinks. And the smell—it was like body odor but somehow oddly metallic.

It was a massive sensory overload. I was so disconcerted that when I first saw her, I figured I might be imagining it.

But then she twisted her head and her eyes met mine. She had straightened her hair, applied heavy makeup, and was dressed differently than I had ever seen her. But the eyes were unmistakably hers—green and luminous, even in the dingy bar.

I was about to walk over to her when I noticed another familiar face: Jesse. He was over by the stage, talking to a tall blonde woman with arm tattoos.

Dammit. It was good to see confirmation that Jesse and Danya knew one another, but I hadn't expected him to be here tonight. I couldn't let him see me.

Thinking quickly, I grabbed a half-full pint glass that someone had left on a nearby table. I lifted it to my lips as if I were drinking, hoping that it obscured my face well enough. While I pretended to take a long draught, I strode toward Sofija and grabbed her arm. As discreetly as I could, I guided her away from the center of the room toward a darkened hallway.

"Sofija! What are you doing here?" I hissed.

Sofija seemed frozen for a second before she shot back defensively, "Trying to clear my name. Just like I told you and Agent Cantrell that I would."

Obnoxiously loud glam rock music pounded through my skull, and a throbbing pain built behind my eyes. *Fantastic. The last thing I need is a poorly-timed migraine.* I tried my best to stave it off and said, "Putting aside the fact that we've warned you against doing this, why are you *here* specifically? Did you know that Jesse would be here? And is what you're wearing an attempt at a disguise?"

"Not that it's any of your business how I dress," Sofija said with a sniff. "But yes. It is a disguise. I don't want Jesse to recognize me if he sees me. He doesn't—he doesn't know that I'm following him tonight."

"Why *are* you following him? Do you suspect him of something?"

Sofija studied me before she shook her head. "I don't have proof of anything."

"Speculate, then."

When she didn't respond, I leaned closer and whispered urgently, "Sofija. It's nice that you don't want to jeopardize potentially innocent people. But please, trust that Cantrell and I will fairly evaluate all the evidence. We won't accuse one suspect just because of another one's hunch. Plus, if you're keeping something from us that could help us catch whoever has been harassing you, or whoever killed Talia, then you're obscuring justice. Can you appreciate that?"

She seemed to carefully consider my words. Eventually, she gave a small nod. "I guess."

"So then tell me: why are you here, and what do you suspect about Jesse?"

Looking up at me, she began talking. "Do you remember, from the report, that my bike spun out because the tires got caught on what looked like ground up asphalt? When I was chasing the biker who left that envelope on my door?"

"Yes, I remember." *I couldn't forget anything that happened to you, Sofija.*

"Well, the company that Jesse hired to pave the Armitage estate's driveway used crushed asphalt that looked identical to the stuff that caused my crash. I mean, I guess most asphalt looks pretty similar. But this was like copy paste—shape, size, even smell. I tried to tell myself it was nothing but-but I felt like it might be something." She paused.

"Go on," I encouraged.

"And then as you know, from a distance the person on the bike looked like Adam, who's a biker himself.

258

Here's the thing: when I was chasing after the biker, Jesse was on the phone with me. He asked me which street I was on, and I told him. Then, less than a minute after I'd told Jesse that I could see the biker in front of me, boom. There was random rubble in the road and I crashed. Almost like someone told the biker that I was gaining on him and he decided to put something in the way to stop me. Do you see where I'm going with this?"

I got the sense that Sofija was still skirting around something, but at least she was talking. "You're worried that Adam and Jesse might be working together to scare you," I said, my voice barely audible above the din of the bar.

"The thought crossed my mind," she admitted. "Though I can't work out a motive that explains both of their behavior toward me. Plus, I have no evidence that Adam wasn't in San Francisco the whole time. So maybe it's a coincidence. Or maybe someone wants me to think it's Adam. I'm not sure."

"And you're here tonight because you've been following the Armitage brothers around? Are you trying to catch them doing something specific, like exchanging money with someone?"

Shaking her head, Sofija said, "I can't follow Adam. When he's in town, he's always at one of three places: his work, his home, or the estate. He would absolutely notice someone tailing him. I'd get caught. As for Jesse…no, I don't follow him around everywhere."

"But you've followed Jesse *here*. Please, Sofija, tell me why. I can tell you're hiding something."

Sofija slowly exhaled a breath I didn't know she had been holding. It cut through the stale air of the bar and washed over my face, a mint-scented caress. I looked down at her mouth and wished I could use my own to follow the source of the pleasant smell.

"It's because of a receipt I found."

Her answer jerked me back to the present. "What?"

She looked defensive as she explained, "Look, the whole gravel thing set me off. After the accident, I just— I really wanted to know who Jesse had hired to pave the driveway."

"So you must be here for Danya," I said, filling in the blanks.

Sofija's eyes opened wide. "You know about her? And that she'd be here?"

"Yes," I replied succinctly. "How did you find out about her?"

"Well, the receipts showed that the driveway paving job was carried out by a company called Smooth Streets, LLC. I went to the Secretary of State's website and saw that someone called Danya Monroe was listed as the CEO and COO. There's only one other employee at the company. The whole thing seemed so weird. When you have a budget of millions, why hire a small, obscure company to do a big job—unless you know someone at the company?"

I was impressed. Sofija's investigative strategy was remarkably similar to the one I had used. But it left me with one burning question. "That makes sense, but how did you know that Danya would be *here*, *tonight*?"

"Are you asking because you're impressed or because you're worried that I did something illegal to get the information?" Sofija asked cautiously.

"Asking questions is part of my job, Sofija. To answer you honestly, it's a little of column A, a little of column B. You're not obligated to tell me anything—I can Mirandize you if you want—but I am obligated to follow up on leads, and you've just given me one."

Sofija sighed. "You're right. I'm sorry. It's just…I'm not proud of how I obtained the information. But it wasn't illegal!" she insisted.

Silently, I waited for her to elaborate. When she realized that I wasn't going to say anything until she did, she squeezed her eyes shut and said, "Okay. Here's the whole story. After urgent care treated my biking injuries, Jesse took me to the Armitage estate. While he was showering, I snuck into the room Frannie uses for administration and found the receipts. I did my search on Smooth Streets, LLC, found Danya's name, and then ran back to Jesse's room. When he came out of the shower I-I—"

"Keep going," I urged when she faltered and blushed.

"*Please* don't judge me," she said, opening her eyes to look at me.

Instead of promising her that I wouldn't, I said, "I know the pressure that you're under. You can tell me."

"I didn't do anything illegal! It's just embarrassing. It doesn't paint me in a great light."

I decided to try a firmer approach. "Sofija, you don't have to talk to me, but if you're going to withhold information, just go home. I'm staying here to investigate Danya. When I'm back at work, though, I will have to look into how you obtained information about her whereabouts tonight. Hacking and stalking *are* illegal."

"Fine! I'll tell you," Sofija huffed. "When Jesse came out of the shower, I suggested that we have some fun to take my mind off the accident."

"Oh my God, did you honeypot him?"

"No!" Sofija denied vehemently. "I just got him drunk on red wine and when he was out, I scrolled through his phone and found his conversation with Danya. They had texted each other some pretty suspicious things, including when Jesse was literally on the phone with me during the bike chase. Anyways, I saw that they had agreed to meet here, tonight, at 7 p.m. While Jesse was still sleeping, I put his phone back in his pocket. He never realized what I'd done. Not illegal," she said, crossing her arms and giving a stubborn pout.

"Unethical, but not illegal. And pretty clever," I added, unable to hide my admiration. "But also very dangerous. If Jesse sees you here, he's going to suspect that you've looked through his phone. You'll really be putting a target on yourself. You know that, right?" I willed her to understand.

"Yes, I do, but like I said, I don't have the luxury of—oh, fuck me," Sofija seethed.

I shot her a quizzical look. My pulse spiked when I saw the genuine panic in her eyes.

"What is it?" I asked, stepping close enough that the lavender scent she always wore cut through the horrible miasma of stale beer, sweat, and greasy food.

"Danya," Sofija replied, worrying her lower lip. "She just picked up her handbag. I think she's coming this way, toward the bathroom. I can't let her see me—for sure Jesse has shown her what I look like." Sofija cast her eyes around, and I did the same. The place was packed—there was nowhere to hide on such short notice.

"There's no way we'll be able to push our way through this crowd before she gets close enough to see us. We have to hide our faces. Quick, kiss me!" Sofija urged.

"But—"

"Now!" Slinging her arms over my shoulders and behind my neck, Sofija pulled me toward her.

As I pressed a featherlight kiss to her lips, I saw her look to the side. Her eyes widened.

"She's almost here!" Sofija murmured urgently against my lips. "This is a dive bar, not church camp! Be more convincing—and angle your head so that neither of our faces are visible."

Even as a debate raged inside me, I understood the real danger of the situation. There was no telling what Jesse would do to Sofija if he found out that she was investigating him. Besides that, I'd be in huge trouble if Jesse told Cantrell that I'd been with Sofija while she was trailing him. Even if I insisted that it was a coincidence, that I hadn't planned it, it would look horrible.

So I put my brain on autopilot and let instinct take over. It was only too easy. I'd been wanting this forbidden thing since almost the moment I met Sofija.

I leaned in and wrested one of her wrists free from my shoulder, pinning it against the wall above her head. She responded enthusiastically, sliding the hand still draped around me down to grasp my collar, tugging me closer. I tripped and fell into her, and our hips collided. Before I could angle mine away to hide my very physical reaction to our improvised spycraft, a few people from the thronging crowd behind me jostled toward the bathroom and got stuck like a ten-car pileup. Sofija and I were locked solidly into place, with little more than wiggle room.

Dammit. She's going to feel how much I like this. A

tightness was building in my lower abdomen and thighs at an alarming rate. We gripped each other a little harder and kissed each other a little deeper. Before I realized what I was doing, I bit down gently on her plush lower lip. She let out a dizzyingly erotic whimper.

On the verge of whispering an apology, a motion cut me off. Sofija had just rolled her hips against mine. Inadvertent or not, I couldn't tell, but the effect was the same. It *broke* something in me.

I buried my free hand into the hair at the nape of her neck and slid my tongue into her mouth. She pressed impossibly close and writhed, like she was trying to fuse into me. Her nipples were so taut that I felt them through her shirt and mine. I was sure that she could feel the tense part of my own anatomy as well.

"Gahh—*fuck*," I moaned helplessly, my uncharacteristic vulgarity barely even registering. I was too painfully aroused to care.

Our little display was par for the course. The bar was full of other patrons grinding against each other. But somehow, what we were doing felt elevated, a class apart. We were keeping each other safe, after all.

I wasn't sure how long we went on like that. It seemed like something outside of time as it was happening, but the minute Sofija pulled away, exhaled shakily, and said, "She's gone now, we can stop," I could have sworn that it hadn't lasted more than thirty seconds.

Gulping, I nodded. "Right. We need to get you out of here. ASAP."

To my relief, Sofija didn't protest. We battled our way out of the hallway. It was like the room didn't want us to leave, like it wanted to enmesh us inside so that we could lose ourselves in each other again. When we finally reached the door and stumbled outside, the cool, dry air felt like a slap. We hurried to the side of the building, away from any windows or doors.

"Umm. Sorry about that," Sofija muttered, eyes averted. "I wasn't trying to cross any boundaries but...I got carried away." She shrugged and looked rather helpless.

"I did too, it-it wasn't just you," I stammered, frowning.

"Please believe me—I didn't scheme to set that up," she pleaded.

My expression softened. "Of course I believe you. This still puts us in a difficult position, though."

"You didn't kiss me for the hell of it. In fact, I initiated it. You just played along to protect me from being spotted by Danya. I don't think you've done anything wrong," Sofija said sullenly.

I pursed my lips and thought. "Maybe the act itself wasn't wrong, given the circumstances. But as you've just seen—"

"Felt," she corrected with a giggle that I silenced with a glare.

"As you've *become aware*, I'm too...responsive to you. Even though I'd still find you guilty if that's what the evidence said, it's just not right for me to have so little restraint. I've been able to keep it under control up until now, but what just happened inside..." I trailed off and shook my head. "And imagine what would happen if we cleared you of all suspicion and then somebody found out about what we just did? Our verdict, the integrity of the case, all of that would be called into question. You might live the rest of your life with a cloud of suspicion hanging over your head."

"Maybe you should make out with Adam, Jesse, Roland, Frannie, and any other suspects and call it even," she quipped.

I stifled a smile and arched a reproachful eyebrow.

Sighing, Sofija said, "Look, it was a normal male response. You would have reacted that way to any female pressed up against you like that."

She sounded a bit sad as she said that last sentence, and I wanted to scream, "No, it's different with you. It's more with you." Tamping down on the urge, I simply said, "Perhaps you're right."

"And if it ever gets totally unmanageable, you could just tell Cantrell that you have some personal reasons for needing to be taken off the case."

"If it ever comes to that," I slowly repeated.

"Right. If."

I knew that my internal battle over this was far from finished, but I truly didn't want to be taken off the case. Not when I felt like I was making some real progress.

"You should get home, Sofija. And might I remind you that you're not supposed to be investigating this on your own. This is an open FBI case."

"Which involves my reputation," she retorted with a defiant toss of her hair. "You know, three of my patients' families have already dropped me. I found out about the third just this afternoon. So while I'm sitting around with all of this extra free time, I thought I might try to salvage my career."

Her words sent a pang of sympathy through me. I wanted to hold her and tell her that it wouldn't be forever, that she would be rehired. But I couldn't. Instead, I said, "Of course, I can't stop you, but take care not to do anything that classifies as interfering or obstructing an investigation."

"Fine," she replied in a clipped tone, folding her arms and narrowing her eyes. "If that's all, *Agent Velasquez*, I'm going to splurge and call TripHitcher, so I can get home as soon as possible." She spun around and started to walk away.

"Sofija?" I called out softly.

"Yes?" she answered, turning her head so that her profile was perfectly outlined in the moonlight.

"My biggest—what I'm most worried—it's about being careful. If you're going to investigate on your own, be careful," I managed.

Even though I could only see half of her face, I could tell that her expression softened.

"You too. You be careful too," she said.

I thought I heard her tack on "Mateo" at the end, but it was so soft that I wasn't sure.

I waited in my car until Sofija's TripHitcher driver arrived, then I drove off. When I got home, I ran the fastest ten miles of my life. The searing pain that burned through my lungs felt like absolution.

Chapter 19

Sofija

After my fraught night at the bar where Mateo and I had kissed, I had a five-hour long patient visit on my schedule. Today, I was extra grateful for the distraction.

Mrs. Tremblay was a regular. The only days I didn't see her were Saturdays, Sundays, Mondays, and the occasional Friday. On those days, her daughter Margaret would come stay with her.

After a home robbery a little over a year ago in which the thieves stole Mrs. Tremblay's jewelry, Margaret had tried to convince her mother to move in with her or into a retirement home. Mrs. Tremblay had refused. "I will not be scared into early dependency," she had proudly declared.

She was a stubborn woman, but a loyal one—which was good news for me. "Thank you, Mrs. Tremblay and family, for not dropping me," I murmured gratefully to my empty apartment as I packed up my nursing bag.

It was a forty-five minute train ride out to Mrs. Tremblay. The last thing I wanted was to sit with my thoughts for the entire ride, so I brought a book with me. After going over the same paragraph four times, I gave up.

Against my better judgment, I pulled out my phone, opened Trawlerr, and typed Mateo Velasquez plus

Massachusetts. A few results that I had seen before popped up—bylines on the University of Gloucester's College of Law student publication articles, blurbs from his old firm. But then I saw a headline that I'd missed the first time I had looked him up. Eagerly, I clicked on the link and read.

During one spring break while at law school, Mateo had done pro bono work at the Alaska Center for Entrepreneurship to help prepare tax returns for rural, indigenous, communities. In the article, he was quoted saying:

"This trip gave me an opportunity to help indigenous people with fledgling businesses, which is something close to my heart, given my mother's background.

"Indigenous people on Turtle Island, from Chile to Nunavut, have had to adapt to imposed legal and financial systems that are oftentimes confusing. Filing taxes is one of the more complicated matters to navigate, especially for new entrepreneurs. Inuit who have launched businesses frequently find themselves bogged down by bureaucracy. Many of them came to the Alaska Center for Entrepreneurship and our volunteer team from the University of Gloucester helped them file their taxes so that they could get the maximum benefits they're entitled to. It's a small way to help, but it was extremely rewarding personally and professionally."

Reading that made me feel tingly. The more I learned about Mateo, the more invested I felt. After our kiss, the hope that I had previously clamped down on was finally pushing its way to the surface. It really seemed possible that Mateo would want to be with me, once this investigation was closed.

My thoughts were interrupted by the smooth voice of the train announcing that we had arrived at my stop. I dismounted and walked over to the bus schedule board.

"Great," I muttered. The bus was delayed fifteen minutes. It would take about that long to walk to Mrs. Tremblay's. It was a beautiful day, so I decided to go on foot.

Mrs. Tremblay was waiting on her porch as I approached. Her lined face crinkled into a smile as she beckoned to me. "Sofija! Come here, my dear."

"Hi, Mrs. Tremblay," I greeted as I ran up the stairs. "How are you feeling today?"

"Wonderful, if only my pancreas would work better."

"I can give you something for that," I said, gesturing inside with a wink.

"You got my doctor's message, right? That new diet and exercise plan has my blood looking much cleaner, so a couple days ago, we reduced my insulin dose."

Nodding, I said, "Yes, I spoke with Dr. Ramachandran about it. I'm supposed to measure your blood sugar at 1 p.m. and again at 5 p.m. after you eat to make sure we've got the dosage right."

Mrs. Tremblay nodded her wizened head and said, "Right. In the meantime, we can sit on the porch and play chess or cards."

I gave her a warm smile. "That sounds like a great plan, Mrs. Tremblay. I can make your special tea and we can play as many games as you want. I have no specific time that I need to leave."

She clapped her gnarled hands together. "Lucky me," she said in her reed-thin voice. "Be a dear and grab the chessboard off the shelf and I'll set it up while you make the tea. Add some of that God awful monk fruit stuff to it. It's better than nothing."

I laughed and did as she said, dropping off the chessboard on the table next to her before heading inside to prepare her tea. It was a mix of black tea, sage, cinnamon, cardamom, and ginger. Every few months when she ran out, I would fish out the fragile piece of paper with the recipe on it from one of her overstuffed cookbooks. Then, I would prepare enough of the mix to fill one of the giant mason jars that lined the counter to the right of the sink.

On my last visit, I had made a new batch, so the jar was full today. I opened it and stuffed two heaping spoonful of the mix into an infuser and inserted it into the opening of the teapot, then sprinkled a little monk fruit sweetener into it. I filled a kettle with filtered water and set it to boil. While it heated up, I called out to check on Mrs. Tremblay.

"The water for the tea is heating up now," I informed her. "Are you hungry for anything?"

"No," she said, shaking her head. "I'm just thirsty. My mouth feels a little dry."

"I'll bring out some water too," I said.

"Actually, I have to use the commode. Would you mind helping me stand?" she asked a little weakly.

"Of course," I agreed, walking over. Something about Mrs. Tremblay's behavior was concerning me, but it wasn't full-blown worry. It was more like a small, annoying pressure at the back of my mind.

Carefully, I guided her inside. When we got to the restroom, I asked if she needed any more help, but she declined.

"Just call out if you need something," I said.

"You know I will," she assured me before closing the door. I stood staring at it for what must have been a minute. Finally, I shook my head and padded back into the kitchen, just in time for the kettle to boil.

I snatched it off the stove before the whistle could grow to a crescendo and turned off the stove. After I poured the boiling water into the teapot, I placed the lid on top to let it steep.

"You all right in there?" I called out.

"Yes, dear."

I grasped the teapot's handle and cradled the spout with a towel that had been lying on the counter. Using my elbow, I nudged open the front door and set the teapot on one of the side tables then went back inside for teacups and a glass of water. Once everything was set up, I walked back inside and waited next to the bathroom door.

The house was uncomfortably silent.

There was a fine line between respecting a patient's autonomy and being attentive. Today, I felt like leaning more toward the latter.

"Mrs. Tremblay? Do you need anything?"

"I'm just coming out now, dear."

I heard a flush and then the sink tap running. The door creaked open and Mrs. Tremblay extended her hands toward me. I rushed to offer her my arm, which she immediately clung to.

"Thank you," she managed. "Don't know what's gotten into me. I've been in and out of the restroom all day. Feels like whatever I drink is going straight through me."

I guided her outside and helped her into her chair before scooching my own so that I was positioned across the table facing her. I poured us some tea and asked, "Ready?"

"That I am. You made this perfectly," Mrs. Tremblay said as she took a sip of the tea.

"I'm glad. I think I get to move first this time—you did last time," I said cheekily.

She gave a dry laugh. "All right, fair is fair."

For about half an hour, we sipped tea and played chess. It was boring, but in a nice way. I was finally starting to feel settled when the sound of something shattering startled me.

I looked up to see Mrs. Tremblay's empty hand extended over air, her shattered teacup on the wooden porch.

"I'm sorry dear. My vision is blurry. I seem to have misjudged where the edge of the table is."

I ran through the mental checklist in my head. *Dry mouth, urge to pee, tired, blurred vision. Textbook symptoms of low insulin.*

"I think we might need to up your insulin dosage a little, Mrs. Tremblay. Let's measure your blood levels a little earlier than usual today, okay?" Hurriedly, I unzipped my nurse's bag and picked up the finger stick blood test device.

"When did you last eat?" I asked.

"Over three hours ago," she replied with what sounded like a huge effort.

"Okay." I cleaned her finger and pricked it. Fifteen seconds later, the reading came out.

"Your blood sugar levels are high. I'm going to give you a small dose of insulin, just like Dr. Ramachandran instructed."

"Do your worst," she joked so quietly that I

struggled to make out her words.

I sprinted into the kitchen. Mrs. Tremblay insisted on keeping her insulin in the fridge along with her food and drinks, despite her daughter Margaret's offer to buy her a mini medicine fridge just for medication. That meant that I often had to root around the shelves to find the tiny vials.

Today was no exception. For at least four minutes, I pushed around containers of leftovers, sourdough starters, and unidentifiable plastic containers full of food. Stamping my foot in frustration, I finally began removing the contents and tossing them on the floor. When I finally found the vials, I snatched one and dashed back to Mrs. Tremblay.

As quickly as I could, I prepared it for injection. Relief flooded me as I watched the clear, liquid barrier between Mrs. Tremblay's life and death leave the syringe. When I was done, I dabbed a bit of rubbing alcohol on the gauze and swiped it across the tiny prick on her skin.

"There," I said soothingly as I rubbed small circles on her skin.

For a tense twenty minutes, we waited. Finally, Mrs. Tremblay began to perk up a little.

"How are you feeling?" I asked gently.

"Fit as a fiddle," Mrs. Tremblay said with a grin. "Although I'll admit, that felt like a close call. Took you a long time to find my vials."

"Well, I hate to say that Margaret and I told you so, Mrs. Tremblay, but that's what you get for keeping your insulin in the same fridge as your food. I—"

It hit me like an unexpected, cold ocean wave.

Sandra had kept her insulin in a medical fridge.

None of it seemed missing or tampered with.

But Sandra hadn't been the only diabetic at the Armitage estate.

Roland was too.

He was a chef, so he rarely left the kitchen. Neither did his insulin. Just like Mrs. Tremblay, he kept it in the fridge alongside the food.

The fridge that the FBI had never checked.

The fridge that Jesse or Adam or anybody could have opened with a perfect alibi: they were looking for a snack.

All the clues started flying together, pulled together by a horrible magnet.

I remembered the strange ending to the exchange between Frannie and Roland that I had overheard. It had seemed harmless at the time. Now, it took on a new meaning.

"Take the reins for a second, Frannie? I've got to use the restroom."

"Again? You went five minutes ago! You've got yourself a stomach bug, don't you? My son knows a great GI. She helped set him right after his summer in the DR had him living on the toilet."

"No, Frannie, it's not that. I—well, to be frank, I've got to piss all the time. Like a pregnant woman. Hell, I've even been feeling tired like one, and God knows I've got the belly."

What if someone had been siphoning insulin from Roland's supplies and diluting it?

I had to check.

"Mrs. Tremblay, I have to leave. It's an emergency. I'm going to call your daughter, because I don't want to leave you alone right now, okay?"

"Of course dear, but can't you tell me what's going on?" she asked, concern deepening the lines on her forehead.

I shook my head. "I'm not sure about anything. And it would take too long to explain. But it's really, really important," I said, already taking out my phone.

Luckily, Margaret picked up. Her work was close by, so she promised to come in ten minutes.

I hailed a car on TripHitcher to get to the Armitage estate—I couldn't wait to take the train. Then, I called the estate. Nobody picked up. I called again. Still no answer.

It made sense; today was Frannie's day off, and Marly often did grocery shopping for the estate around this time. Roland should have been in the kitchen, though, meal prepping or cleaning. The fact that he wasn't answering was concerning.

He could just have his earphones in. He loves listening to loud jazz.

While I tried unsuccessfully to reassure myself, the TripHitcher driver and Margaret pulled up, one after the other.

"Sofija!" Margaret said. "What's going on?"

"No time to explain," I said. "By the way, your mom was a little low on insulin. I'll talk about it with Dr. Ramachandran, but you should monitor her blood sugar."

Before Margaret could reply, I hopped in the car and instructed, "Drive as fast as you can."

For the entire ride, I kept calling the estate, praying for someone to pick up.

Nobody did.

****

I hopped out of the car and sprinted up the gravel side path so fast that I nearly tripped. Throwing open the door, I screamed, "Roland? ROLAND?"

"Kitchen," came his feeble reply.

Seconds later, I was standing in front of Roland. He had collapsed into a chair, his arms and legs drooping toward the ground.

"Thirsty 'n tired," he mumbled.

Squatting down in front of him, I took his massive hands in mine. "Roland, I don't want you to panic, but I think there is something wrong with the insulin you've been taking."

His face turned even more ashen than it already was. "Like poison?"

I squeezed him comfortingly with one hand while I dialed 911 with the other. "I don't think so. More like it's been diluted."

A dispatcher picked up almost immediately.

"911, what's your emergency?"

As calmly as I could, I said, "Hello, my name is Sofija Zammit and I was the nurse for the late Mrs. Sandra Armitage. I'm at the Armitage estate now. It's 15 Maple Run Drive. The chef here, Roland Courville, is in trouble. I think his insulin supplies have been watered down with something because he's presenting signs of hyperglycemia. I'm going to give him a glucose test as soon as I hang up, but I'm pretty sure that's what's happening. If his vials have been diluted, I don't know by how much, so I don't know what the concentration is. That's why I'm scared to give him a supplementary dose. Please send an emergency dispatch to the Armitage estate as soon as possible. Have them bring insulin. We'll be waiting in the hall, just inside the entrance."

"Okay, ma'am. The address is 15 Maple Run Drive, correct?"

"Yes. *Please* hurry," I implored.

"We will. What number can we reach you at?"

I rattled it off from memory.

"We'll have an ambulance out there in fifteen minutes."

"Thank you so much," I said.

When I hung up, I looked at Roland's face. He looked panicked but wasn't saying anything.

"Let's get you to the front hall," I said. I slung his arm over my shoulder and used my left arm to grasp his waist. We slowly stumbled to the front door.

Both Roland and I were huffing by the time we got him situated on the divan in the hall. He reclined and closed his eyes as he muttered, "Water."

"Of course," I said as I dashed back to the kitchen. Skidding to a stop in front of the cupboard, I threw open the doors and grabbed the first glass I could. As soon as I'd filled it with water, I slammed off the tap and ran back to Roland.

Thrusting the glass at him, I said, "I want to do a quick blood test, okay?"

"Go ahead," he breathed.

I grabbed the device and pricked his finger. The results confirmed my fears.

"Roland, you're hyperglycemic right now. Like I said, I think there's something wrong with your insulin supply. I want to pop back into the kitchen to look at it, okay? See if it looks off. First, though, I'm going to help you drink this water and then I'll bring back more."

"Thank you," he whispered. "You're a good one, Sofija. Those asses at the newspaper are wrong."

I smiled a little, holding back tears. I carefully tilted Roland's head back and helped him drink down the water. When he was finished, I ran back to the kitchen and threw open the fridge doors.

Roland's vials were lined up neatly in one of the fridge shelves. I retrieved one and held it up to the light.

Sure enough, there was a subtle but noticeable difference in the opacity of the solution.

I put the vial back with trembling hands.

Some of Roland's insulin had been siphoned away and replaced with something else. It was a perfect crime; the fridge was covered in DNA from everybody, and there were no cameras inside the kitchen.

It seemed almost certain that someone at the estate had used the insulin they'd stolen from Roland to kill Talia by inducing hypoglycemia. It was probably Adam or Jesse—or both.

Roland's faint moan cut through my reverie and spiked my adrenaline. I was so nervous that I felt like all five-foot-two of me could have scooped him up and run him to the hospital myself if the ambulance didn't come soon.

I dialed Mateo to tell him my theory. While the phone rang, I carefully placed the tampered-with vial back in the fridge and started to fill up Roland's glass with water. It occurred to me that maybe I could give him a microdose of Sandra's insulin supply, if it hadn't already expired.

"Hello, Sofija," Mateo answered after two rings. He sounded cautious, maybe because of our encounter the night before.

"Agent Velasquez, hi. I—" a loud creaking sound came from the direction of the door that connected the kitchen to the side porch. "One second," I said.

"Sofija? Sofija, what's going on?" Mateo demanded, but my attention was glued to the door. I set my phone down on the kitchen island and grabbed one of the chopping knives.

As I crept toward the door, I heard a shuffle and a creak. I braced myself and gripped the knife tighter as I rounded the corner.

The sound of a gun safety clicked next to my head and Jesse's voice, menacingly soft, said, "Scream and you're dead. Got it?"

I bit my lips and nodded, trembling.

"Here's what you're going to do. You're going to pick up the phone and tell Velasquez that you're sorry for keeping him waiting—you had to use the bathroom. Then you're going to tell him that you've been feeling so much guilt lately. You're sorry for lying to him, but it will all be clear soon. And then you're going to tell him that it's too late to fix things, so you're saying goodbye. Say it just like that. Understood?"

Panic and rage coursed through me. I shook my head as much as I could, given the gun at my temple.

Jesse pressed the barrel deeper and hissed, "I swear to God, Sofija, it won't just be you. It'll be your father too. Don't think I wouldn't. One less old man who already has one foot in the grave doesn't matter to me. People wouldn't even suspect it was anything but an accident."

"No," I whimpered.

"Then walk and talk," he commanded.

Slowly, I trudged over to my phone. Jesse's gun never left my head.

"Sorry, Agent Velasquez. I had to dash off to the

bathroom."

"It's okay. Is everything all right, Sofija?" Mateo asked, the concern in his voice bleeding through the phone.

"It's—no it's not. I've been feeling so guilty lately. I'm sorry for lying to you—it will all be clear soon. But it's too late to fix things, so goodbye…Mateo"

"Sofija!? Sofija wait—"

I hung up and glared at Jesse.

"Not a bad performance, Sofija," he said with a grin. Then he wound back a balled fist and everything went dark.

Chapter 20

Sofija

A piercing sensation on my right mandible radiated out in painful throbs. Eyes still closed, I opened my jaw experimentally and hissed. Something was coiled around different parts of my body so tightly that I thought it might be cutting into my skin.

"Morning, babe," came Jesse's voice. I'd heard him say those exact words many times before. In the past, they had made me melt. Now, they sent a shiver down my spine.

I opened my eyes and he slowly came into focus, along with our surroundings. We seemed to be in an abandoned gym. Basketball backboards were mounted at each end of the room. Shreds of nets hung limply from the hoops. The bleachers and the floor were covered in a thick layer of dust, except around us, where it had been disturbed enough to reveal shiny hardwood.

Jesse must have guessed my train of thought, because he smirked and said, "Bet you were shit at basketball, huh, Sofija? Bit on the short side." He looked down at my feet as he said it. I did the same and saw what I felt: coils of rope fastened me tightly to a chair. My feet didn't even reach the ground.

"Fuck you, Jesse. You're everyone's worst impression of you and then some."

"Sorry, Sofi, but that's going to be *your* legacy, not mine," Jesse said smugly.

I blanched. "What do you mean?" I asked, though I had a grim idea.

Jesse tapped his finger on his chin as if in thought, then swatted the air in front of him with a grin. "Ah, what's the harm? You might as well go out knowing how you'll be remembered once you're gone."

Cold sweat beaded on my forehead and dripped down my back. I waited.

Jesse leaned back against what must have been the scorekeeper's table and said, "As we speak, one of my associates is on his way to your apartment. He's bringing the vial we've been using to store the insulin that we stole from Roland. He's going to plant it in your fridge, right next to that awful smelling kombucha. When you've been missing for a couple days, the FBI will go search your apartment."

The script he had made me recite to Mateo was making more and more sense. I felt like I was going to throw up.

"They won't just find the insulin, though. When they open up your laptop—thanks for sharing the password with me, by the way—they'll find a *very* moving suicide note. You want to hear what it's going to say, Sofi?"

I shook my head.

He laughed, a cold, empty laugh. "I think I'll tell you anyway. In the note, you're going to admit to having manipulated my mother. You'll also confess that you were jealous of Talia, because you'd caught me having sex with her. Talia isn't alive to contradict it, and I have a certain reputation when it comes to women. Nobody will question it. You'll say that your jealousy drove you to kill her, but that you didn't want to make it bloody. Nurses know how insulin works, and you had easy access to Roland's. But the guilt drove you insane, so you decided to drown yourself."

He gave me a heart stopping smile and used his foot to nudge a huge bucket full of ice next to him.

As I struggled futilely against the ropes, I fumed, "How the hell did you even know that I would be at the Armitage estate today?"

Jesse reached into his pocket and fished out my phone. He tapped the screen and said, "Zero-click spyware. With enough money, you can do anything. As it just so happens, I have enough money. And it's going to stay that way. You know why, Sofija?"

I twisted my head away to look anywhere but at him.

"Because when you're declared dead, whatever you would have inherited will be evenly split between me and Adam," Jesse announced triumphantly.

Whipping my head back around to face him, I demanded, "Why not just kill me from the beginning, then? Would have saved you the trouble of pretending to like me. And it's not like you hesitated to kill Talia."

"I only killed Talia because she was looking into the receipts for the estate maintenance jobs. What if she'd shared what she found with the police? Or with you? If my own mother cut me out of her will when she found out I was grifting her through these jobs, what would you have done? You wouldn't have shared a single dollar with me."

When my only response was a glare, Jesse continued. "But no, I don't *prefer* killing, Sofi. It's messy. It forces me to answer questions that I'd rather not. That's why I pressured you to just finalize the inheritance and split it with me. I tried to do this nicely. But you've suspected me for some time, haven't you? You weren't going to share it with me. So when honey fails, vinegar it is."

My body was shaking. I took deep breaths and finally managed to ask, "Is Adam in on this with you?"

Scoffing, Jesse replied, "Adam has no idea. I did have my associate dress up like him to confuse you and the FBI. I even had him do that around Talia in the days leading up to her death, just so people would see someone who resembled Adam and mention it to whoever asked. Throw everyone off the trail, you know?"

"Brother of the year," I muttered sarcastically.

He waved off my comment. "Please. Adam was never in danger of actually being found guilty. Seeing a tall, pale man with dark hair is such circumstantial evidence that a lawyer would be laughed out of court for presenting it. Especially if they went up against the kind of defense that Adam can afford. Plus, I assume that the FBI will eventually assume that you hired an Adam lookalike to harass you so you'd seem innocent."

"And what was your plan if I had caught your friend on the bike after he left that envelope on my porch? It would have proven that it wasn't Adam harassing and stalking me. Also, the FBI might have questioned him until he gave you up."

"You were never going to catch him, though. I arranged beforehand for him to carry a big sack of crushed asphalt from Danya's company. One cut to the bag and boom, it came tumbling out. I knew your shitty secondhand bike couldn't handle it."

"Wow Jesse!" I seethed. "Did you come up with that all on your own, or did you use Saturday morning cartoons for inspiration? And they call Adam the genius brother. He's got nothing on you and your beautiful mind."

Jesse's expression twisted into a sneer. "That's not all I did, Sofi. I'm the one who leaked your story to the newspaper. Bet you'd never have guessed that, huh?"

I stayed silent.

"Answer me!" he bellowed, kicking my shin.

"Fuck," I whelped in pain. "No, I wouldn't have guessed that."

"That's right. I'd hoped it would scare you into thinking that you couldn't shake the scandal for the rest of your professional life. I wanted you to feel like taking the money and living off of it was your only option. Any smart person would have done that. But you're not too bright, are you? So deluded, thinking that any schools would want you, with your trash reputation. You know, Sofi, I'm being generous by killing you. Now you don't have to live through the pain of being tossed aside and rejected, watching your dream slip away."

Jesse's words hurt. They struck right at the heart of my deepest fears over the past few weeks.

"Oh Jesse, if you'd put that much thought into your failed companies, you might not be so dependent on murdering women to maintain your lifestyle. You could have been more than a useless leech."

At the mention of his failed businesses, Jesse's face darkened and he took a step closer.

"You don't know when to fucking quit, do you Sofi? Just like Adam that way. It could have been you, me, and the money. We would have been set for life, if a little bored. But Adam had to be his usual obsessive self. He had to run to the FBI, like he always ran to mom when he thought I was screwing up. And then you had to pick at the whole thing until you left me no choice."

I was about to retort when my self-preservation instinct pierced through the thick fog of my fury. *Bond with your captor. Make him see you as human.* It couldn't hurt to try.

"Fucking Adam. He should have never gotten the FBI involved in the first place. It's not like he needed the money. Fucking Adam," I repeated. Jesse looked up at me. He seemed almost pleasantly surprised.

"Yeah. Fucking Adam," he agreed.

This is good. Keep it up.

"You know, Jesse, it could still be that way."

Squinting, he took a step closer. "Be what way?"

"You, me, and the money. We don't have to be boring. We can travel, even live anywhere you like. Show me how to live life beyond Massachusetts. Beyond America."

At this, Jesse lunged at me, a snarl distorting his features. He grabbed my shoulders and shook me. "You think you can trick me? I'm not a fucking moron, Sofija. Even before today, I knew that you didn't feel the same about me anymore."

Tears spilled from my eyes. I was going to die if I didn't turn this around. "Why do you say that, Jesse?"

He released my shoulders and crouched down so that our noses were almost touching. I could taste the whiskey on his breath. "Because Sofi, I've *never* felt that way about you, and like recognizes like. You're just playing now. I know because that's all I've ever done with you."

A choked sob escaped me. "But Jesse, I *did* love you at one point! You-you never did?" I hated how needy and pathetic I sounded.

Jesse drawled, "Come on, Sofi. Think about the timing, about when we started getting close. Think about who I wanted to keep us a secret from."

I bowed my head and sniffed.

"Sofi," Jesse said gently, just the way he used to.

"What?"

"You were a *really* good lay, if that makes you feel better. I'm being totally honest about that."

My last thread of hope unraveled. I sobbed in earnest now.

"Too bad Agent Velasquez will never experience that."

Shocked, I whipped my head up. Jesse was giving me a disgusted look. "Thought I was blind? I saw the way he was around you when he first came to the estate to question us. Saw the way you practically fucked in the bar when you were following me last night."

I gasped. He continued. "Yeah, I saw that little display. Real classy, Sofi. I wonder, if you two hadn't been worried about getting caught, would you have stopped there? I'd put my money on you leading him off to one of the bar's dark corners and letting him have you against the wall. You really are trash."

We had passed the point of no return. There was no way I was getting out of this, and I wasn't going to spend my final moments alive letting this piece of shit drag my name through the mud.

"You're not going to tell me who I am right before I die. I know who the hell I am. Seems like you're just jealous that you've never had instant chemistry with someone like I have with Mateo. Well, fuck you, Jesse. I hope you burn through the money on more of your shitty companies. God knows you're good at *that*."

A dangerous fury lit Jesse's face and he opened his mouth as if to yell. But instead, he chuckled and taunted, "Lot of heat behind those words. Let's see if that hot little mouth of yours can melt these in time for you to breathe." With that, he spun around and grabbed the bucket of large ice cubes, a clothespin, and duct tape.

"Wh-what are you going to do?" I asked shakily.

"I'm going to have a little fun, Sofi, and then I'm going to drown you in your seat. That's how you die, remember? Then when everyone is asleep, I'll dump you in the pond on the estate. Hey!" he said, eyes lighting up with a malicious gleam. "The estate was going to belong to you, but now you're going to belong to the estate. And that's a special pond for us, isn't it Sofija? This really is coming together so nicely."

A memory of us sitting on the pond's bank, watching the ducks swim in the new spring world, flashed before my eyes. I let out a scream of frustration and hurled out, "It's going to be so obvious that there was foul play."

Jesse shrugged unconcernedly. "You'll have water in your lungs. That's how people drown."

"They'll find my body and see these rope burns and the bruise on my jaw."

"The fish will have cleaned most of your flesh off by then. Massachusetts is full of bodies of water. Your letter isn't going to specify which one you used to kill yourself."

"But—"

"Enough talk," he snapped. "You'll want to save

your jaw strength for what's next."

He approached me and held my head still as he fastened a clothespin on my nose. Then he said, "Open wide, Sofi," and pried my mouth open. He began stuffing me full of ice cubes.

I gnashed my teeth as I tried to crunch through the ice and breathe. The clothespin was doing an alarmingly good job of sealing my nose shut. The impulse to breathe through my mouth was all-consuming.

Jesse smirked cruelly as he surveyed his work. "Be a good girl now, Sofi. Less teeth. I know that I've told you that before."

Tears of humiliation and rage streamed down my cheeks as some of the ice finally began melting and cold water slithered down my throat. I clawed at anything I could reach, which wasn't much, given how tightly Jesse had fasted my upper arms, waist, and thighs to the chair. My feet flailed helplessly, just far enough from the ground that I couldn't run away with the chair still attached. Even if I could have, I wouldn't have gotten very far.

"What's wrong baby? You're a drooling mess. I can't understand a word you're saying."

A cube of ice melted enough that it started to slide down my throat. I gagged and felt bile shoot up my esophagus. Everything tasted acrid, I smelled like sweat, and my face was sticky with tears. The small amount of air that made it through the blockade of ice wasn't enough. I was rapidly becoming dizzy.

Suddenly, Jesse's phone rang. It was the same tune that I'd picked out for him just weeks ago, curled up with him on the couch in front of the TV. That seemed like another lifetime.

I watched through watery eyes as he listened, said "Just a second," then tapped mute. "This is important. You don't mind if I put this," he gestured toward me, "on *ice* for a bit, do you?" He barked a cruel laugh. "Good thing I'm getting rid of you. Your terrible puns and who knows what else are starting to rub off on me." He grabbed a cloth, hastily wiped my lower face, and then sealed my mouth with several strips of duct tape.

I was now completely unable to breathe. Everything was narrowing to a black point.

Thankfully, Jesse removed the clothespin and I frantically inhaled through my nose. He gave me a mocking wink and tugged at the ropes, as if to check that they were still digging into my skin. "Sit *tight*, now, Sofija. Jesus, two puns in a minute? You really are a terrible influence."

He straightened and picked up his phone from the table. "I'm back," he said. He listened for a minute and replied, "Yeah. Yeah they're in my car. No, I'm not going to sort through all of them just to check this for you. I don't have time for that. Come on, calm down— oh for fuck's sake, fine. Just chill. I'm going to check them now."

He mouthed 'sorry' at me with a mocking grin and walked toward the exit.

Frantically, I strained against the ropes to little avail. They loosened, but not nearly enough. Jesse had tied them too snugly for that.

I looked around me, but nothing was near except the half-filled bucket of melting ice, which sat a few inches in front of me.

That's it! I thought. It was a longshot, but I had no better play at this point.

Jesse dragging me into the gym, combined with his pacing, had cleared some of the dust from the floor around my chair and the table—enough that water would be difficult to see against the high gloss finish.

Wriggling and rotating, I managed to angle my left foot toward the right one and push down until my right sneaker fell off. I did the same for my other foot. Once I was shoeless, I slipped my socks off.

To the extent that I could, I slumped down and extended by bare foot toward the rim of the bucket. On my first attempt, my toes slipped and the bucket teetered perilously back and forth. For one horrible second, I thought it would fall. Eventually, it settled back down.

Thank God.

I tried again, and this time, I managed to hook the rim of the bucket between my big toe and the next one. Using my other foot to steady the bucket, I tilted it slowly, lower and lower, until some of the melted ice water ran out of the bucket and onto the floor. I tightened my muscles and held the position until my legs were shaking.

That'll have to be enough.

Carefully, I righted the bucket and used my toes to slip my socks in my shoes and my shoes back on—and not a moment too soon. Just as I finished, Jesse's voice echoed through the empty gym. He was nearly back.

I slumped down and hoped that I looked defeated.

As Jesse walked toward me with an infuriating swagger, I peered out through narrow, tear-stained eyes. When he was close, I lifted my head and whimpered through my nose, trying to draw his attention to my face.

Don't look down! I prayed.

Thankfully, he didn't.

"Got something to say, Sofi? Speak up." He reached down and ripped the duct tape off of my mouth. I screamed in pain. Once the stinging subsided, I took a deep breath and put my plan into action.

I started whispering gibberish and laughing gleefully.

Jesse narrowed his eyes. "What's so funny? What the fuck could you possibly have to be laughing about?"

I whispered nonsense again, making sure it was just quiet enough that he wouldn't be able to make out that it was meaningless. Then I giggled provocatively.

Scowling, Jesse asked, "Did the ice somehow break your throat and mouth? Because I can't understand anything you're saying. But you're going to tell me what's so funny."

Jesse moved to close the distance between us, leaning toward me. The minute his foot touched the wet floor where I'd poured the ice water, I kicked out as hard as I could and headbutted him.

My head smashed into his and the tip of my shoe connected with his shin. He howled in pain, and his foot failed to find traction on the slippery floor surface. Flailing wildly, he fell and hit his head on the table behind him with a sickening thud. When he landed on the floor, he was unconscious. His head lolled back and forth until it finally stilled.

"Taste of your own medicine, brought to you by nurse Sofija," I shouted triumphantly.

Now it was time for the hard part, part two. If I failed, then when Jesse woke up...well, it was a safe bet that he'd make sure it hurt when I died.

I rocked forward and to one side and then forward and to the other in the chair. It was tricky, trying to balance not tipping over with working up enough momentum to shuffle toward Jesse's unconscious form.

Slowly but surely, me and the chair inched toward him.

After what must have been five minutes of that, I was panting but right next to Jesse's body. I took a few seconds to collect my breath before I once again shoved off my sneakers and socks.

I straightened my leg and pointed my toes until they made contact with the slick screen of my phone, which was peeking out from Jesse's jean pocket.

Over and over, I swiped my foot, pulling the phone closer and closer until finally I was able to clasp it between my toes. I knew my feet wouldn't be able to reach the screen if I let the phone drop to the floor, so I carefully placed it on top of Jesse's chest, praying that the pressure wouldn't rouse him.

With one foot, I held the phone still. With the other, I pressed the button to wake it up. When it did, I felt like weeping tears of joy.

There were seven missed calls from Mateo. Even though I was by no means in the clear yet and death was still a real possibility, knowing that Mateo cared that much made me smile.

It also made what I had to do next much easier.

I pressed on one of the missed call notifications to initiate a call back. As expected, the screen prompted me to unlock it. I tapped out the numerical passcode.

Seconds felt like forever as I waited for the call to start. When it did, I pressed the speakerphone button.

I knew it was a gamble. The noise might wake up Jesse—but I couldn't think of an alternative.

"Sofija? Is it you? Are you all right?" came Mateo's

panicked voice.

"Mateo," I sobbed. I needed to call him Mateo right now. "It was Jesse. He killed Talia and he forced me to say those things to you. Then he knocked me out and brought me to some old gym. I'm tied up. I managed to knock him out, but he's going to wake up at some point. He's going to kill me, fake a suicide note, and dump me in water somewhere."

"Share your location with me. Can you do that?"

"I can try." I fiddled around, swiping clumsily through the little app icons on the screen until I found the messages app and opened our conversation. I finally managed to press share location.

"Got it?" I asked in a quavering voice.

After a second, he replied, "Yes! I'm coming for you, Sofija. I'm already running to my car. I'm going to call 911 and Cantrell on the way, but I'm coming."

"Hurry," I squeaked. "I'm going to hang up now so you can call them. And I don't want to make more noise than I have to and risk waking Jesse up."

"Good thinking. I'm coming, Sofija. I've got you."

The click that told me that Mateo had hung up sent a wave of dread through me. I knew it meant he was calling 911 and was on the way, but hearing his voice had made me feel safe.

There was nothing to do now but wait—wait and hope that Jesse didn't wake up.

Time seemed to creep by, slow as cold honey. Jesse began to stir, and my heart sank.

It took all of my self-control not to cry or to call Mateo back.

Sofija Maria Zammit, stay quiet!

I sat as still as I could and stared ahead. The dust,

undisturbed for so long, must have been stirred up from our movements. I could see it suspended in the air as it passed through the weak beams of sunlight that filtered through the dirty windows.

Suddenly, I felt the need to sneeze. I held off for as long as I could, but the urge became too strong. Closing my mouth and nostrils, I muffled the sneeze as best as I could. It hurt my sinuses, and it wasn't stealthy enough, because Jesse stirred again. This time, he groaned.

Fuck.

Jesse rotated his head and slowly reached up to cradle where it had hit the table. He moaned in pain and slowly opened his eyes. At first, they were unfocused and he stared blankly up at the ceiling.

Gradually, though, he seemed to become more aware of his surroundings. He pushed himself up and scooted back against one of the legs of the table.

Then his eyes met mine. I'd never seen Jesse look so menacing as he did now, even in his weakened state.

"Good news, Sofi," he rasped.

"Oh?" was all I managed to croak.

"Yeah. That right there," he said, gesturing to the puddle I had used to trip him. "That's the last mistake you're ever going to make."

Gulping, I screwed my eyes shut and willed Mateo to get here faster.

"I was going to torture you just a little more before I drowned you. But seeing as you've dumped my supplies, looks like I'll have to suffocate you the old-fashioned way and then pour the water down your lungs."

The mental image that painted had me sobbing and screaming, "MATEO! Mateo please hurry!"

"He's not here, Sofija. If he ever sees you again, you'll be half eaten by the fish and worms."

With that, Jesse grabbed the edge of the table and hauled himself up. He grabbed the duct tape and approached me unsteadily.

"Deep breath now, Sofi," he sneered as he clipped the clothespin back on my nose.

The duct tape made an awful tearing sound—louder and sharper than seemed possible. Just as he was about to seal the first strip over my mouth, Jesse roared in pain and fell to the ground, grasping his foot.

Confused, I looked up and saw Cantrell standing at the entrance of the gym, his gun trained on the spot where Jesse's foot had been.

But most of my focus was on Mateo, who was sprinting toward me.

"Sofija, thank God," he panted as he skidded to a stop in front of me and removed the clothespin.

"You came," I whispered. Tears were running down my cheeks in such strong rivulets that they cut through the mix of sweat and dust that clung to my skin.

Mateo set to work untying the rope binding my thighs to the chair. "Of course I came," he said.

I was about to respond when I saw movement in my left peripheral. "Mateo, watch out!" I screamed.

Jesse's fist sailed through the air toward Mateo's head, but Mateo managed to block the punch and elbow Jesse in the face. Cantrell was lumbering toward us at a surprising clip. Before Jesse could recover from Mateo's blow, Cantrell had pinned his arms down and was cuffing him.

"Ms. Sofija, you can consider this the end of our investigations into you," Cantrell stated. "I'm going to take this," he said, thumping his hand down on Jesse's shoulder, "to the Boston office and get his statement and make mine."

"Cantrell," Mateo began. "Is it okay if I take Sofija to urgent care and then follow you once she's gotten medical attention?"

"Sure is," Cantrell said. He looked down at Jesse and grabbed my phone from his pocket. "This yours, Ms. Sofija?"

"It is," I confirmed. "But you can keep it for evidence."

"No need for that right now," he said, handing my phone to Mateo since my arms were still bound. "We've got two eyewitnesses and a mountain of new evidence."

Cantrell began pushing Jesse, who was limping and groaning in pain, toward the exit. "By the way, Ms. Sofija," he added, "if you need a day to recover before you come in for a final statement, take it. And take care of yourself."

"Thank you, Agent Cantrell, for helping save my life," I called out after him.

"It's my job, but you're also most welcome." He and Jesse disappeared around the corner.

And then it was just me and Mateo.

Chapter 21

Mateo

After Cantrell had left, the gym was silent except for the gentle rustle of the rope and creak of the chair as I untied Sofija from her bindings.

Desperate to hear her voice and assure myself that she would be all right, I said the first thing that came to my mind. "I recused myself from this case earlier this morning. Just a couple hours before you called me, actually."

"What does that mean?" Sofija asked, the high vowels of the last word pitching up into a squeak as the rope fell off of her wrists. Deep, raw indentations marred the surface of her otherwise smooth skin. A whimper escaped her lips as she rotated her ankles and wrists and massaged the sensitive areas. To my horror, I noticed a little blood trickling down, pooling in the crease of her elbow.

"Sofija, you're bleeding. We need to get you to urgent care."

"No," she stubbornly insisted. "I don't have the best health insurance right now, and I've already been to urgent care once this month. I just can't afford to go again. I'm not a millionaire yet."

"Then I'll get you what you need to treat your injuries," I proposed. "Iodine, antibacterial cream, bandages, gauze. I'll stock you up so well that you'll have the best supplied apartment in the city. A mini urgent care of your own."

Sofija grimaced, but I could tell it had more to do with the tenderness of her newly-freed ankles than it did to my offer.

"You don't have to do that for me. It wouldn't be appropriate anyways, would it?" she murmured sadly.

Ruled by instinct, I reached out and tipped her chin up so that her eyes met mine. They were tired, but still shone like bottomless jade.

"What I would really like to do is pay for your entire urgent care or hospital stay, but I do think that'd be pushing it, since I only just recused myself today. But nobody is going to blink an eye about some band aids and antibiotic ointment."

Sofija's breathing had turned shallow, each gentle puff gently breaking on my nose. We were so close, nearly as close as we had been last night at the bar.

"You keep saying you've recused yourself. What does that mean?" she asked softly.

"It means I'm no longer part of this particular investigation. Not in an FBI capacity. I realized that there was just no way I could stay on it, not when I feel the way that I do."

Her expression brightened and her gaze flickered to my lips. She gently took my hand and flipped it over so that it was facing up. I thought she would lace her fingers into mine, but instead, she ran her thumb over my palm, a butterfly touch, so light that I glanced down to confirm it was really happening. "Does that mean that we can..." she trailed off.

"It does," I said, self-control fraying at an alarming

rate. I forced myself to lean away. Sofija's look of disappointment broke me. "But for appearances' sake, we should wait a few weeks before we, you know…"

"Finish what we started last night?" she provocatively supplied.

Groaning, I said, "I'm going to have to call you a ride to take you home separately if you get me thinking about that in too much detail."

A giggle escaped her, and she leaned back. "Fair enough. So I have to wait two weeks to experience the FBI's finest. It'll be a struggle, but I can manage."

"I think I said a few weeks, and two is a couple," I grudgingly corrected. "Cantrell's advice. It would be zero weeks, in an ideal world."

Sofija's coquettish expression faded into one of concern. "I don't want to get you into trouble."

"You won't," I quickly assured her. "I just want to be by-the-book about this. To the extent that I still can, at least."

"But what happens if you're still fired?" she fretted.

Stilling her hand from its gentle tracing of my palm, I engulfed it in between my own. "In that absolute worst-case scenario, I'd go back to practicing law. I wouldn't lose my bar affiliation over it. I haven't broken a law; it's just not great in terms of optics. But you let me figure that out."

It wasn't clear whether what I'd said really reassured her, but Sofija nodded nonetheless. "Okay. So we can pick back up in five or six weeks."

"Five or six?!" I spluttered. "A few can also mean three or four, you know."

Smiling, she replied, "Four and a half. A good solid month."

"Fine," I conceded.

We sat there in happy silence for a minute before she arched her eyebrows. "I may be imagining things after everything I've been through today, but did you say earlier that Cantrell knows about us?"

"He does," I confessed.

"Then how are you here?" she asked, the confusion plain on her face.

"Cantrell couldn't stop me from coming here on my own, in my capacity as a concerned civilian. But he had to be the one to take down Jesse and book him. That, and I'm really not a good shot for an FBI agent," I admitted with a small chuckle.

"I guess I should have noticed that you weren't wearing your FBI jacket. But I wasn't really in a state to register anything but pain."

Her words struck me. "Sofija, you've been through a lot. You'll need time to heal. I don't want—the last thing I want is for you to feel rushed into something physical, or even romantic with me. If a month comes and goes and you've changed your mind, or you need more time, you need to communicate that to me, okay?"

At that, Sofija's grin became downright sinful. She leaned forward, her nose just brushing the shell of my ear. I shivered. Even though the sweat glistening from her neck had that cortisol-heavy scent, something about her still smelled sweet to me.

"Mateo, some people recover from trauma by taking a break and slowing down. That's fine, but it's not me. I'm one of those people who recovers by diving back into what I like. I refuse to let someone like Jesse ruin my life. Despite his best efforts, I'm going to come out of this mess stronger. "

She paused for a second, then dropped her voice to a silky murmur. "And speaking of ruining things. I want you to do that to me. In a *very* different sense of the word, though. Do you get me?"

Gulping, I squeezed my eyes shut and nodded.

"Since I didn't hear a response, *Agent Mateo Velasquez*, let me be absolutely clear," she purred. "In a month, I want you over at my apartment, eating the mediocre Maltese food I'm going to cook for you. I want you to pretend that it's the best thing anybody's ever made. Then I want you to help me wash the dishes while we sip on wine, and when we're done, I want you to follow me into my bedroom and *ruin* me." She leaned back to face me, her eyes flicking down to my pants, which had gotten tight to the point of slight discomfort during her little monologue.

Then she made a little humming noise, like she'd tasted something unexpectedly delicious.

"*Sofija*," I moaned, gripping the chair on either side of her thighs. I wanted to nuzzle into her, inhale her.

She gave a self-satisfied grin and leaned in again to add, "And if we break any of my cheap furniture in the process, even better. I've got some money coming in, so I'll buy replacements."

I abruptly stood up and retreated to stand behind the table, desperate to put some kind of obstacle in between us. "Stop teasing me like this. It's too much," I managed to say, my voice sounding hoarse even to my own ears.

"Is it?" she asked innocently.

"I'm trying to do the right thing. Trying so, so hard."

"I bet you *are*," she murmured.

"Sofi!" I choked out.

Tucking a curl of hair behind her ear, she smiled

slyly at me. "I'll try to behave." She moved to stand, but crumpled the minute she put weight on her foot.

"Dammit," she cursed, forehead scrunched in obvious pain. "It's my left knee. I can't remember what happened to it though. Maybe I fell on it when Jesse knocked me out."

In a second, I was by her side again.

"Be careful, Sofija," I admonished. Without waiting, I leaned down and draped her arm over my shoulder so that she could hobble along without putting too much weight on her leg. "Let's get you to my car and back to your place."

She buried her face in my chest, and I held her there, stroking her tangled hair. When she looked up, her eyes were gleaming.

"Thank you, Mateo," she said softly.

"For helping find you? It was the only thing to do, recused from the case or not."

Shaking her head, Sofija said, "No. Well, thanks for that too, of course. But what I meant was, thank you for believing me throughout this whole thing. Because you did, didn't you?"

For the first time since the case started, I could finally tell her the truth. "Always."

She didn't say anything in response; she just squeezed my shoulder with what I suspected was all the force her weakened form could muster. We made our way toward the exit.

It was slow going, especially when we got outside and had to make our way across the pothole-ridden parking lot. Eventually, though, we arrived at my car. I shifted Sofija slightly and bent over so that I could lean down and open the door without dropping her.

Once we'd maneuvered her into the passenger seat, I rested my arms on the roof just above the window and looked down. "I'll always believe you, Sofija."

I gently closed the door and walked around to the driver's seat. After I'd started the engine, I looked over. Sofija was real, sitting there and smiling. Reassured, I pulled out of the parking lot and put the building in our rearview.

She slept for at least fifteen minutes, but when we pulled off the highway and onto streets that had more stops and starts, she stirred awake. "I know what I'm going to do with the money," she announced with surprising post-nap clarity.

"Oh?" I asked curiously.

"I'm going to keep enough for nurse practitioner school and to pay off my brother's med school debt. Then, I'm going to buy my dad a vacation to Malta. I'm going to buy myself a new table, some new chairs, and a new bed. I think I'll donate $1 million to the National Institute on Aging. They're doing some exciting research on Alzheimer's."

Smiling, I said, "That sounds great, but that's not eight million dollars. Are you going to invest the rest?"

Shaking her head, she said, "No. I'm going to give $200,000 to Talia Portnoy's family and $100,000 each to Frannie, Roland, and Marly. The estate, I'll give to Adam. That reminds me—hold on." She placed a hand on top of mine and picked up her phone from where I'd placed it in the car's cup holder.

I rubbed my thumb slowly over her hand as she placed a call.

"Hi, Adam. I need to tell you something."

****

I parked outside the pharmacy and ran inside to buy the first aid materials. By the time I came back, Sofija had hung up. She looked like she was in shock.

"How'd he take it?" I asked.

"Well, he was grateful that I'm giving him the estate. About Jesse, he wasn't happy. I mean, they weren't on perfect terms, but it's his brother. He was upset. Not really surprising."

"But *you* look surprised. Why is that?"

"Umm…because he invited me and my dad to Christmas dinner this year."

My eyes bugged out in disbelief. "Adam Armitage?"

"Well, his husband Xiaoming did, but Adam didn't stop him. So I'm counting it," she said, laughing.

Her laugh wasn't musical. It wasn't delicate. It was hearty, surprisingly so for having been produced by such a small body.

It was perfect for her.

"I guess I'll have to ask my mom to push back our Christmas dinner by a day so that you can make both," I said without thinking.

Sofija gave a small gasp and I swallowed. "That was a little fast of me, no?" I mumbled, mortified.

"A little. But after the past year, I land firmly on the side of preferring a man who wants to introduce me to his family as his girlfriend too soon rather than too late. Anyways, we can see how this goes and reevaluate in December—but I'm going to say yes," she said, eyes twinkling.

I was equally confident that my feelings would have only gotten stronger by then, but I decided to keep it light. "That gives me a little time to teach you Spanish."

Sofija nodded enthusiastically. "I would love that!" She gave me a sly look. "Maybe we can work out some kind of reward system. I have it on good authority that with the proper motivation, I could be a *hispanohablante* in a matter of months."

I chuckled. "Whoever told you that sounds like he knows what he was talking about."

"Agent Velasquez," she teased. "I don't recall saying it was a he. Are you privy to inside information, or just keeping tabs on me?"

"You caught me." I leaned in a little closer. "Impressive detective skills. I look forward to learning your other talents, of which I'm sure there are many."

Her eyes lit up, lambent pools of green mirth. "I don't know about that. But I'm nothing if not an enthusiastic, hands-on learner." She sunk back into her seat and observed the effect of her words with a mischievous smile.

Shuddering, I took the car out of park and we drove off toward possibilities I hadn't entertained as more than wishful thinking.

Chapter 22

Sofija

We didn't get to experience my average home cooked Maltese meal, or the cheap bottle of wine.

The day the four and a half weeks were over, I answered the pounding at my apartment door to find Mateo.

He stood outside, cracking his knuckles, wearing nothing but a fitted plain white tee and jeans.

"Hi," he said, sounding rather agitated. "Can we—I didn't want to just barge in here and ask, I know our date is for tonight, but…" he trailed off. I'd never seen him so worked up.

"Yes," I quickly assented. I dragged him inside, shut and locked the door, and barely turned around before Mateo's lips were on mine.

"Sofija," he moaned. "I've wanted you for so long."

"You can have me," I murmured against his lips.

He pulled his shirt off and I did the same. I turned and practically ran into my bedroom. His footsteps assured me that he was close behind.

As I slipped out of my skirt, I watched Mateo take me in. His glazed-over smile faltered as he seemed to remember something. Reaching into his jeans pocket, he retrieved a shiny packet. "Condom?" he asked in a husky voice.

Blushing, I said, "Whatever you're comfortable with. I'm on the pill and...in preparation for this, I took an STD test last week. All clean. I mean, I was always safe with-with—"

Jesse's name sat heavy in my mouth, bitter when all I was primed for was sweet. I shook my head, determined to push out all the bad memories with something better. To that end, I stepped closer to Mateo. "But I took one, just in case. I've got the results, if you want to verify," I said, snatching up the paper on the chest of draws to my right.

A hungry grin crossed Mateo's face. He closed what little distance still separated us and plucked the paper from my hand. After giving it a cursory glance, he set it back on the chest of drawers. "I like that you're prepared. So good, aren't you, Sofija?" he hummed as he threaded his fingers through my hair. I met his eyes as he studied my reaction carefully.

I responded with a relaxed smile and nod. He sighed in relief.

After what I'd been through, I'd given a lot of thought to what I'd be comfortable with today. Jesse had always called me good, and I had gone back and forth about whether I could hear that from another man's mouth without it sending me spiraling.

At exactly 12 a.m. last night, I had pressed send on a text that I had been composing and editing over the last few weeks. The first part of the message was a heartfelt letter of appreciation to Mateo for believing in me.

The second half was far more nerve-wracking to send. I had asked Mateo what he liked, and I had given him a long, detailed list of my own. There were things I knew that I liked; things that I thought I might never like and didn't want to be asked for; and things that I wasn't sure if I could still handle, but that I wanted to try.

Being called "good" fell firmly into the last category.

Mateo's smooth voice pierced my thoughts, like a cold knife through jam. "You liked that, I take it?"

Beaming at him, I confirmed, "I did. We're *good* to go." I grimaced a little at my cheesiness, but he grinned.

"Thanks for that," he said, gesturing to the drawer where the lab results rested. "So nice of you, Sofija." His grip in my hair tightened infinitesimally. "So, *so* good."

He regarded me with a satisfied smirk as I shivered at his words. Every part of me, from the surface of my skin to deep inside, felt taut.

Mateo spoke again. "I did the same." In a flash, he used his free hand to fish into his back pocket and pull out his phone. After a few taps, he held up the screen with his results.

"All clean," I said happily. I took the condom that he'd placed on the bedside table and tucked it back into his pocket. "So no need for that."

He exhaled slowly and closed his eyes. "You have no idea how many times I pictured some variation of this, Sofija. And not just this past month—from the minute I saw you with your patient. What was that? Less than a week into the investigation? And already I was gone for you."

We walked back toward the bed until my knees hit the side and I fell onto it, bouncing a little. Mateo slid out of his jeans, and then his boxers. He stared at me, almost reverently. I shimmed out of my underwear and reclined, delirious in anticipation.

He slid over me, propping his torso up with his

hands while everything else lay flush against me. "I knew I should feel guilty, fantasizing about you. I felt like I was a bad agent. Like I had no control. But you know what, Sofija?"

"What?" I trembled under him.

He leaned down and licked the space between my breasts all the way up to my neck. As he hovered next to my ear, he guided my hand down to where he was hard. "I couldn't stop then, and now? Now I'm going to have the real thing," he growled, sliding his hand between my thighs. When he hit my center, I arched into him and he started rubbing, deliciously slowly.

I kissed him hungrily. He pulled back and looked down to where our hips touched and licked his lips. "Do you want me to…"

Without thinking, I cried, "NO!" He looked shocked, so I reassuringly caressed his upper arms. "I mean—I do like that. A lot. But I don't want it now. I just want to be *together*."

Mateo groaned, and after a flurry of aligning and gliding, he was where I needed him. As he started moving, I gasped. "Ahh—I just—I need a second to adjust," I said.

He immediately stilled and kissed me gently on the lips. "Sure you don't want me to take care of you first? I'd really, *really* like to."

I shook my head stubbornly. "We can do that another time. I need *this* right now. Just give me a minute."

There was pain like what Jesse had made me feel with his ropes and ice cubes that day in the warehouse, when I thought I would die. That pain had made me suffer. It had terrified me. It had drained me.

The stretch that I felt now was different. It filled me, and not just physically, though there was that too. What I felt now filled me with power, because I knew that I set the terms for any discomfort. Mateo would only give what I wanted. That both thrilled and calmed me.

I gazed up adoringly into his eyes. They were so liquid right now, as if he were fighting not to tear up. I could almost imagine some of the golden color escaping and dripping down his nose, splashing onto my bare skin, washing over me like the sweetest honeyed rain.

Mateo reached down to just above where we were joined and began rubbing his thumb in lazy circles. It sent little shocks through me. "Take as long as you need. I'm not going anywhere," he said tenderly.

Feeling more powerful than I had in weeks, I pulled his head down for a kiss before I said, "You weren't the only one who fell fast, you know."

Raising his eyebrows, he said, "Oh?"

"The first time you came over to question me…" I trailed off.

"That *is* fast," he said in a low voice. I felt him twitch inside me.

His reaction triggered a dam break in me. "You were this stunning FBI agent who was also so respectful. You acted like I was worth believing. I couldn't help it. It made me feel guilty because I was still with *him*. But all I could think was that if I got off and walked free, I wanted to walk straight to your house and get *you* off."

Mateo laughed, the shaking of his own body reverberating through me. Anything resembling discomfort was rapidly fading. Only a faint echo of it remained.

"You think I'm cheesy," I giggled.

"You are, and it's wonderful. Also, remind me to thank Cantrell for making my personality look sparkling by comparison on that first day."

I rolled my eyes, before turning serious. "Mateo? I'm ready."

"Yeah?" he asked, giving a tentative buck. It had me thrumming.

"Completely," I urged, my voice breaking on the word.

"I think I can feel that," he said as he began thrusting in earnest.

We clung to each other and forged months of frustration into something both infinitely thrilling and soothing, like the rocking of a boat on the boundless sea.

And finally, my future felt the same—boundless.

A word about the author…

Rebecca is a travel-obsessed linguist and wannabe archaeologist who has lived in Boston, Toronto, Amman, Detroit, Cincinnati, Jerusalem, and Cairo. She's worked in everything from tech to media, but her real passions are writing and hiking—and brewing almost overly-pungent kombucha, much to her husband's chagrin.

https://rebeccalynnbyrne.com/

Thank you for purchasing
this publication of The Wild Rose Press, Inc.

For questions or more information
contact us at
info@thewildrosepress.com.

The Wild Rose Press, Inc.
www.thewildrosepress.com